By the Sea

Nikki R. Flionis

Rudiyat Press

For
Nick and Pat Flionis,
Anne Carrabino,
the young people of MissionSAFE,
who made it all possible.

By the sea, by the sea,
By the beautiful sea...
Oh, how happy we'll be.

Prologue

He heard the gun go off. He didn't know at first what it was. He had been asleep in his corner bedroom. It was not yet dark and not yet time to meet his boys. As always here, he was bored, feeling a bit down. So he slept. The explosion was followed by screaming and a slightly burnt smell. Suddenly he was fully awake. It had been loud and there were no more shots. Was it his gun?

Chapter One

JaQuan

September 2002

In Boston, subway riders making the trip from downtown to East Boston travel an underworld deep below cubic tons of ocean. They ride an escalator up from the depths of Maverick Station blinking like newborns in the sun.

For JaQuan Miller, the ride under the harbor was a pilgrimage to a new land. Fifteen years old and full of a sinewy restless strength, he sat now with a hoodie pulled over his head in East Boston's Piers Park, on the edge of the Atlantic Ocean. He didn't need his hoodie, but it made him feel less exposed. He marveled to himself as he watched sunlight dancing on the restless water, and airplanes rising from the airport on the island's other end.

He'd never truly realized that his home sat right on the sea. He'd known only one or two sections of Boston intimately, and neither of them looked like this. The air was warm for early fall, soft-fuzzing the edges of the Boston skyline across the harbor from him. He felt energized and confused.

***

"I can't believe you've never been here, man. You know it's not just white people anymore. Eastie's full of brothers now too."

Matthie gave JaQuan a playful push as they ran from the Blue Line subway train up the steep escalator of the dark and musty T station. They burst into the light of Maverick Square, with its roaring bus engines, cars, blowing grit, litter, and the surrounding plaza of mom-and-pop stores—once all Italian and Portuguese, now Latino and Asian as well.

"Follow me, Q."

They walked to the park, where some moms and their babies were hanging out.

"Damn, MD! What the fuck. I don't believe this!" JaQuan took a deep breath. The Maverick projects behind him, bleak and square, were more like what he was used to.

"Yo, man, it's dope, right?" Matthie, aka MD, stopped beside him, looking out at the ocean and skyline too. "Man, I could sit here and smoke all day just staring at it. Never go back...'cept in winter." He laughed and gave JaQuan a light punch on the arm.

"Aight, Q. Just chill here, okay? I'll be back soon as I find Jesse and see if he's okay with getting me some more. It'll be better if I see him alone."

Matthie crossed over to the bricks to find his cousin and Q chose a bench that let him watch the ocean and the bricks. They had come to score weed. JaQuan—Q as his boys called him—didn't know whether Matthie's cousin would be able to get them enough. Jesse sold to college students over by Fenway, and to Matthie for his own use. But JaQuan had convinced Matthie that they had nothing to lose by asking for more.

JaQuan had found the money to front it. He was a natural entrepreneur. None of his crew had jobs. They were too young to be hired and sometimes they didn't focus all that well. Their moms had nothing to give them, maybe a dollar here and there, which, in JaQuan's case, meant no money at all. From time to time they acted as impromptu lookouts for dealers a few blocks away or did a quick purse-snatch or in-kind pick-up from a convenience store in another neighborhood, which they could then sell.

Q was an idea man—he was sure they could move a little weed right on the block where they were, just a couple of days a week. They already did it informally from time to time, using Matthie's personal stash. He was also sure that if his homies kept snatching purses and stealing from the bodegas, they'd get caught. His boys didn't have his kind of vision, he knew. He'd have to take care of them. And he needed them to be there for him. They had saved him from his aunts and their attitude. His boys were his family now.

As he huddled on the bench, he thought: *This city's right by the sea, but where I live you'd never know it.* He glanced around at the park and back out at the ocean. *At least these homies can see it and smell it. I wonder if it makes any difference.*

Mesmerized by the fluidity and sparkle of the harbor water, JaQuan felt the charge of energy again, but also a sadness as he watched the motion and limitless horizon of sea and sky.

He looked around for Matthie. The bricks were quiet and he hoped Jesse was there. Sometimes he and Matthie hung out with Jesse, and they had met some of the college girls where he sold his weed. Jesse was handsome and the girls—mostly white—were always trying to get him to "grow into his potential." The girls, he told Matthie and Q, were always telling him, "Do it for you, you're worth it." And Jesse would answer, "I am doing this for me. I want to find out who I am and what I can do, but I need to support myself while I do it."

"They're talking shit, but they mean well," Jesse told Q and MD. "If you're rich, man, ok—you can grow into your potential. You got mommy and daddy with plenty of white money to make sure you don't fall."

JaQuan understood. No matter what, in his world you had to be taking care of yourself, there was no one else. And you had to be doing something for your peeps, because they were your supports, they kept you safe. And you needed them because otherwise you were like a balloon floating in air, unconnected, not sure why you were here, and about to float away into nothing. You needed the connections, man. It was the only way to remember who you were.

A jet lifted off from Logan, and from here he was close enough that he could almost read the airline name. The jet soared, lifted and banked away toward the north, toward Revere Beach. He looked back at the Boston skyline—glittering across, and reflecting in, the bright water. He thought of the Emerald City in *The Wizard of Oz*, seen from a distance—big, bright, hopeful, mysterious.

JaQuan didn't know what happened in those high buildings in downtown but he wondered now, as he sometimes let himself, what it would feel like to belong in one of them, to work there and to have work friends. To be a player in the world that called the shots. He'd once wondered that aloud when he was at Downtown Crossing with his crew. His boy, Snake, had lashed out at him.

"What the fuck you care, Q. Those m'fuckers bow down all day to some boss so's the corporation make money. Then he come out here beaten down and fucked, and fucks us up."

"They jealous, Snake," one of the boys answered, "'cause we so dark, good-looking and sexy. Them pale holed-up white folks, eating pale white food, pushing piles of white paper in those buildings—'course they try to fuck us."

JaQuan said nothing more. He had learned to pick his fights with Snake. But truth was, though some of those folks looked miserable, a lot of them looked pretty happy and well-dressed, and not all of them were white. He knew, of course, there were companies—banks, insurance companies, and companies that he had no idea what they did. But his question really was, what did people actually do in those places, for eight hours every day, all dressed up. And if you ever wanted to do whatever they did, how did you get in? One of his uncles had managed to get in, though Q didn't really know what he did. Since he got in, they never saw him.

JaQuan knew his teachers or white people would say: "School, that's how you get in." But where he lived, he'd never seen school make any difference for anyone he knew, even if they finished it. Course now, more and more black folks were talking college, like that would make the difference. He shrugged and looked back across Boston Harbor. Maybe it would.

As he looked back out toward the ocean, sadness again swamped him. He had loved the sea when he was young and his grandmoms would pack a lunch and take him to the beach. They had done that at least once a week in the summer. His grandmoms had loved the beach all her life. "My dream," his grandmoms had told him once, "would be to have a house right by the sea, where I could smell that fresh air every day, go to sleep to the sound of the waves, and wake up to those old seagulls squealing with happiness every morning."

In those days, the sea had felt like freedom and happiness to him. He felt it still whenever he went up to Revere Beach in summer with his boys. But then he forgot about it, the feeling didn't last when he moved back into his real life. Boston was street and bricks to him. The sea was from his childhood.

He imagined what it would be like to fly over that water, or take a cruise. He guessed that if he could see across the big vast ocean, he would be looking at England—because after all, all those English folks—Pilgrims and Puritans—sailed here to Boston when they left England. But he remembered from geography in middle school, that he really looked across to Spain—if he could see it: bull fights, matadors, guitars and everyone speaking a different Spanish from his 'Rican friends.

JaQuan turned back to look at the Maverick projects. He sighed as he saw Matthie coming toward him across the street. He turned back to look out at the sea, letting his mind go free one last time. When he looked, he could imagine different ways his life could be if he traveled to Africa, Spain or France.

The sea calmed him, his heart slowed. He felt bigger and smaller at the same time. He could lie on a beach all day, even if he was alone, and everything else in the world, for those few hours, just wouldn't matter.

Matthie came up behind him and punched his shoulder.

"I got it, Q. He had plenty. We are in business, my brother!"

Chapter Two

Shelley

September 2002

Shelley Colabro loved living in Revere. Her eyes barely open from sleep, curly hair tousled, she walked out onto her front porch with a cup of strong, hot coffee in hand. As she sipped, her eyes moved above the long window boxes full of petunias, impatiens and marigolds, across the tiny, empty road in front of her house, to focus on the early sunlight sparkling and leaping on Broad Sound—the patch of Atlantic Ocean that was her real front yard. Seabirds did graceful balletic swoops above the shoreline, and she could hear periodic cracks, as they dropped their beakfuls of clams and mussels from the sky to break open for breakfast.

She was content. Sunday, towards the end of September, the end of summer, in her house in the tiny, private beach neighborhood where the Pines River met the sea. She didn't love living here when she was young. It was a difficult neighborhood for her when she hit adolescence. But her parents had left her the house when they died, and she finally understood why they'd stayed.

"What an incredible day!" Her partner Carolyn eased open the screen door and stepped out, carrying a handmade wooden tray with scones, more coffee and the Sunday papers. The screen door slapped shut behind her. She put the tray down on the teak table they had found at the Mill Stores, and faithfully oiled each spring and fall, and took her own coffee over to stand beside Shelley. Both watched as a jetliner descended toward Logan, and a small lobster boat headed out toward the point. They waved as the elderly ex-marine from down the street did his daily morning jog.

Carolyn had been up early baking the scones, a specialty and favorite stress-reducer of hers, and the smell of baking and coffee contrasting with the smell of the sea was comforting and heady to them both. Carolyn was almost the same height as Shelley, an inch shorter than Shelley's five-foot-eight. Both women were athletic, but while Shelley had hazel eyes, curly hair the color of honey, and skin that tanned easily, Carolyn's eyes were a deep blue, her hair short, straight and almost black, her skin fair and easily burned. Carolyn had been Shelley's partner for almost seven years now. She took one final glance at the sea, then settled down at the table with the *New York Times*, leaving the *Boston Globe* for Shelley.

Carolyn was a photojournalist who traveled the world doing her job. Shelley was a public relations consultant, and her current assignment was closer to home. Her boss at a prestigious public relations firm, Tim O'Riley, had made an offer to the Mayor and Boston Police Department that he could help them reverse the bad publicity they were garnering as youth violence continued. After back and forth negotiations, Shelley had been placed with the Boston Police Department for this past year as part of a two-year, and potentially ongoing, contract, with the goal of working behind the scenes to help the department improve its image in the community through an aggressive marketing strategy, and provision of more and higher quality information to the press.

"Buck up, Colabro. Trust me, you're the person for this job," Tim had told her. "You've got the chops and you'll be able to charm that son-of-a-gun of a commissioner into letting you do the job they need. They'll give you sh—, but don't let it get to you."

And it was an uncomfortable position for her. The department had gone back to having their communications function led by police spokespeople and had eliminated the civilian position of Director of Media Relations. The police department did not take kindly to a civilian coming back into communications, even in this advisory role, and they were uncomfortable with the access to crime scenes that she needed for the strategy to work.

John O'Brien, her immediate supervisor at the department, had quickly welcomed her, but her acceptance had been more grudging for others. O'Riley worked behind the scenes, staying in touch with the Mayor and helping the Commissioner place op-eds that Shelley helped create in Boston's main newspapers—and he worked with Shelley finessing PR strategy behind the scenes. The department had been dealing with a surge in youth and young adult violence, much of it fatal, and there was a growing feeling in the city that the police were failing in their attempts to deal with that surge. The days of the Boston Miracle in the late '80s—as the work of the police, ministers and street workers was known—was behind them, and another surge of violence with different, and sometimes younger, players was emerging.

Shelley joined Carolyn at the table and scanned the *Globe*'s headlines and political stories (that part of her job never eased up), pausing to sip her coffee and watch another lobster boat, while a high-speed motorboat skimmed toward the Harbor Islands. Out beyond Broad Sound, which was bounded by Revere, Nahant and Winthrop, she watched an ocean-going container ship move slowly and majestically from the South Boston waterfront through the deep shipping lanes just beyond Nahant. From her front porch, with her binoculars, she could see the Great Blue Hill over in Canton and the wind turbine down in Hull on the south shore. On New Year's Eve, when they were home, she and Carolyn placed beach chairs on the sidewalk, with a bucket of champagne between them and, dressed in parkas and gloves, watched the midnight fireworks in Boston, shooting up from Boston Harbor. There truly was no place she'd rather be now.

From inside the house, the telephone rang. Carolyn looked at Shelley.

"It's a little early for your crew to be bothering us, isn't it?" Carolyn lifted an eyebrow. Shelley was always on-call for when the BPD needed her assistance, but it was their standing, admittedly morbid, joke that most of the gang members slept in, so usually those calls came at night.

"I sincerely hope so," Shelley answered, pushing herself up out of her chair. "I'll bring out the watering can when I come back?"

Letting the screen door slam behind her, Shelley followed the ring to her office, where she had a separate line for work-related calls. She picked up the receiver.

"Hi Shelley, it's John. I'm sorry to call you on a Sunday morning, but we've had another shooting." John O'Brien, Shelley's immediate boss on this project, was kind, thoughtful, understated, and for some reason didn't resent her presence. She could hear pain in his voice.

"What's the deal, John?" She didn't really want to know.

"We've had a fatal shooting—a seven-year-old accidentally shot by his six-year-old cousin."

"Oh, God."

"And if that wasn't bad enough, the family involved is one of the IP families in the Roxbury-Egleston area and we're going to have to handle this gently." Along with the pain, Shelley could hear something else in his voice.

"I'll be there as quickly as I can. Give me the location." Shelley grabbed a notebook and wrote as John gave her the information. She remembered that John had a wife—outgoing and funny—and two young children, ages six and eight. She had met them briefly at a department cook-out. This shooting would have hit close to home for John. She hung up the phone and walked back out to her porch.

"You have to go in, babe?" Carolyn had been with Shelley long enough to see it in her face.

"This one's worse than usual. Two young children, cousins, one accidentally shot the other."

"Oh, Shel, that's horrible." Carolyn put down the paper and looked at her. "But why do they need you for that? It's tragic, but it's not a gang-related shooting."

"The boys are part of one of the families known as Impact Player families," Shelley answered. "That means several people in the family have been involved in ongoing shootings and street crime. Impact players cause a disproportionate share of the violence that goes on. So, the fear is that this case may still need some very delicate handling. Listen, I'm going to shower, I need to get down there right away and I'm not sure when I can get back. I'm sorry."

Carolyn rose, moved to the porch railing, her back to Shelley. "You do remember that I'm leaving tomorrow for two weeks. This was going to be our weekend, Shel."

Shelley moved to her and put her hands on her shoulders. Carolyn shrugged her off, then turned to her. "It's not like you love this job, Shel. It gets you down, it takes all of our time because you're so thorough, and it's not making any of the shootings stop."

This theme had been developing between them for the last few months, and it annoyed Shelley. She wasn't sure exactly why.

"Car, come on. I'm really sorry. I don't have a choice here." Shelley looked out at the sea and back to Carolyn.

"Don't worry. I'll just hang out, do some laundry, take a walk. I need to finish packing anyway. And I'll water the plants," Carolyn said curtly. Dismissively, she went back to reading her paper. "See you whenever you get back."

"Stop it, Carolyn. I feel bad enough that we can't spend the day like we planned. I'll get back as quickly as I can, all right?"

"I've heard those words so many times before. Just think about it, Shelley, ok? It might be time to ask for another assignment."

Shelley bent down, put her arms around Carolyn and whispered into her ear. "Be patient with me, ok? I'm patient with the traveling you do."

Shelley felt Carolyn tighten again with anger. She let go and kissed the top of her partner's head.

"I know it's not the same, Car. This job isn't my passion in the same way your job is, but it is important to me. I'm just asking you to be patient for a little longer." Shelley turned and went inside.

Carolyn was heading out of the country on a ten-day photo shoot, but with travel and follow-up would be gone a full two weeks. Yesterday they had gone into Boston, checked out bookstores, gotten haircuts, met some friends for drinks and dinner. Today they had hoped to spend time quietly together, maybe walking the beach, maybe a drive up the north shore coast, maybe cooking an elaborate Sunday dinner or wallowing in a video brunch date. They hadn't decided.

Shelley poked her head back out. "Maybe we can go for dinner at Antonia's or The Tides when I'm done. Or I can pick up sushi and a movie. I'll call you when I'm heading back." She didn't wait for an answer from Carolyn.

After showering and dressing, Shelley lowered the top on her dark blue Mini and directed it toward Boston. Thinking about Carolyn and about this shooting tamped down the pleasure of the ride. Still, she could smell the sea until she hit the rotary.

She took the Tobin Bridge into the city. From its height the skyline, the inner and outer harbors of Boston, the islands, and parts of Charlestown were visible. It was a view that always moved her. Boston was still very much a working port as well as a gentrified harbor of cruises and high-end restaurants and hotels. The skyline had doubled in size since her childhood and was impressive to her, even though she drove this route almost every day.

Shelley paid the bridge toll and descended into what she thought of as the real Boston, with its small winding streets, shaded alleys, blowing bits of litter and trash, the rush of downtown workers, and the pockets of poverty and misery often sitting less than a mile from the affluence and beauty of downtown, Back Bay and Beacon Hill neighborhoods.

She headed out Storrow Drive, cut through the Fenway and Mission Hill and drove through Roxbury out to Egleston—one section of Boston seeing regular shootings—and took a few more turns. When she reached the crime scene, she pulled her Cooper alongside a row of police cars. She took her notebook and pens, locked the car and went over to join the official throng in front of a brick apartment building.

Chapter Three

Shelley

C rime scene tape cordoned off a chunk of sidewalk in front of the building. The Police Commissioner, whom all the staff called Chief, stood talking to a small group of officers and detectives. Other cops were interviewing, searching, standing, yawning. The Crime Response Team was on-site. All around her, Shelley witnessed the familiar organized chaos of a crime scene. She could tell from the lack of tension that the ambulance had gone. Her boss was one of those in conversation with the Chief. Flashing her police-issued ID, she walked over to join them.

"Hey, Shelley," the Chief said, spotting her. "Thanks for getting down here so quickly. I'll let John fill you in."

"Good morning, Chief," Shelley said, then she and John peeled away from the group.

John O'Brien was a former uniform cop, six feet tall, handsome, blue eyes, dark hair beginning to gray. An ex-football player, college-educated, thirty-six years old, he had been an up and coming uniform. He was badly wounded on the job a few years back and put on medical leave. When he returned, he was taken off the streets and moved into the Commissioner's office as spokesperson since he had a facility with words. Shelley had learned early that he still carried that complex mix of street cop responses—compassionate, opinionated, empathetic but not to be challenged. Today, though, he looked ill—pale and drawn. Shelley remembered his children's names: John's son, Michael, was eight and his little girl, Janine, was six.

"What happened?" Shelley asked.

"Two young cousins, Ishmael and Antwon Miller, live in this building." John's tone was flat, just the facts. "Ishmael was seven years old, Antwon is six. They were playing and somehow got hold of a loaded gun. It went off. Antwon was holding it. Ishmael is dead."

The Chief's group had broken up, and he rejoined Shelley and John.

"The six-year-old is in shock—I don't think he had any idea the gun could really do damage." The Chief, too, looked pale and his hound-dog features looked even sadder than usual. "As of this moment, unless something else turns up, we are considering this an accidental shooting. But, as John probably already told you, this family is on our list of impact players, so you two have to be on this every second. The gun probably came from someone in the family—there's an older cousin staying here, and, we understand, a couple of boyfriends. Both mothers deny there was ever any gun in either apartment or any boyfriends hanging around."

"They also deny," John broke in, "that any of their boyfriends, sons, daughters, nephews or nieces have ever been involved in violence or gangs."

"Cool it, John." The Chief took the conversation back. "We need to find where the gun came from and we need to be very careful how we present our investigation and our finds each step of the way. These were two little boys—innocent victims, no matter what their families have been involved with. We have to treat this very carefully."

"Because God forbid we should look like we're railroading a family who sells drugs, uses drugs, has relatives in prison and gets involved in gang warfare."

The Chief frowned. "For the last time, John, that's enough. We're all feeling this, but now is not the time. For now, I want you both to work on some press releases that cover the bases, depending on how this goes, and come up with a press strategy. I'm going to have to talk to the press again by the end of today and I want you to have several options ready for me. Right now, we're still investigating and don't have answers." He paused, looking at Shelley and John. "I have to make some calls and talk with the Mayor, he's on his way down. Get to work on this and keep your emotions in check." The Chief laid his hand on John's shoulder gently, then walked away.

John turned to Shelley. "The kids found a weapon, no one seems to know how, were playing with it and it discharged." He continued his recitation, outlining points they would use in the release. "The bullet went right through the seven-year-old and lodged in the wooden window frame. The boy died instantly. His cousin is in shock, as are the mothers of both boys." He paused, breathing deeply, and looked pensively at the scene.

Shelley knew John well enough that she could see he was rigid with anger but trying to let it seep away with each breath. She knew how he doted on his children. He would be furious with adults who put a child in danger. When she first met John, he told her he had come to desk duty reluctantly, after being shot chasing suspected drug dealers in Roxbury. His personality, though controlled, seemed always to be just below a boil.

"Everyone denies there was a gun anywhere around," he continued. Unsaid in his tone was, *of course*. Shelley understood John's cynicism. "We were able to retrieve the bullet in fairly good shape. It hadn't hit any bone and the window frame was old and soft. The Chief sent the bullet off with the gun to ballistics, with a rush on it. He wants information as soon as we can get it, while this case is hot. The Chief is right—as if this isn't enough of a tragedy in its own right, it could explode in our faces."

Shelley nodded. "The old police insensitivity and the laying of blame automatically at the feet of any person of color."

"We've issued only the barest facts at this point," John continued, not responding to her words. "Seven-year-old dead, apparently shot by accident by his six-year-old cousin while playing with a gun.

"Do your interviews, Shelley. I've gotten you clearance to talk with the moms, even though this is still an active scene. Get a feel and let's talk again in an hour or so about how we want to approach this with the press."

John wandered off to make a couple of calls to his office staff and to talk informally with press as they arrived, setting up a conference time, and giving the standard "this is what we know—no other comment—it's too soon" statements. Shelley watched the action around her, took some notes, and prepared to enter the apartment building, still cordoned by officers gathering information and quietly keeping press away from the family. It was her practice to interview family and friends of any victim. It had taken several shootings before the Chief agreed to let her try it, since she wasn't police or a psychologist. But Shelley had years ago trained and practiced as a social worker until she discovered she was better at telling stories, and moved into public relations. The Chief had known her dad back in the old days. And he, like the Mayor, was friends with her boss. After seeing the difference it made in press response already, the trust had been cemented and the Chief agreed to allow the interviews as long as they didn't compromise the investigation.

Shelley still got resistance from the uniforms and some detectives. She was a civilian, not one of them, and should not be at the crime scene. Nobody understood or cared that it was painful for her as well, nor did they understand that it allowed her to nuance her writing with empathy for them—the cops—who had to witness and deal with the results of fatal shootings far more often than any human being should have to. This practice also, she thought, gave a little bit of power back to the victims' families, to be able to tell some of what they were feeling.

Shelley looked around her. The sun was shining and it showed the neighborhood to good advantage. Shelley knew most non-residents—students, tourists, and the workers who commuted into the city, as well as many white residents—saw only the downtown part of Boston and its closer neighborhoods and institutions, which were lovely and historic: the Common, Beacon Hill, the North End, Faneuil Hall, Charlestown with the USS Constitution and Bunker Hill Monument; Back Bay, the South End, the Fenway. But Shelley by now was aware of the beauty and history that could be found in all the city's neighborhoods, even when desperation and poverty obscured them. The sun shone on the deep crimson brick of the four-story traditional apartment buildings around her and made them look calm and prosperous.

The part of Roxbury where Shelley stood was just past Egleston Square, where Roxbury and Jamaica Plain collided and where the old elevated used to roar overhead hundreds of times a day. She stood just off Seaver Street in one of the side streets before Franklin Park. The Boston theme of brick rowhouses that began in Back Bay continued on a more modest scale here, and Franklin Park, just down the street, was another Olmstedian gem of green space, trees, trails, cultivated beauty; and home to the Franklin Park Zoo. City and state officials had worked hard over the years with non-profit and for-profit partners to restore the area and the buildings, making them livable for people of modest means. In the early 1980s many of these buildings were burned out and boarded up. Many sections of Roxbury, Dorchester and Jamaica Plain had looked as if a great war just ended.

Shelley walked up to the building to talk briefly with officers and detectives on-scene and prepare her questions before she met the family.

Chapter Four

JaQuan

JaQuan Miller sat hunched in the corner of his room, lights off, in the darkness by the open closet door. Headlights from cars threading their way toward or up Seaver Street toward Blue Hill Avenue periodically brightened, then faded, on the wall behind his bed like storm waves against a shore. *I am a man*, he told himself, *I am strong*. It was his own fucking fault. Then he wept. He had never felt more like a child. And he was scared.

"JaQuan—get the fuck down here! How many times I have to call you?"

"Ma—leave him. His lights are off. I don't even think he's up there."

"Fuck he's not. Goddamn motherfucker. JaQuan!"

***

JaQuan had been upstairs in his room when the gun went off. Sleeping. He had been living with his aunts for two months. He slept a lot when he was there because it was clear he wasn't really welcome. His

Aunt Miriam had given him a room of his own, though. He had first taken cover, not sure where the gunshot had come from or if there would be more. Then he registered how loud the explosion had been, and he heard his aunt.

"Oh, God. Oh, God. Ishmael! Baby. Oh. God."

The wail that followed was inhuman but he made himself go down. In the living room, little Antwon sat unmoving, a gun on the floor near him. Ishmael lay a foot away, still. JaQuan felt his body go cold. He started toward Ishmael but couldn't move.

"Fucking call 911," he heard himself croak. His Aunt Miriam was on the floor now, cradling her son. His other aunt, Naomi, was dialing.

"That yours, 'Quan?" Naomi, call completed, stared hard at him.

"I swear I never used it, I hid it...He couldn't have found it..."

Naomi slapped him hard. "Get out of here, boy!"

"I'll get the gun," he said mechanically.

"Don't touch it!" Joseph appeared, tall and solid, and squatted to hold Miriam and Ishmael's little form. He was Miriam's longtime boyfriend. "They don't find a gun, cops'll be looking through everything. This way they'll see it was an accident. You can say the boys found the gun outside." He looked toward Naomi. "Where's that Sticky?" Joseph asked, referring to Naomi's new boyfriend.

"He ain't here." Naomi was defensive.

"Well, he better stay gone."

Miriam looked up. "Joseph, you go too. Go! Them cops find you here, you know what's gonna happen."

Naomi whipped around and saw JaQuan. "What you still here for, boy? Go!"

JaQuan turned but didn't leave. He ran up the stairs to his room. Locking the door behind him, he dropped to the floor and curled himself up, still cold, too stunned to move.

***

He heard sirens, then the police and paramedics crashing around the front hall. Voices, banging, and scuffling. Orders shouted. More sirens. More voices. Finally, he heard his aunt scream for him and knew he had to move.

JaQuan eased open the window, leaned over toward the porch in back, reached out and caught its railing with his arms, pulled himself out and shimmied down to the tiny dirt and weed backyard behind the building. He'd done it often before. He brushed himself off, adjusted his pants and slipped through the loose plank of the fence. On the other side, he sauntered, cool to the world, looking for his boys. He erased all hints on his face of what he was feeling inside and walked the two blocks to the park. He stopped beneath a tree at the edge and closed his eyes. Then he gave a low call.

"Hoo-Hooooo."

He did it again. This was the call they used to summon each other. When he opened his eyes again, he saw them coming toward the playground and basketball courts. He stepped from behind the tree.

"What up, Q-dog." Jonathan, his lieutenant and best friend, was known as J-Nice. They tapped their closed fists together in greeting. Cool. Giving dap.

"Some weird shit, man. My little cousin, he shot my other little cousin. He's dead."

There was silence for a beat.

"Aw, fuck, Q, you aight?" Jonathan was a few inches shorter than JaQuan, who was already five-foot-ten. He took off his do-rag and ran his hand over his head, then re-tied it.

"I'm straight, man, yeh, I'm straight. It's hard shit though, man, he was a cool little dude."

"Man, ain't no place really safe." J-Nice was stunned. He motioned to three others, who were smoking blunts in the corner of the lot, quietly watching. They came over to Jonathan and JaQuan, and Jonathan filled them in.

"That sucks, man," Cameron, JaQuan's other crew chief, chimed in.

"That really sucks, Q, yeh, man, it does. Really sucks." Matthie Dobson, known as MD, the doc—for his initials and for his ability to score the weed they used to cure all ills, and sold. Snake, the last of the inner circle, gave a nod of his head in agreement.

"You look like shit, Q," he said.

MD broke in again, feeling the emotion. "This is deep, man, this is really bad. What you wanna do, dog?"

"Q, you wanna go down the center, play a little ball, take your mind off? Chill?" J-Nice tried.

"No. Q, what about we go fuck up the MIC boys—they bitches been spreading shit they gonna jump our girls." Snake was short for Snake-eyes, because he always carried a pair of dice. He was the action man.

JaQuan stood listening, hands in his pockets, his right hand caressing the closed 10-inch hunting knife he always carried in there for protection. He felt as if a steamroller had run him over, his neck, his shoulders, his head—it felt like someone had beat him. But he was the captain of his posse, he wouldn't let it show.

"Let's just chill. I don't feel like ballin' right now, man, and I can't go messing anyone up. My little cousin. He gonna be buried, I gotta be straight for that, can't go getting into any new shit."

"That's righteous, man," MD said. "But I know what will help. I got some serious stuff near my crib. Let's hit my stash."

"Q, man," J-Nice finally said, "shouldn't you be with your aunts and cousins now?"

JaQuan flashed on his aunts' home and their last interaction.

"Man, I can't handle it. They be cops all over that place. They trying to figure out where little man got the gun."

"Shit, Q. Man, they'll be lookin' for you, huh."

"Probably, man. I gotta stay on the down-low for a while."

"Word," Cameron said. "Let's bounce."

Chapter Five

Shelley

After talking to the officers in front, Shelley slipped her ID over her head and walked into the apartment building. She knocked, then walked into the living room where the two mothers were sitting. A social worker and an officer were talking to Antwon near his mother and aunt, and Shelley watched as the social worker got grudging permission to talk with him alone in a corner of the room. Antwon hesitated and threw himself into his mother's arms. She said something softly, and he nodded, crying, and walked to the other side of the room.

Shelley listened as detectives interviewed the weeping mother of the dead child—who began to scream and sob—and the weeping mother of the six-year-old shooter, Antwon. Antwon's mother began to wail as well. Shelley felt her heart squeeze—she could only imagine what they were feeling. And she tried not to think about what Antwon would be feeling when a little time had passed. She looked over to the corner, where Antwon sat in shock with the social worker, looking stunned and as if he were about to start crying again.

"We didn't know he had no gun! Ishmael! My Ishmael's done passed," Ishmael's mother screamed. "But I know Antwon didn't mean no harm," she choked out. "Ishmael and Antwon, they like brothers."

"We don't know how he got no gun, Antwon; they's no guns here," Antwon's distraught mother whispered.

Both women were average height, about five-five or -six, and thin. Ishmael's mother wore her hair shoulder length and straightened. It was a dark brown, almost black. Her eyes were deep brown, her face thin, with prominent cheekbones, the color of coffee with a little bit of cream. Her sister, Antwon's mom, was a little fuller in the face and a little darker. She wore her dark hair up, held in place with a large barrette and the ends sticking out. She had a dark red, almost purple streak in her hair that went from her part, over to the right and spurted out of the barrette with the rest of her hair. Her eyes too were a deep brown and she wore long red acrylic nails.

Out the windows, Shelley could see children, the other siblings, cousins and friends, all crying, and adults, mostly women. A few teens and young men were trying to comfort the women and girls, but stood sullenly whenever the officers tried to speak with them. Shelley turned back and made eye contact with the detectives.

"Ma'am and ma'am," Detective Mulroney said, "we're gonna let our PR person talk with you a little bit. She's the one can help tell your story."

The second detective, a woman Shelley hadn't yet met, looked hard at her and said nothing. Shelley moved closer, nodded to the detectives and pulled up a chair to talk with the two grieving women.

"My name is Shelley, Shelley Colabro." Shelley sat down as she spoke and looked each woman in the eye. "I do the press releases for the police department. And I'm the one who makes sure people hear what you want to say, how you want Ishmael remembered, what you want people to know. But first let me say how very sorry I am for your loss." Shelley looked first at Ishmael's mother, then at Antwon's.

"You got children?" Ishmael's mother looked at her.

"No," Shelley said.

Ishmael's mother looked away.

"Meaning no disrespect," Antwon's mother said, "but how you gonna tell our side of the story, what we want people to know, if you're with them." She nodded her head toward the officers at the door.

"I don't work for the police department, I work with them," Shelley said. "I'm an outside consultant and my job is just this."

"And you think they're really gonna print what you say?" Antwon's mother asked.

"That's why they hired me. They don't always get it right."

"Amen to that," said Antwon's mother.

"And what I write," Shelley continued, "goes out to all the press people, so they hear your feelings whether or not they get a chance to talk to you."

Shelley led the women slowly through her questions, pausing to let them add. Naomi Miller was Antwon's mother. She had an edge that softened as she told her story. Ishmael's mother, Miriam, said very little until it came time to talk about Ishmael.

"First thing," Naomi said, "we know folks out there think this is just gang-land where folks of color live, you understand? Well, there are problems, sure, what you expect when people got no jobs, no money. But we just people, trying to live our lives. Sure, there be gang stuff, violence and all, but we got to live with it, too. We just families trying to love our children and make it. You understand that? And Ishmael and Antwon—they was like brothers. They played all the time, they loved each other."

Miriam spoke for the first time, smiling sadly. "They are sweet boys, were, I mean, Ishmael..." She caught herself and breathed deeply. "Let me tell you about Ishmael. He was the one made us all laugh. He loved to tell jokes, he loved to do pranks. He was already reading good in school, his teacher told me, he was a smart boy, could do his letters, add real good. He loved to draw..."

Her sister saw her start to falter and stepped in. "He and Antwon would play together all the time. Sometimes they would be making a pretend movie, sometimes they would be teasing all the girls. They would make people laugh, especially Ishmael. And he and Antwon were close as this." She crossed her fingers.

"What you gotta tell people, miss, is this is a family filled with love. We take care of each other, and these boys...I don't know what my Antwon gonna do without his cousin."

As Naomi said these last words, Miriam started to weep again.

"Lady, if this enough for you, I think we hafta stop talking now," Naomi said. "This too hard for Miriam."

Shelley closed her notebook.

"Thank you both, I know how hard this is for you. I just want people to know what a wonderful boy Ishmael was, and what a wonderful boy Antwon is. Thank you for talking to me."

Shelley shook hands with both women and repeated with real emotion, "I am really so sorry for your loss. I can't even begin to understand what you're both feeling but my prayers will be with you and your families."

As she walked away she heard the whispers behind her.

"Goddamn right, she don't have a clue, white bitch, she think she know? Not a fucking clue."

"Calm down, Naomi, she mean well."

Shelley went back outside and took a deep breath. She couldn't take it personally, she knew that. The women didn't even know her. And they were hurting. She wanted to weep, for Ishmael—what a senseless tragedy. For Antwon—this would never go away for him. For the distrust and rage she heard in Naomi's words behind her back. But she didn't weep. She returned to her car and made some quick edits to her notes. She added some things she had learned, and transcribed her own responses, feelings and descriptions. She would do a further edit when she got back to the office and then sit down with John.

She reviewed what she'd learned from John as well as from the two women. Miriam, Naomi and their children lived in two apartments in this same building. Their front doors faced each other across the first-floor hallway. Both units were duplexes taking up the first two stories, the rent paid by Section 8. One cousin lived in each unit, going back and forth as children do. One room upstairs was another cousin's, JaQuan Miller, son of Naomi and Miriam's other sister. Another room housed two older female siblings. Shelley also knew from the detectives that two boyfriends stayed there, but were not on the lease. She knew she'd see the reports back at headquarters, but then she spotted the Chief's second-in-command, Superintendent Paul Boyle, or Supe, as he was called, standing nearby. She went over to see if he could give her a little more background.

"This family, Shelley, as you know, is one of the fifty families we're tracking for the IP Project. Eighty-five percent of the impact players come from these families, who make up fewer than one percent of all the families living in Roxbury and Dorchester, and they create over ninety-five percent of the street violence and crime out here. Think about it, the IP's are less than one percent of the population in these neighborhoods. But this situation's a little different, the IP stuff isn't an issue here. Even though the Millers are an IP family, this shooting seems to have been just a horrible accident. The issue is where the child got the gun."

Shelley noted the phrase, "these neighborhoods." As in war, she thought, the cops needed a way of distancing, of objectifying: these neighborhoods; these people.

The IP Project had been underway for a year now. Shelley had learned enough about it to understand that it was not normal policing, it was meant to be a more comprehensive approach. Impact players, the theory went, generally came from families that were so messed up, it was no wonder the children made bad choices. These families combined many of the "indicators" that could predict a child's path toward violence—any of the variations of multi-generational joblessness, drug use, prison time, drug dealing, domestic violence, alcoholism, bi-polar and other mental illnesses, lack of education, and a variety of physical diseases. The police would still arrest, but they also worked with agencies to get these families case management and resources.

More press had arrived, including the TV field reporters and anchors, and the cameras were clicking and rolling, waiting for the family to make a response. Uniformed officers held them back behind the line. The sun was bright and more neighbors gathered outside the line. Press members took comments from them. Cars whizzed past in a steady procession—low-riders, tricked-out Hondas, Escalades. They all slowed slightly as they passed. Shelley saw John O'Brien and went over to consult with him about the immediate message. They agreed on a strategy for now—the truth, actually: *One cousin shot the other. The family denies knowledge of any gun. The family is grief-stricken and in shock. We are trying to find out where the gun came from. We'll notify you if the family decides to speak out. Stay behind the crime scene tape, please. There will be a full press conference at 6:30 tonight.*

There was a sudden murmur through the crowd and press around the scene. The Mayor had arrived. Almost immediately, he, the Chief, Supe Boyle and the B2 captain were in conversation with two of the detectives. Then the Mayor detached from the group and walked with the Chief and captain to talk with the family. "Shelley, John, join us please," Boyle said, still standing by the two detectives.

"Supe?" John used Boyle's formal title.

"Detectives, fill them in please."

Detective Mulroney, the older one, did the talking. "The Chief told the lab to put a rush on ballistics and we'll get the results tomorrow. But even without them, it's clear this is an illegal gun. The registration has been filed off. It looks well used. We don't know who it belonged to in the household, but we're not ruling out that it might be a 'community' gun that was stored here."

John cut right to the chase. "Do you know how the gun got here?"

Supe answered him. "There is one boy missing, a fifteen-year-old, JaQuan, who is cousin to the shooter and the victim. From the gang unit, we know he's involved with a group of kids calling themselves 33 Deep. They're relatively new, and young, street gang wannabes who think they own the six blocks around here, though as far as we can tell—again, according to the gang unit—they only sell small amounts of weed and have not been engaged in any gun violence. We're thinking JaQuan might have gotten hold of a gun and hidden it in the building. Or it belongs to one of the boyfriends. If JaQuan hid it, we don't know why and we need to find out. It might be a shared community gun, or his little posse is going in a new direction. If it's a boyfriend, we need to find out who they are and what they're into. We need to find these actors. In the meantime, come up with a strategy for the press, will you? Especially before things start leaking." Supe strode off to join the Commissioner and the Mayor.

Shelley consulted with John, then left the scene to return to head-quarters and create several informational releases, and a draft strategy for briefing the press, depending on what turn events took. She ate a stale sandwich and drank some tea as she worked, sending off a quick email update to her boss. She finished at four o'clock and went over the drafts with John, as well as the list of reporters and editors to brief with key background points. She left the drafts for him to make any further changes before tonight's press conference. She would review her strategy brief again Monday, before their meeting with the Chief. Finally, she called it day and headed out toward Revere, several hours of daylight still ahead. She and Carolyn would watch the news tonight—she had to—maybe then walk the beach or go to dinner. She called Carolyn from the car as she drove.

Chapter Six

Shelley

Shelley was to get a great deal more information to work with. Over the next few days, after more questioning of six-year-old Antwon, this time at headquarters, without his mom, and with a psychologist present, detectives unearthed that he had found the gun hidden in the front hall closet under a gym bag and some shoes. Ballistics revealed that the gun had been used before, though the Chief was being close-mouthed as to what those crimes were. As the Chief predicted, the press got hold of some of this information and the police upped the heat on finding JaQuan. They had interviewed one of the boyfriends as well, and were still looking for the other. It was interesting to watch the play in the press. They tried to straddle the line between the prurient—was the family, especially the missing JaQuan and the boyfriends, but his aunts as well, responsible for the death of this young boy?—and the sympathetic: the family was grieving this horrific loss. The churches, ministers and youth groups in the neighborhood had no such line. They defended the family and JaQuan as additional victims.

"A tragic accident. Two young cousins who lived together, played together, loved each other. This family and young JaQuan Miller are as much victims as the two cousins," Minister Paul Behrendt intoned at the funeral and to the press. "We need to put away the people who bring weapons into our neighborhoods. We adults have to make sure kids like JaQuan feel safe enough they don't need those weapons. And we need to support this family now, as they mourn this tiny life that had been so full of joy, of love, of potential. This tiny life, now gone from us, but safely in the arms of his Lord."

Members of the Peace Initiative arrived to meet with and support the family after the police finished the interrogation, to do their good, but painful, work. They were a group founded by a mother who had lost a son to murder and made up of other women who had lost children to murder. They visited every newly bereaved mother they knew of in order to offer ongoing support, and help with funeral planning as well as the other little things that accompanied these tragedies. They also spoke out, marched, lobbied against gun violence and advocated at the State House and City Hall for more resources to end the violence.

Carolyn and Shelley watched the first news reports at home Sunday night and then again Monday, before Carolyn had to leave. They had managed not to fight for the rest of the weekend, but Carolyn's resentment was clear.

"You resent this job because it means I don't put all my focus on you anymore," Shelley had said to Carolyn, blurting it out in anger.

"That's not true," Carolyn had replied, hurt. "I don't like to see you in this much pain. This job is getting to you, it makes you hurt and it's not even what you really want to do with your life."

They had called a truce then, but Shelley thought—*it's true this is not what I had planned to do, it's not my calling. But it's important right now and I'm good at it.*

It was just as well, Shelley decided, that Carolyn would be gone for the next ten days. She'd be spending most of her time this week at work. Yet it was during cases like this that she needed Carolyn the most. She needed the emotional support, she needed the distraction. Of course, that was probably another reason why Carolyn didn't like her doing this job. When Shelley was working straight corporate PR, she didn't bring it home. They saw friends more, played golf, had season tickets to the theatre. And at home, her attention was completely on Carolyn and her work. This job had shifted the emotional dynamics.

Shelley's attraction to Carolyn, when they met seven years ago, had been immediately and overwhelmingly physical. It had never happened that way before for her. For the first two years that they dated and courted, her own passions and interests were kept in the background. Carolyn fascinated her. She was confident, in control, centered on her work, and passionate about the causes she traveled to photograph. She was renowned for her work and it was a heady combination for Shelley. For the most part, they were complementary in their personalities and Shelley, while having her own successful professional life, made her main function supporting Carolyn in her work, creating special welcomes for her returns, promoting her any way she could. This changed after she took the assignment with the Boston Police Department.

With Carolyn out of the country, Shelley submerged herself in her job—press releases about the Miller case and other potentially sensitive cases as well as working with John to prepare press statements about cold cases, a very public internal affairs issue, and the recurring problem of evidence issues from some old cases.

Four days later, as the first round of intensive press coverage on the shooting of Ishmael Miller diminished, his cousin, JaQuan, was still unaccounted for. His disappearance and the inability of the police to find him, Shelley knew, would make the story a front-page sidebar to every new shooting or murder in the 'hood. If he wasn't found soon, the story would be perfect fodder for an up-and-coming investigative reporter to pitch to his or her editor—why can't the police, in a city as small as Boston, find a fifteen-year-old boy who may have been involved in his cousin's shooting? The Chief certainly didn't need that kind of publicity for the department he was trying to transform.

JaQuan's young cousin had been buried and JaQuan hadn't shown up for the funeral—everyone had been fairly confident that he would, in the background perhaps, disguised, but that he would come. Street-workers, church workers, the gang unit, were everywhere. JaQuan had not been there.

What Shelley didn't yet know was how right she was. The story would continue to pop onto the front page as the police made discoveries—that JaQuan's aunt and mother knew he had brought a gun home, though they claimed they didn't, and they still claimed they didn't know where he kept it; that the new boyfriend, Richard "Sticky" Raines, who had a long police record, had also disappeared. The Department of Social Services investigation into the family would be re-opened. But Shelley was already nursing the thought that as long as the story was going to keep appearing, they should use it proactively to try to goose JaQuan out of hiding. It was a dangerous strategy and she wanted to think it through some more before she presented it.

And Carolyn was certainly right about one thing, Shelley thought. She was feeling the cumulative weight of these shootings and murders. The interviews she did with families of the victims, though useful, filled her with a grief she hadn't expected to feel. She was painfully aware that her role made her a voyeur. She was not helping in any tangible way. She was also aware of the racial disparity. The majority of families she interviewed were people of color and she was a white woman. Ishmael's shooting, so poignant and awful, could be a tipping point for the department and for the neighborhoods if she handled it right. Everyone felt empathy in this one—a seven-year-old boy, an innocent. But it was only a matter of time before the weight of new youth and gun-related homicides finally wiped the Millers and little Ishmael out of memory.

And Carolyn was right about something else, too. Shelley had come to hate how this job made her feel, beyond the grief. Writing about these shootings—a seventeen-year-old Cape Verdean boy, a 71-year-old shopkeeper, the rape and murder of a sixteen-year-old girl, a drive-by injuring two and killing three black teens, the shooting of an eleven-year-old middle school boy—was toxic. The list went on and on, and she knew from listening to friends and acquaintances that compassion, after all these years, had deadened. The response had become: *as long as it's contained in Roxbury and Dorchester...since there's nothing we can do.* And, she realized now, that also meant: *as long as it's "them," not us.* Shelley had really never been conscious of racial issues until this job. If she had missed it before, it was now in front of her every day. Though no one would say this, it was clear to her that there was a demarcation—some people mattered, others didn't. There had to be a way, in this job, that she could help change things. Otherwise, she knew she couldn't take much more. She'd give it another few months and then argue for a new assignment.

***

Saturday morning, with five more days until Carolyn's return, Shelley rose early, ate breakfast and headed over to the Revere Boat Club.

Wedged between a Dunkin' Donuts and a lobster restaurant, the small marina on the Pines River sat across from the commuter railroad and Saugus Ironworks. *Ah yes,* Shelley thought, *the scenic waterfront in Revere.* But secretly she was grateful. There might be no Starbucks, the scenery surrounding the water was early industrial and auto body, but this meant she could afford her house, she could afford a boat slip, and once you rounded the Pines River into the Sound, it was beautiful. Nahant to the left of the channel, the shipping lanes to the left of Nahant and, after you passed Winthrop on your right, a straight shot down to East Boston, Charlestown, the main Boston harbor.

Shelley had grown up in Revere. Her father had bought this house when Revere prices were even lower. Shelley had grown up in the house, one of four children. Her father had sold it to her for a dollar, when he and her mother decided to move to a smaller place. She had been the youngest, the only girl, and unmarried. It was her parents' way of assuring she had some financial stability until she married. Her brothers were all older and already married. They had houses and families of their own.

Shelley had never planned to stay in Revere. That may have been another reason her father gave her the house—he knew it might be the only way to keep her there. She'd had many friends in the neighborhood as a young child. Together they raced up and down their small streets on bikes, combed the beach for shells, flew kites, made bonfires at night in summer. But as she grew older, she knew she was different. She couldn't talk about it, but Revere felt claustrophobic. She didn't fit in, she couldn't be herself, even though she wasn't yet sure what that meant. By the end of high school, she had put a name to it: she was gay. And she didn't know what to do with that in a working class, Italian town. In Revere, you were expected to get married and have children, to work hard and do well economically, but not too well. And you were not expected to be too intelligent or to put on airs—which even meant too much love of art, theatre or literature. Yet those unspoken rules were in complete contrast to how her parents raised her: be open and fair to everyone, the world is yours, you can be anything you want to be.

"Hi, Jerry," Shelley called to one of her neighbors, who was out early washing down his boat.

"Hey, Shel, how's it shaking?"

"Good, Jerry. You?"

"I'm good. You taking her out?"

"Yep."

"Not too many days left. Enjoy it!"

Shelley waved and got to work uncovering the old lobster boat her father had refurbished. She inherited it after her parents died, and the time cleaning, polishing, and maintaining it, as well as the occasional boating parties and her own solitary cruises, was one of the ways she kept their memories alive and herself sane. She was glad Jerry was busy and couldn't wander over. He always asked her if she was still working down in that dangerous city—"Worse than some parts of Revere, you know, now that Revere has changed." He would laugh. She would ignore him and make small talk, or soon he'd be talking about those black neighborhoods. "Are those negros still killing those negros?" he'd say. It was a side of Jerry she'd never seen until she started this assignment.

She swabbed the boat down, checked the levels, warmed the motor, and when all was ready, released the ties and slowly backed her out. She pushed the throttle to forward and gunned the motor enough to clear the marina, then opened her up and headed for some open sea.

Chapter Seven

Monique

It was another balmy, end-of-summer September day in the South End as Monique Sanders tried to wake up. The air outside her window felt soft, the sky was clear and blue. The brick of the townhouses surrounding her building shone deep red in the sparkling air, and it felt like it would be another 70-degree day. School began at 7:30 a.m. so she had a half hour to shower and have breakfast, and 45 minutes to get dressed and make sure her hair was right. She would stop on the way to school for a snack and coffee, since her mother still didn't let her drink it at home.

Monique was a high school sophomore—five feet, three inches, lithe and athletic, almost always smiling, yet with a dry and quick sense of humor. She was bright, curious and an honor student at Boston Latin. The trials of high school dating were just beginning to affect her and with her parents' hardline stance, it all felt awkward and difficult. Her dad was from Trinidad, her mom born in Boston—in a block of rowhouses in lower Roxbury not so far from their home now in the South End. They were adamant that she was too young to be dating, so all her dates had to be at her home and chaperoned. Needless to say, she hadn't had many formal dates. Her mom was always reminding her to be careful.

Her mom and dad were always telling her stories about the old South End. It was a very different place now, they said. To be honest, that old South End sounded like a place Monique sometimes wished she had grown up in. Neighbors looked out for each other and they partied a lot more—block parties, jazz clubs, old-fashioned barbecues. She was thinking of that as she walked down Tremont Street.

"Hey, Monique." The voice came from an alley to her right. She stopped.

"JaQuan—is that you? You are in so much trouble! What are you doing around here?"

"Yo, Monique. Get over here. Hey girl, you gotta keep quiet now, all right. You can't let anyone know you've seen me."

"Q—you know me. I ain't gonna tell a soul! You couldn't even go to your cousin's funeral. You can't keep just hiding, you know—you're not going to have a life."

"Shit, girl, I don't have a life now. You got time to go get some food with me?"

"Naw, Q, I've got to get to school." Monique shifted her backpack as she looked at him. He looked as handsome as ever, his clothes freshly washed. But he looked tired.

"Monique, you know you never miss a day—you know how you are. Do this just this once for me, huh? Come on, I need to talk to you. You know I'd never ask you if I didn't need your help."

"I can't, Q. I would, you know, but I really can't. Not right now." She sounded to her own ears like her mother. "You want me to get you something to eat from the store down the street? I can do that."

"Naw, I can get something where I'm staying." He looked her in the eyes. "I just wanted to talk to someone really smart I can trust."

"You know you're really smart, Q—and I am sorry, but I can't be late. I'll meet you later—after school if you want."

"I don't know if I'll even be around later, girl, I'm thinking I gotta go stay with friends in Springfield maybe, or Providence."

"You got friends there?"

"I got friends who got friends."

"JaQuan—you got depth, you're smart; you got something, you know? Why do you do this stuff?"

"What else I'm gonna do, Monique. Come on—you know I don't really do school anymore and now, man, cause I'm down with the Deep, fuckin' cops aren't gonna listen to me, give me any kind a chance. You know it too. Shit—there some cops...come on, Monique—give me some cover."

"I gotta go now, JaQuan. I'll stand, you take off, they won't see you. Call me, ok?"

"I'm out. Thanks, Monique." JaQuan melted back into the alley. Monique stood adjusting her book bag as the police cruiser rolled by. She stepped into the roti shop on the corner to get a savory and coffee. She tucked the meat pie into her bag and drank the coffee, with three sugars and cream, as she walked. The day felt like anything was possible. She wished JaQuan could know that feeling. He used to know it, they all did way back. A beautiful September day—it was still summer, the air was warm, but if you paid attention the smell of fall was in the air. The sky was the kind of deep blue she could swim in. The new school year had just begun. Monique rounded the corner from Tremont onto Mass Avenue and headed to the Mass Ave. MBTA stop. She'd catch the outbound to Ruggles, then grab the Number 8 bus to Avenue Louis Pasteur, where Latin sat, hemmed in by three colleges—Simmons, Emmanuel and MassArt—as well as the Museum of Fine Arts, Gardner Museum, and the hospitals of the Longwood Medical Area.

She had known JaQuan Miller since grade school, when they both went to Hernandez Elementary on East Concord Street. They had played together and been in the same class. They had done art classes at the Harriet Tubman House, and summer camp together.

She didn't know him anymore—he was known as Q now. He scared her a little. Not him, actually. JaQuan was always sweet and thoughtful to her. He was very sensitive and cared about people he loved, and cared about animals. And he could be funny. But now, she was scared of what was around him, and how he acted sometimes with his boys. He had put himself in a place where he couldn't control what might happen to him, or to anyone around him. He hardly ever went to school—he said it was too dangerous—and she knew he often hadn't had a place to sleep till he had moved in with his aunts. She knew he would say his boys were just for protection, and they needed him. He would say as a young black man he had no control anyway, whether he ran with a posse or not.

But she felt guilty, too, for the way she'd acted just now. She should have stopped to talk to him. She knew JaQuan, he had to be torn up about his cousin. He needed someone to talk to, but she wasn't ready. She looked back, but JaQuan was gone. He was in deep trouble, she'd seen the papers. Everything had changed when he left the South End.

"Hey, girl!" Lakeisha and Kimberly fell in beside her.

"You have to be dreamin' 'bout some boy, you walk right by us like that!" Lakeisha laughed and gave her a playful poke to the arm. Kimberly laughed with her.

"Well, if I am, you ain't never gonna know, are you!" Monique responded. The three of them reached the T stop and pulled out their bus passes. They dodged the early rush of commuters and headed into the subway stop. The school day had begun.

***

JaQuan had watched Monique leave with a deep feeling of sadness. He'd been feeling that a lot lately, a lot more than he usually did. It had been over a week since he'd seen any of his boys, or his family, and he'd missed his cousin's funeral. He couldn't risk it. She was right. The way he was going, he wasn't going to have any life left. At least not any of the life he used to know. And he was numb, all the time. He couldn't let himself even think about Ishmael, or Antwon. He felt empty, but he couldn't show it. He was just moving, doing what he needed to do to stay out of jail. He had no life right now: no friends, no girls.

He knew that's how most guys got picked up, by going back to hang around with their boys. JaQuan hadn't meant to let his life become what it had. But what choice did he have? It was easy when you were young. When he and Monique had been in pre-school and school together, it was fun. You played, you set up pranks on the girls. Life seemed easier—even though it was hard when he was at home with his moms.

Eventually, he had ended up completely with his grandmother, and though she was very stern, he felt safe with her and protected. There was always good food and she didn't have boyfriends around all the time like his mother had, boyfriends who took advantage of her and then dared to talk to him as if they were his father. But when you got older...well, no one could protect you from what was on the streets, and you had to use the streets. Then, too, when you got older, the street life got into the schools. It seemed like, if you were lucky, life could only be fun when you were young. He could still remember times from his childhood so clearly. He had felt safe and happy back then.

Chapter Eight

JaQuan

1⁹⁹⁵

Jakey (which is what JaQuan's friends called him) loved the mornings—even in winter—though especially in summer and fall. He was in third grade.

"Jake! Breakfast! Come on down!" Grandmoms called the same thing every morning, but JaQuan never woke easily and her second call, always the same, always came within ten minutes. "Rise and shine, my little love! It's a beautiful day!" And if he still took his time, he heard, "Last call, boy, or I'm taking it all over to Mr. Horsley at the market!"

Grandmoms always woke him to a big breakfast. Sometimes it was grits, sometimes her own special hotcakes—big as a plate—or French toast, with bacon and eggs. It was different every morning but always hot, always plenty, and they ate it together. Grandmoms always had a cup of hot coffee and when he was halfway through his breakfast she would start the conversation, partly to slow him down. This was their talk-time, in the morning. She'd ask some questions: How was school? What was he excited about doing today? How did he like his teachers? What was he going to do with his friends? Then mostly she would listen.

"How you feeling today, Jake?" she asked as she poured him some orange juice. The sun poured in through the large grated windows. The skillet was heating on the stove and Anna Mae Miller opened the back door and put down a small bowl of milk for the stray cat that roamed the neighborhood. "Mm-hm. That sun feels good today. How about hotcakes this morning!"

Jake was smiling. Hotcakes were his favorite, but with the pitcher of batter ready on the counter and the way Grandmoms was heating that skillet, he'd already known that's what it was gonna be.

"What are you doing at school today?" she asked him as she poured batter into the pan.

"We got a quiz in arithmetic today." Jake watched her flip the hotcakes in the skillet. "We're doing painting today in art class. Mr. Crite from down the street is coming in to teach us. Then we're doing a spelling bee."

Anna Mae set a pancake on his plate and poured another one. She watched him as he talked and her heart filled every time she saw his energy and excitement. She had wanted that so badly for her girls. The timing just hadn't been right. And she'd been part of the problem. Those had been her drinking days. She was determined that JaQuan would not get caught up into that world of drugs, alcohol and giv-ing-up that had taken her girls.

"You know," she said, "Mr. Crite has his paintings on exhibit this weekend up at the Harriet Tubman House. Why don't we go Saturday to see them and then we can walk down to Charlie's Diner for lunch. Would you like that?"

"Oh yeah, 'Moms, that'd be great." JaQuan ate happily as his grandmother bustled about in the kitchen and then poured her coffee to sit with him at the table. Their house was a traditional South End brownstone with the kitchen and dining area in the basement, opening out the back door onto a small fenced-in yard with a flagstone patio and tiny herb and flower garden. The first floor was the parlor floor, the second floor were the bedrooms. Anna Mae rented out the third and fourth floors to good quiet people. That allowed her to keep up on the taxes, oil and repairs.

Grandmoms had taken him to the Museum of Fine Arts, she had taken him to the Gardner Museum, and she had taken him to Chinatown for real Chinese food. Every time, she got dressed up, and held his hand as they got on the subway or the bus. She could be strict, but she also was fun and he knew she loved him.

Grandmoms was stern, that was how she said it, only when she had to be. She said, "My rules, young man, are to keep you safe and to teach you to be respectful to older folks." She was always there for him, he never felt lonely with her. She would walk him to school when the weather was good or have one of his friends' younger parents pick him up, if it was snowing or too cold for her to go out. She always made him lunch and had a hot snack waiting when he got home.

He had a lot of friends. He had known Monique, Colin and Kenny the longest, but there were also Jimmy, Charles, Sharon, Boo, Rachel and Joey. They were his closest friends, his crew. Joey was his best friend of the boys. Monique, of the girls.

And school, he loved school. It was a warm and wonderful place to be—they were always learning new things. The school was close to the Harriet Tubman House's Art Center. His class went there a lot. They drew and painted and made sculptures and were taught all this by real artists. His grandmoms talked about it all the time.

"One-two-THREE; come out Ja-KEY!" A chorus of children's voices came through the window into the parlor where he was doing his homework of letters and arithmetic.

"'Moms—can I go play? PLEASE!" JaQuan pleaded.

"Let me take a look at that homework, little Jake." She ruffled his head. "Mm-hmm. Those sentences look pretty good to me. Let me see your sums."

Grandmoms picked up the papers and looked closely at his work.

"This is very good work, young man. You go ahead and play with your friends, but I want you home for supper, you hear? It's a school night. And you know you have to stay on these two blocks."

"Yes, 'Moms, I know. Thanks." He gave her a solemn eight-year-old's hug, then ran upstairs to get his sneakers and jacket.

"HI-HO-JAKEY!" came the childish yells under his window.

In his bedroom, JaQuan stopped tying his sneakers and threw open the window. "I'm coming!" he yelled. He slammed the window shut, finished tying his shoes, and ran down the stairs and out the front door.

The neighborhood JaQuan lived in was a great one—full of things to do, full of friends. His grandmother lived on West Concord Street in a brownstone that her father, a railroad conductor, had bought for $2,000 a long, long time ago and that was now worth a lot—and her grown children, including JaQuan's moms, were always after her to sell it. When her friends came to visit, it was one of the things the adults always talked about—how the neighborhood had changed and how all these lovely old brownstones were going to speculators for ridiculous prices but how the old folks and the black folk were being cheated. According to Grandmoms, a lot of her old friends were gone because they had sold their homes, way too cheaply and then couldn't find another place to live in the neighborhood. But quite a few had to sell because the banks wouldn't lend money to help black folks keep their houses fixed and warm, and they were kind people—they couldn't believe the sincere young man who talked them into selling would have cheated them so badly. Some of those who had bought their homes for $2,000 or $3,000 like Grandmoms' dad were offered fifty or sixty thousand dollars and thought they had done well, but these developers then turned around and sold the very same building, with no repairs, for $300,000. And as speculators drove rents and prices up, Grandmoms' old friends who sold could not afford to stay.

But though she was grieved over the changes, Grandmoms always made new friends. She was, he had heard her friends say, very civic-minded, and when she felt well enough, she volunteered at the settlement house, played bingo, had coffee with friends and talked politics. She was a member of the 400 Club over on Mass Ave.—a service club of other educated and civic-minded black women—and was proud of that. And Jakey felt safe with her ever since his own moms had gotten sick and he'd gone to live with Grandmoms.

"Let's go to Sparrow Park," Colin said, "I've got the kickball."

***

Tonight it was Colin, JaQuan, Jimmy, Boo, Joey, Sharon, Kenny and Monique. Enough for a good game. They were the lords of their territory. The South End was a great place for them. Even though, as Grandmoms had told him, regular folk could hardly afford to live there anymore, most neighbors were civic-minded like Grandmoms and watched out for one another and the kids. The Harriet Tubman House had two buildings, one on the corner of Mass Ave. and Columbus Ave., two blocks from West Concord, and the other over near his school, on Rutland Street, where they had the Art Center. There were parks, like Sparrow on West Newton and the tennis courts down by Dartmouth. And where Grandmoms said there used to be railroad tracks separating the colored folk and the poor whites of the South End from the la-di-da's of the Back Bay and Beacon Hill, now there was a long park of grass and bike paths that stretched from Dartmouth Street to Mass Ave. Of course, now there were la-di-da's in the South End too. That, said Grandmoms, was both good and bad. So, JaQuan and his friends all knew where they could go and where they couldn't. They weren't allowed down near the Copley Mall or over on Mass Ave. or by the hospital on Albany Street or down by the A&P. All those places could be dangerous—there were young gangs now, like the Hornets. And always they had to be careful crossing streets. Cars raced down Columbus, Tremont and Washington like they were trying out for the Indy 500, that's how Jimmy's mother described it.

"Let's buck up for who goes first," Colin said. The teams were always the same: Colin, Jimmy, Sharon and Kenny; JaQuan, Monique, Joey and Boo. If Charles and Rachel had come, they would have had to buck up for sides too, to be fair, since neither of them were regulars. Colin and Jimmy were best friends. Sharon and Kenny liked each other and had kissed once already. JaQuan liked Monique, but Monique was independent, she said. Joey was his best white friend. Grandmoms said one of the best things about the South End was that people respected one another and could be friends whether they were black, white, Spanish or anything else. There were Greeks, Syrians, Lebanese, French, Italian, English, Irish, Puerto Ricans, Dominicans, northern blacks and some Southern blacks in the South End. There were artists and musicians too, though it was harder for everyone to stay because now there were people who were just rich, gentrifying the whole neighborhood, which meant making it too expensive for regular folk.

But, Grandmoms would say, *there's always good and bad.* Things were more expensive now and you didn't know all your neighbors (*those rich young professionals*, she said, *just work all the time and don't really care to know people*) but, then again, the streets used to be full of no-account drunks who never worked. *There's always something.*

JaQuan's team won the buck-up and went first. Colin rolled the ball to JaQuan. Colin always pitched, Kenny took first base, Jimmy took third and Sharon played second. Jakey was the fastest runner of them all, and he loved to run. He had a good kick too, and when he was up, chances were he'd get at least to third. Jakey got a good kick off the first roll and made it to second. Jimmy was fast and stopped it just past third, then ran toward second ready to throw. JaQuan had stopped there. Monique was up next.

"'Nique! You can do it! Hit me home!" JaQuan screamed his encouragement, happy to be out in the soft September dusk, confident because Monique was almost as fast a runner as he was and loved it every bit as much. Monique kicked foul her first try. Her next kick was hard toward first. She flew toward the base, but Colin hit her with his throw. JaQuan made it to third.

Boo came up next. Boo was the mysterious friend. He was a quiet dark-skinned child whose smile was so beautiful it completely changed his face. All the kids liked him, but no one had ever been to his house. He was tall for his age, agile and graceful, but his eyes were slightly crossed and he was not always accurate in his throwing. He had power and speed, and when he caught the kick just right, the ball would be gone. Colin rolled him two balls he didn't like, but Boo caught the next roll perfectly and the ball spiraled into the sky toward shortstop, then lifted over their heads to the outfield. JaQuan was home in a flash and

Boo's long-legged lope brought him in before Jimmy had even reached the ball. In a screech of car tires and a blast of horns on West Newton Street, the game was forgotten and all of them raced across the park.

"You god-damn kids, watch where you're kicking that ball! I could have been killed!" A short white man in a dark suit had gotten out of his car, which was skewed slightly sideways and stopped in the middle of West Newton Street. He was yelling at Jimmy as they ran up. The man had the ball in his hand.

"Don't your parents teach you anything—safety, manners? Brats! Were you all born in a barn?"

JaQuan stepped forward. Boo, the kicker, quietly disappeared.

"We're sorry, mister," JaQuan said. "He just got a good kick. We didn't mean for it to go all this way."

The man stared at him. "Then you have to be careful. You're lucky I didn't hit one of these parked cars. I would have sued your families for medical bills and damages, you got that? The man walked toward them as he spoke. He was about five foot seven, with dark hair cut extremely short. He wore a dark suit and a tie and his face was red and angry.

"And see this ball?" He put it down on the ground, held it with his foot and took a penknife out of his pocket. "We'll make sure it does no more damage."

With that he reached down and jabbed the ball, then stomped on it repeatedly until it was flat. He flung it back at the children.

"It's getting dark. It figures in this neighborhood, you're all just running around, no supervision, no common sense, no respect, parents who don't teach you anything. No fathers, right? Drug-addict moms. Well, I don't give a shit. Get out of my face, go home. I don't want to see you around here again."

Behind the man, on the other side of the street, Boo signaled them frantically to run. Then he disappeared. At the same time, Jimmy and JaQuan noticed that the man's car was listing to the right. Cars were starting to back up behind him, horns beeping. The man gave them the finger.

JaQuan whispered, "Let's get out of here." Like one they took off, running fast, in different directions. As they disappeared from view, they heard the angry man in the distance. "You goddamn fucking kids. Who cut my tires? I'll get you for this. Come back here! I want your names!"

They re-grouped near JaQuan's.

"Can you believe that man?" Colin said.

"Man, he was mean," Monique said.

"Hey, but Boo almost got us in real trouble," Sharon said.

"Boo shouldn't have done it, but that man deserved it," said JaQuan.

"Do you think he'll really tell our folks?" Sharon asked.

"Come on, he doesn't know who we are or where we live," Jimmy said.

"I have to go in for supper anyway," JaQuan said. "See you tomorrow, and no one tells on Boo, right?"

"It's not right he has a knife," Sharon said.

"Come on, Sharon, we swore, remember? We're all blood friends forever. No telling," Joey said.

"Yeah, Sharon. Joey's right. Swear?" JaQuan said.

Sharon hesitated, then they all put their hands together in the circle. "Blood!" they yelled, then dispersed quietly toward their homes.

Chapter Nine

JaQuan

2 ^{002} JaQuan shook his head as if to shake away the memory. Things had changed so much since he was eight. Maybe if he'd been able to stay with Grandmoms... But even if he had, when you got older...well, no one could protect you from what was on the streets, and you had to use the streets.

The first time he got jumped, he was twelve. He and his friend had gone to watch a baseball game near the Lenox project. They were challenged by some boys there. Were they representing, reppin', Cathedral? JaQuan and his friends said no, they were just here to watch the game. They weren't even from Cathedral, but it would have sounded weak to say so. The Lenox boys promised to jump them anyway, on their way home when the game was over.

Q and his friends knew instinctively if they backed down, they'd be in trouble, so they put on hard faces, stayed at the game, and on the way home jumped the Lenox boys first. The tension and fear of not knowing when they'd be jumped had built throughout the game and kept Q and his friends agitated and nervous. So they made the first move and started the fight. From then on, there was a beef. Would the Lenox boys really have jumped them? Or had they just been posturing? Because they'd jumped the Lenox boys first, Q and his friends would never know. They just knew Lenox was their enemy now.

JaQuan circled through several alleys and came back out onto Tremont Street near the roti shop Monique had gone into. It was run by an old West Indian couple. The cops were gone, so he went in.

"How are you doin' this beautiful day!" the old woman asked him as he decided what he wanted.

"I'm doing OK." JaQuan smiled at her and nodded to her husband, who sat reading the papers in the corner of the shop.

"You must be runnin' late for school, I'm tinkin'. Tall, handsome boy like you should be in school, you know. Make a good future for you. Make your mama proud. What can I be gettin' for you?"

JaQuan bought four meat pies and a soda. He wolfed down two pies on the spot and wrapped the other two in the bag to take with him. Monique and her family had introduced him to these. And he had some Spanish friends—Puerto Rican—who had their own version of meat pies. *Pasteles*, he remembered. His people didn't have meat pies, they had fried chicken, gravy, greens, biscuits, mac and cheese. He had met Miguel and his friend Pedro while hanging out with some friends of his cousin in Mission Hill. Now he couldn't go to Mission Hill or, if he did, he had to call Tyrone and be sure he got an escort. Mission had a beef with the Deep that started a couple of years ago over who was dating some girl. Mission also had beefs with the Egleston boys, and the new Dorchester gangs—the H-Block—named for the seven streets (all beginning with H) in their area. Mission pretty much picked beefs everywhere—they used to even have beefs with each other, but the blacks and Spanish there, at least some of them, had learned to get along—it made it safer.

But where JaQuan was living now, with his aunts, blacks didn't mix with the Spanish. You stuck with your own. Who were your own, though? In school, when he'd been going, you mixed with everyone, you had to, and sort of got along. But outside of school, in the 'hood, the Haitians didn't mix with Cape Verdeans, Dominicans stayed away from the 'Ricans, everyone beat on the Somalis. Some of the schools were bad, too. He'd been at South Boston for a while, and at Dorchester High. And he had friends who went to Charlestown High—forget that. In Charlestown they had to have a police presence every day when school let out. Wherever you were in this city, you could get jumped on your way to and from school, and if you weren't careful you could take a beating inside if you stepped into someone else's territory. There were plenty of spots the teachers couldn't see.

The teachers didn't get it at all—or if they did, they had no way to stop it. And it was the same on the streets. Adults tried, some of them actually cared, his grandmoms, his moms and aunts when they weren't all stressed out, some of the teachers, even some of the white and Spanish ones. But no matter what they said, once you were out of their sight, you were no longer safe. Adults gave you rules, but in return you got no safety, no money, no learning you could actually use. Once you were out of elementary school, you got nothing except maybe a meal and a place to sleep.

Here in the South End, he had to be careful, too. He had no beef with Villa or the Hornets, but he did have a beef still with Lenox, and the Hornets were down with Lenox. The Villa boys were just paranoid. Black or Spanish, you had to be careful with them if they didn't know you.

It was crazy, but it was just the way it was, and if you didn't have your own posse to run with, you had no protection. You weren't safe anywhere.

JaQuan had worked his way back down West Concord, past Methunion Manor, the church-built housing project, and over to West Newton Street. He would cross St. Botolph Street and come out at the back of the Prudential Center. He thought he was pretty safe walking through there. Then he would hole up in the Copley Square main branch of the public library until dark. He had come to like the library. His 7th grade class had gone on a school field trip there years ago. Everyone else thought it was boring, but JaQuan liked knowing there was a big public place that he could go to for free, listen to music, read magazines, look up stuff if he needed to, and not have to go home—he was back living with his mother then. If he got bored, there were some fancy liberal churches all around the library where he could sit, or hear jazz—he was getting to like jazz—or have some food when the concerts were over. No police would expect him to be in these places and there were just enough black folk that he didn't stick out. The gangs he had beefs with rarely came here, they mostly stayed at the Copley Place Mall or the Galleria Mall in Cambridge. It was so much better roaming here than being home.

Of course, he couldn't go home now anyway. The cops were watching his crib and were watching his boys. He had talked to Cameron and J-Nice once each. But he mainly kept his phone turned off. For one, he didn't have many minutes left and, for another, from all the television shows like *CSI*, *Law and Order*, and *Without a Trace*, he was afraid that they might really be able to track him through his cell. Triangulating, it was called.

At the library, he met nice girls, though mostly they were white. Talking to them and helping them with homework, pretending he had homework, it kept him occupied so he didn't think about Ishmael. He could flirt and talk, and for now that was enough. He didn't want to risk one of their parents recognizing him. He missed his girl, Sharena. Before Sharena, JaQuan had been seeing a Spanish girl, Bianca, who was down with a hip-hop afterschool group. She was fine. But the Deep girls, and his boys, had been on him big time: why wasn't Q down with one of them and why didn't he stay with his own kind—what was wrong with black girls? He had told them, they were too fine, and if he picked one of them the others would be jealous. His job was to protect them, not go out with them. And, he said, they had to stop being prejudiced. Still, he quit seeing Bianca and hooked up with Sharena. She wasn't with the Deep, but she was a homegirl. He missed Bianca a lot, he missed Sharena, too. But he couldn't risk calling either of them.

JaQuan had done some research the first day he was at the library and had found other places he could get into free on certain days and times—art museums, science museums, even the aquarium with a little bit of work. He didn't have a plan, but he knew he had to stay hidden till he did, or until something changed.

He'd had time to think during these hours alone, and realized he didn't want to be a street player. It had just happened. But he didn't know what else to do. He was a wanted man now. He wouldn't tell 5-0 anything about how or where he got the gun. He wouldn't give up his boys. They would arrest him and he would go to prison. It would be like the streets but with no place to go to escape. His friends, and the OG's they knew, pretended it was cool to go to prison—you were tough if you survived. The OG's—Original Gangsters was what it meant, but JaQuan realized that now it should mean Older Guys, because they all were—the older guys who'd been, and come out, talked about prison as: *Yeh, it was tough, but it makes you tougher.* A lot of people admired them 'cause they had made it through and came out tougher and with new tricks.

And you had to come out tougher—'cause while you were in, someone took your girls, your corner and your business. Everyone knew prison was inevitable for a young black man in his neighborhood and you were cool when you got out because you had taken what the Man threw at you, and you were still alive. A person had to really trust someone to let them know how bad prison was. It wasn't cool to talk about how scared and lonely and bored you were in there.

JaQuan finished his meat pies as he walked down Boylston Street. He would call Monique. She couldn't talk to him this morning but she liked the library, too. She would come here to meet him. Or maybe she wouldn't. They weren't as close nowadays as they had been growing up. And she shouldn't bring her friends with her, but she might, then everyone would know one of his hiding places. He could maybe ask one of the girls he met at the BPL to have dinner with him at Uno's or Fridays, but he knew he had to be careful there, too. His picture had been in all the papers. Plus, he was stealing money anytime he could—from backpacks, wallets, purses—in the library. Little bits of cash at a time so no one would really notice, or if they did, they'd think it was the homeless guys who hung out there. He didn't like doing it, it felt low, but he couldn't move product anymore and he needed something to live on. He had to contribute. He wished he could sleep at the library, but that wasn't possible.

Chapter Ten

JaQuan

"You got something to contribute to the crib, little man? It don't have to be money, you can help out." His host smiled. Emilio was an OG, retired. He was thirty-two, had spent a decade of those years in prison and was trying hard to figure out how not to go back and yet make a living. He wasn't a bad man, JaQuan thought. He had a good heart and let young people crash at his place whenever they needed to. You had to bring your own food sometimes and you had to help out with trash and stuff. But you had a place to sleep.

"Look, man," JaQuan's cousin Tyrone from Mission Hill had told him. "It's getting too hot for you here." JaQuan was crashing at Tyrone's moms' place then. It was tricky cause Tyrone's moms might be evicted if management found out. And it was tight because of Tyrone's little sisters. One day, JaQuan had had to hide in the closet when local officers came around. They had a warrant for him, but not a warrant to search, so JaQuan had covered himself with extra blankets and squashed at the rear of a closet stuffed with clothes and shoes and hardly dared to breathe. The officers sat at the kitchen table for the longest time asking questions. After that, Tyrone had gotten another friend in Mission to put JaQuan up for a few days, then another.

No one would give him up, even if they had a beef with him, no one did that. They would take care of you themselves. But Tyrone had interceded for him, and he had sympathy, having lost his young cousin and still being blamed for it by the cops. After a bit, though, even friends wanted some payment to cover the risks. Tyrone had made all kinds of friends and acquaintances in Mission over the years. Some black, some Haitian, some Spanish. He introduced JaQuan to Emilio, who was Spanish, from Mission, but living in a tiny basement in Charlestown. They figured that was far enough to throw the cops off the scent.

Vivianna yelled out to all of them, squashed into Emilio's tiny living room watching television and smoking the weed JaQuan had managed to contribute. "All right, you assholes, come and get it. And I ain't cleaning up, either."

Vivianna came into the living room holding a plate heaped with rice and beans, chicken, and mac and cheese. She was the only girl staying there right now. Four boys, including JaQuan, and Emilio filed into the tiny kitchen to fill their plates.

"*Mi casa*, show a little respect." Emilio pushed by them all to the front of the line, loaded up his plate and grabbed a beer out of the fridge. "No beer for y'all, you're too young, you get soda."

It was Emilio who had friends in Providence. Unless he could think of something else, JaQuan would be in a strange town with a lot of Spanish and black folks he didn't know, living in places filled with the smoke of blunts and cigarettes; filled with drinking and partying, but drinking and partying that he didn't control and wasn't a part of. And JaQuan wasn't much of a drinker, smoker or party-goer. Maybe it was the memory of his moms being stoned on crack for half of his young life; the arguments she had with her boyfriends and his aunts when she was drinking. But he was not a party sort of guy. At least at his aunts', he'd had his own room and a way out of it. He could have quiet when he wanted it and could leave when he needed to.

After dinner, he, Hector and Ricardo got to do the dishes and put the food away. Luis got to take the trash out to the dumpster down the street. Emilio was strict on food and clean-up.

"Man," he would say, "I don't be havin' money to throw away on this shit and you all don't bring in that much. We need to be careful with the food, and I don't want to be seeing no cockroaches around here."

He was strict about school, too. After supper he would always ask who had homework and make them sit down and do it. And if he woke up early enough, he'd take anyone who needed a ride to school. While they sat down with homework, or cards, or a pad to draw in, Emilio would shower and change in his small bedroom and take off for the night.

"I'll be back in a couple of hours," he'd say. "Finish your homework. If you go out, lock up, and I don't want anyone out after midnight." He ran a tight ship. Smelling strongly of his aftershave, Emilio would head out, trusting them to keep his crib clean and in order if they wanted a place to stay. Sometimes he'd return by eleven and start a card game with any of them who were there, and often, even though they had to go to school, they didn't finish playing till two or three in the morning. Sometimes he wouldn't get in himself till three or four in the morning and smelled strongly of booze. But if you had girl troubles, or home troubles, or just something bothering you, he'd be there to listen and offer any advice he had. Emilio was a good guy.

JaQuan rolled up in his blanket with a small pillow and tried to sleep, but the nights were hard. That was when he would see it all again. Ishmael on the floor, bleeding. Antwon. The gun. He pushed it out of his head every time. He had to survive. He had to keep busy.

He still hadn't come up with a plan for himself, and if he didn't get one soon, he'd be down in Rhode Island. And if he went to Rhode Island, he'd be in the game, there'd be no getting out. But tomorrow was the first day of his new job with Emilio. That might keep him here long enough to figure something out. JaQuan wasn't contributing enough to the kitty, Emilio had said. If he wanted to bunk down longer, he'd have to help bring in more. But Emilio wanted him to study, even if he couldn't go to school. A contact had gotten him some old GED books and he had started JaQuan studying them. This would only be a couple days a week, Emilio said. Since Q wasn't in school right now anyway, he could spend a couple of days earning, then a couple of days learning.

"This is easy work, man, but you gotta be good at it, or it's my ass...you understand? You're gonna be my main lookout. But there's some game to it, man, if you don't want 5-0 to spot you.

"I don't want you getting in this business, you understand, I'm getting out. But sometimes when you just need to make some fast cash, this works. You understand me?" Emilio finished up. He ran a small heroin business in Charlestown. Heroin was cheap now and it was the drug of choice in the Town. It seemed to Q that everybody used it—Spanish, black but especially those white townies: kids, parents, grandparents. He'd never seen anything like it, even back in the 'hood.

JaQuan understood what Emilio was asking him to do, and he was nervous. Heroin was big time. As far as he was concerned, he had never done anything they could arrest him for, though it was clear after Ishmael passed that cops would arrest you for anything. He and his boys moved a little weed to some regular customers a couple times a week, but that was nothing. He had runners and look-outs too, he knew the gig. But they never touched heroin, or crack. You had to have some kind of income, but weed was like beer, harmless, and it relaxed people. They carried knives, but that wasn't against the law, and you needed some kind of protection. They didn't carry guns, JaQuan drew a line there. The gun that Antwon and Ishmael had found, well, he thought he'd been doing something good, hiding it.

And if they fought with other blocks, well, that was self-defense. You weren't tough, you got crushed. The cops would never get it, Q and his crew weren't bad, they were just trying to survive. The cops didn't see it and they didn't care. You were a ghetto kid, you were bad, simple as that. Even if you did something good, it was just an accident, they thought. They didn't even begin to understand. Emilio understood, he had lived it; he got it.

"Q, man, nobody understands your life but you and your boys, you know. You can't expect it. The cops, the government, even your moms and family, they don't really get it. You're male, you black, boy, you know?" Emilio laughed, talking street. "We 'Ricans are black, too. You know that? We're a mix. The Dominicans, too. On the islands they had the Tainos, Indians, man; the blacks from Africa who escaped being slaves, and those Spanish warriors. So you look at me: I'm black, I'm white, I'm Indio, you know.

"But those cops, they're all white and all male—even the blacks and the women, man—they're all blue, all the same. If they look black or Spanish or female, don't let it fool you. They hearts is white. So they going to be lookin' to bust you up for anything. And your family, man, they love you and all, but they don't know what it's like to be on that street not knowin' if you gonna get jumped by the Man, by the niggas down the block, by someone thinks you made eyes at their girl...so 5-0, he thinks he gotta keep you runnin' and keep you in line, and these ignorant niggas from down the next block, they want to jump you before you wise up and get them... You gotta have your boys, man, and you got to have protection...just to drink your coffee in peace."

"Yo, 'Milio, I hear you, man. But you livin' by yourself, you ain't got no posse, you ain't got..." JaQuan answered, talking street too.

"With all respect, little man," Emilio interrupted, "you don't know what I got. I know everyone in this 'hood. I got my protection when I need it, that's how I can do my work when I need to. You just don't see it." He sat back and continued. "I'm going to explain a little about how to do this and then I'm gonna give you an opportunity to help me out. You need to be contributing a little more to the house, man, 'cause I'm sensing you need to stay here a little longer, you're not down with Providence. Am I right?"

JaQuan was pleased to see that Emilio was a fair employer. In three days of work with him, simply standing lookout, he had made seventy-two dollars. Not bad for a few hours' work with practically no risk to himself. It was during the first week working with Emilio that JaQuan met Janet. He ended up working almost every day that first week. He met her walking through the project with her girls. They were all white, but they were ghetto white, you could hear it in the way they talked. There was something about Janet, and he could feel it back from her. He might never see Sharena again, and a man just couldn't be alone all the time.

Chapter Eleven

JaQuan

A cold rain had drizzled over the city all morning, but the sky was simply gray as JaQuan sat with a magazine, staring out the tiny windows of the library. It was his last day here. He'd started to make friends in his few days here and they wanted to know more about him: where he lived, about his family, his school and other friends, things that would be harder to lie about as they went deeper. Plus, he'd been working with Emilio. Hanging out in Charlestown, he'd met Janet. He thought maybe he could care about this girl and she was into him big time.

The library was warmer than it needed to be, making him drowsy. The constant pedestrians and street traffic outside livened the view from his window. He waited. At any moment, the curtain would rise and he would be on.

"Malachi? Nathaniel? Help!" Christie came running to where JaQuan sat reading. Malachi, his middle name, was the name he used here. "Malachi, my cell phone is gone. I think someone stole my cell phone."

JaQuan got up and hugged Christie briefly. She was blond, with shoulder length hair, warm brown eyes and a tall, athletic build.

JaQuan had a crush on her, a little one, he told himself, and there was no chance anything good would come out of it. It was another reason to stop hanging out here.

He answered her. "Come on, Chris, are you sure? You didn't forget it at home or something?"

Nathaniel and her other two friends, Joanie and Tamara, were coming back from the computers. "What's up, Christie?" Nathaniel asked.

"I think someone stole my cell phone from my bag."

"Man, Christie, you can't leave your bag lying around," Nathaniel said.

"It wasn't that far from me, Nate, and I was only away from it for a minute." Christie was close to tears. "And that's just what my dad's going to say. He'll be angry."

"Christy, it's only a pre-paid. It's not like you lost an expensive Blackberry."

"Which now I'll never get." Christy plopped down in the chair.

"You sure you didn't leave it somewhere?" Joanie asked. "Why don't we look around?"

"OK, let's look, but I tell you, it was in my bag."

It was after six when they all left the library. Christie and her friends said goodbye to JaQuan and took off for their homes in Jamaica Plain and Roslindale. JaQuan walked with them toward the South End, but turned around as soon as they went down to the Orange Line trains at Back Bay Station. Walking back to Copley Square, he pulled out the small pre-paid phone and dialed. A voice came on the other end.

"Who?" It was J-Nice, his second in command.

"Nice, it's Q."

"Whoa, man, we've been worried 'bout you. Where you calling from?"

"It's OK, man, it's a pre-paid. Listen, I need you to meet me and stay on the down-low, OK? Here's what I need you to do."

JaQuan gave J-Nice the details he had worked out after talking with Emilio. He was going to have them meet him at Janet's place in Everett. She wouldn't mind, he was pretty sure, as long as he showed up when her folks weren't around. He had gone there alone a few times. They had a code. He'd get there first and let her know his crew was coming, maybe she could make them all some food. She really liked him, he thought. He gave Jonathan directions on how to find him and what route to take so they weren't followed. He knew J-Nice wouldn't be happy, they'd rather take a ride than the T—you never knew who you were gonna meet on the T. But for this, the subway was safer.

He finished his conversation and terminated the call. He walked over to the Burger King on Boylston Street to get some dinner to go before the next phase of his plan. He'd thought about this a lot and finally confided in Emilio. They had worked through the details together. Emilio had a philosophy, though he didn't call it that.

"Look, Q, my man, there is no other way. You keep your friends close to you, you keep your enemies closer. You get that? That way, you always have your boys when you need 'em, your women too; and you take care of your boys, you know? They're there for you 'cause they know you take care of them.

"But your enemies, that's even more important. You throw 'em off, and they can't really get at you behind your back, 'cause you're always there."

JaQuan protested. "Man, I can't hang around anyone who's ever jumped us."

"No, man. That's not what I mean. They wouldn't let you anyways. No, I mean the ones who're really evil to you, the ones might want to snitch you out, or take over your turf, or some girl you screwed, you know."

Emilio explained his theory in greater detail, with examples. It was after this talk that JaQuan had come up with his idea. It was better than giving up and going to Rhode Island. And he couldn't stick around Charlestown acting lookout for Emilio. He missed his boys, they depended on him. He was a nobody now, running. He couldn't let anyone know who he was. If he didn't do something soon, he'd be running all his life and wouldn't ever be able to let anyone know the real JaQuan—at least, as much of the real JaQuan as he himself knew. The first thing he had to do, though, was reach out to his boys and meet them somewhere safe, somewhere they couldn't be followed. To reach them without being traced, he couldn't use his own phone. He had come up with the idea of borrowing Christie's and he hadn't told Emilio. That was none of Emilio's business.

Chapter Twelve

Shelley

Shelley's Mini made the trip to the new Boston Police Headquarters at One Schroeder Plaza, Roxbury, in just under thirty minutes during the fresh early hours of morning, four days after Ishmael's death. She had left the house in Revere at six a.m. Carolyn was still on assignment in Israel and these quiet mornings were an inducement to getting in to work early.

Shelley had her choice of parking spaces when she finally reached the huge, unpaved field between Whittier Housing Project and the back of Madison Park High, where Nelson Mandela had once addressed Roxbury crowds after his release from prison in South Africa. BPD now used it as a parking lot. By eight o'clock this makeshift lot would be completely full as officers and city officials filled up the huge modernistic box that made up One Schroeder Plaza. The old headquarters on Berkeley Street had become a high-priced boutique hotel. The new headquarters had been built at a distance from downtown and close to Roxbury as a gesture of good faith toward the minority communities and an example to real estate developers of the city putting its own money where its rhetoric was as it urged developers to invest in these areas.

By seven a.m., Shelley was banging away at a series of new press releases and strategy notes for John to comment on and edit. They had to address the leaks around the community gun and crimes in which it had been used. The police so far had been unable to find JaQuan Miller. He'd missed his cousin's funeral and in spite of other criminal activity going on in the city, it seemed this story wasn't going anywhere soon. People were saddened and concerned that a six-year-old had gotten hold of a loaded gun and shot a seven-year-old. It was something even families in the suburbs could empathize with, since many of them owned at least one gun. But even more, Shelley thought cynically, they were waiting for the rest of the story. This wasn't some suburban family. This was a family up to its neck in gang members, violence and other criminality. Everyone was waiting for the other shoe to drop.

"Good morning, Shelley. You're in early." John O'Brien strode through the door at eight-thirty with his cup of Dunkin' Donuts coffee in hand.

"Hey, John. I wanted to finish up these releases before the phones started ringing so we could sit down with them."

"Good. The Chief wants an update. He scheduled a meeting with us, the Supe and the case detectives to go over what we have on this. The media's really keeping this one alive."

"Well, anyone can identify here. A six- and seven- year old. Every parent feels it. And those suburban folks, a lot of them have guns at home, too, and they identify with this on some level. No one identifies when it's just teen on teen."

"You're right. The last time suburbia was this interested was the random shootings we had along Columbus Ave. when one of them was killed."

"It made it real," Shelley said.

"That's right—you're one of those suburban folks, aren't you? Other days aren't real."

"Oh, cut it, John." Shelley sighed. He always gave her grief like this. She never quite knew if he was joking, or deep down resented an outsider. "What time is the meeting?"

"Ten o'clock. Why don't you refresh your coffee and join me in the conference room so we can go over those releases?"

Shelley finished re-reading the pieces on her computer and sent them to print. She dumped her coffee, grabbed a donut from the box John had brought in, then poured a fresh cup from the pot. She nibbled the donut as she watched the printer spit out the press releases. This new headquarters had all the personality of a corporate building. She liked the clean lines, big windows and soft gray carpeting, but had to admit that it had none of color, boisterousness and atmosphere of the old headquarters at Berkeley Street. On the other hand, it also had none of the cramped quality, yellowed linoleum or smells of mold and fear that had seemed embedded in the old building. Maybe it was just a matter of time.

She took her coffee and her print-outs down to the conference room where John was opening the blinds. They sat, and got down to it.

Chapter Thirteen

Cassie

Cassiopeia Rock sat on her back porch and watched as the sun streamed through the trees. She held a vodka tonic and sipped slowly as she sat back and watched the sunset developing to her right, and the glimpses of the Boston skyline peeking through the leaves to her left. This porch on the third floor of her Linwood Street home had been part of two years of renovations to insulate, repair and make this house livable. She loved this porch. It still had a fresh wood smell. She'd installed screens that slid open—she had them open now—to allow her a full view of the city and the sky. In winter she replaced them with triple-pane storms, that with her small heater allowed her to sit out here all year long. The porch functioned as a fire escape as well. A small trap door in one corner could be unlocked and opened to access narrow ladder stairs that led down to the second-floor porch, which had its own trap and set of stairs leading down to the first floor.

Cassie had been saving for years to be able to buy and she had long wanted to live on Fort Hill. It was a real neighborhood, a tight-knit community of people who watched out for one another. And it was slightly bohemian—artists and musicians lived there, gay folks felt welcome, there were some white families. So when this old brick townhouse was being foreclosed on, Cassie was there with cash to buy it outright. She had basically camped in the building for the first year and a half. Her two daughters were grown. Curtis was out of her life—the divorce had been painful—and the house was her symbol of stability and peace for herself. All the things she wanted and hoped she would enjoy when she retired, were here.

And the renovation process had helped keep her sane during this time: the divorce, the move into Homicide, the intense emotions of each burned out by the constant physical labor on this building. The emotions from her work in Homicide were still intense, but she was learning how to manage them and now her home was no longer her distraction, it was her sanctuary.

This porch was her private space, an extension of the comfortable master suite that took up the whole third floor. When she'd finished her day and locked up the house down below, she retreated here to sit literally above it all. And in time, she might find a man worthy to share it with. *In time*, she thought. *One step at a time.*

Working at the Boston Police Department for a decade, Cassie had finally made Sergeant Detective in Homicide a year ago. It had been a long haul; the exams were rigorous. She was a latecomer, drawn in during the department's aggressive recruiting of minorities and women. It had been her dream to move to Homicide, where she felt she could really do some good, but the adjustment had been as hard as the work she had done to achieve it. She had wanted Homicide because she could no longer stand by and do nothing as youth of color killed one another day after day. But at first only the exhausting physical work on the house could take her mind off what she saw and felt. It had taken time to learn to manage the emotions she felt, the grief and horror that surrounded each case.

Her first year in Homicide, she was essentially a rookie again, partnered with a more experienced detective, learning the practical ropes of investigation, and largely in the background. She had seen the results of drive-by shootings, domestic murders, a variety of horrible things. At the end of each workday, whatever time it finally did end, she would throw herself into whatever renovation work was on her list for the day—knocking down walls, blowing insulation, hanging doors, scrubbing and cleaning. Now she was a Sergeant Detective, with a team of two: Mulroney and Hal Fischer.

At the end of each day, and the end times still varied, she would come out to this spot with a glass of cold white wine and watch the sun set, or the moon rise, the play of the floodlight on the rippling leaves, or in winter, glistening snow. Tonight, however, something stronger was called for, as it sometimes was, and the vodka tonic was the first of a couple she would probably have.

Seeing a seven-year-old boy dead, shot, even though accidentally, by his six-year-old cousin, had rattled her in a way she hadn't been rattled in a while. It wasn't her usual case, they knew who the shooter was, but the sadness and the waste of it brought all the horror and sorrow of every murder she investigated into focus. And it was her case this time, hers and the team's. She wasn't in the background anymore, she was calling the shots. Her first case as lead, and it was this.

She was still angry at herself for letting Mulroney take the lead with that PR consultant from the department. Her instincts were against letting anyone who was not a cop talk to those women. It was important to find out where the gun had come from, how a six-year-old had found it, why it was loaded. Mulroney sensed her anger at this intrusion, but the Chief had given standing orders, so he'd smoothed the moment.

Cassie ran her hand over her hair and took another sip from her drink. A tall woman, six feet with black hair, a soft natural, cut short, Cassie was striking. Her skin was the color of mahogany, she had high cheekbones, almond-shaped eyes, the irises a dark chocolate, and she was fit. She ran and lifted on a regular basis. Cassie was also extremely intelligent and organized. She had won the respect of colleagues. College-educated before she joined the force, she'd been building a career in financial services. That was where she'd been able to save up enough money to buy this place. She was good at her job, and between the salary and her bonuses, she had left in fairly good shape.

She was grateful she hadn't let Curtis influence her financial habits. What a disaster he had been. Mocha-colored skin, blue eyes, very buff and an exquisite dresser, it had been lust at first sight for her. He was a developer, influential, contacts at the city, and as cultured a man as she had ever met. With Curtis, she spent time at the Museum of Fine Arts, and the Museum of Contemporary Art. They had seats at the symphony and were sponsors of the black community's annual All That Jazz fundraiser for black philanthropic causes. They had Sunday brunch at Bob the Chef's and listened to intimate jazz at Wally's. When he proposed, Cassie was sure she had finally found a soulmate. They were a handsome couple, respected in the community, and shared the same tastes and values. She thought.

After they returned from a Hawaiian honeymoon, she discovered she had married someone she didn't know at all. Curtis was controlling, he preferred she stop working and become hostess for dinners with prospective investors, bankers and his developer partners. He began to drink heavily, or she began to notice his drinking more. He wanted them to have a joint bank account and when she refused to put all her savings into it, he accused her of not loving him. His ambition, she realized, was not to help build Boston's black community into the safe, prosperous cultural enclave it could become, ensuring a good education to all its children, preserving some of the old traditions, supporting its artists and musicians. His ambition was to earn enough money to move out to the exclusive white suburbs—Weston or Dover; to have not only his house in Oak Bluffs, but a villa in the Caribbean, which he wanted her to buy for them with her savings.

Eventually they devolved into shouted arguments, Curtis's drunken rants and, finally, physical violence when she attempted to walk out one night during one of his tirades. He did not make the divorce easy, but she had found a very good lawyer. She knew there was a tiny part of becoming a cop that had to do with Curtis knowing she carried, and could use, a gun.

So, why did having that white PR woman, what was her name?—Shelley. Why did that white, Italian, public relations consultant from the department bother her so much? Cassie didn't think of herself as biased about people, but wary. Experience had taught her to be careful. It bothered her, she thought, because of the assumption this woman seemed to be making that she could understand the experience of the Miller sisters, and tell their story. It rankled too, she had to admit, that the Chief felt the department could not stand on its own, that they needed a PR consultant to get the public on their side. Finally, she didn't know if she was more angry thinking this woman would mess up her investigation by gaining sympathy for the Miller women, who might well have been partly responsible, or that gaining sympathy for them would backfire if Cassie ended up having to arrest them. Reluctantly, she admitted to herself that she might have to go talk with this woman and explain the ways her work could mess up the investigation. She downed the rest of her drink.

It was time for bed. Cassie closed the screens on her porch, but left the French doors slightly open as she went into her bedroom. She had designed her master suite for herself. The bedroom had a huge king bed in a recessed alcove near the French doors, and a skylight so she could be awakened by sun and birds and go to sleep to the moon and stars. A gas fireplace sat in the wall next to the alcove, facing a small seating area with a loveseat and two comfortable armchairs, each with a reading lamp beside it. Across from the seating area was a large and lavish bathroom with a Jacuzzi, a freestanding shower, a double sink and dressing table. The bathroom picked up the cream colors of the paint in her bedroom and accented them with peach and a soft gray.

A door from her bedroom led into her private library/office—the walls painted a federal blue and offset with cream on the moldings. Cassie loved books and paintings, and while most of her collection was in the library and parlor on the lower floors, she had her current reading, and current favorites, in her private room. A large rolltop desk held pride of place between the two front windows so she could write or do her bills gazing over toward Mission Hill and beyond it, the Fenway and the Charles River. One wall was built-in bookshelves done in cherrywood. A richly colored oriental rug made the room warm. A loveseat near the bookshelves and roll-top was one of her favorite morning places to read. Original oil paintings and photographs hung on the remaining walls.

The door to her suite was through the library/office, and from there one could walk out a short hallway with a window seat and street-facing window, just before the stairs leading down. There had been a small dumbwaiter installed between the hallway and the bathroom. She had boarded it up on every floor but kept the space. It would be her next project. The day might come when she would need a small personal elevator to reach her hideaway. She planned to grow old in this house. If she ended up in a wheelchair at age 88, she would still be here, where the world felt beautiful and safe.

She adjusted the hot water and ran a bath for herself. Her latest book sat on the bedside table and she moved it to the small settee beside the tub. As the water ran, she did a walk-through of the house to make sure it was locked up for the night. She ran her palm along the hand-carved old banister as she started down. This place gave her pleasure in every way.

Chapter Fourteen

Cassie

Cassie Rock pulled her Prius into the formal police lot next to headquarters. Because she was Homicide, she got to park here when the lot wasn't filled and didn't have to use the field across the street. She was early enough today. She had just finished her bath the night before when Mulroney called. He had been updating the investigation case file, adding the results of Fischer's canvasses, and seen the note the Supe had left that the Commissioner wanted a ten o'clock meeting with them today. The public relations folks would be there as well. She would have her chance to talk to this Shelley person after all. Cassie took a deep breath. She'd have to let go of this anger. She had only met the woman once, and Cassie had to admit the department had been doing a terrific job getting info out and keeping the press on their side.

"Morning, Detective." Officer Brannon looked up from his *Globe* as she walked in. She nodded a greeting. Brannon had been manning the metal detector ever since he'd been accused of sleeping with mothers of the kids he arrested on drug and misdemeanor charges. He'd denied it, and it had never been proven conclusively, but the Commissioner's office believed the charges and felt they had enough internal proof. If not for the union, Brannon would have been gone. Oddly, Cassie had always liked him. Whatever he had or hadn't done, he'd always given those kids in his Roxbury area second and third chances to get straight before he took them in.

Cassie pressed the elevator button for 4, the Commissioner's floor. Mulroney was on his way up with the investigation case file. She made it non-stop to the fourth floor and met Mulroney in the hall, jawing with the assistants at their desks and finishing a glazed donut. He fell in step beside her, and they walked down to 4 South and presented their badges to the guard on duty.

Eva Papadoulis, the Chief's executive assistant and an old hand, greeted them cheerily outside the office and escorted them inside.

"He'll be right in," she confided to them, in the way only Eva could, as though they were so important, she felt it her duty to tell them that little secret. "There's fresh coffee and a little spread I put out. Help yourselves."

John O'Brien and that Shelley person, as Cassie thought of her, were already seated and going over some papers in front of them. John looked up.

"Detectives," he said. They both nodded. Mulroney put the investigation case file on the conference table opposite the public relations staff and joined Cassie at the coffee cart. Cassie poured coffee for them both, added milk to hers and took a bagel with some light cream cheese (bless Eva), then sat down at the table. Mulroney sugared and creamed his coffee, grabbed a cinnamon roll, then joined her.

As if they had been waiting for that moment, the Commissioner and Superintendent Boyle entered from the Chief's inner office and sat down.

"Good morning," the Chief said. "Let's get right to it." He looked at Mulroney and Cassie. "You both know John, of course." They nodded. "And this is Shelley Colabro, she's been helping us out with PR strategy on these tough cases for the last year."

Shelley smiled at them. Mulroney smiled back. Cassie acknowledged her by looking straight at her.

The Chief continued with introductions. "Shelley, this is Detective James Mulroney and Detective Cassie Rock. This is their case. Detective Rock is lead. Detectives, why don't you update us, then we'll go over next steps."

As Detective Mulroney opened the case file and began detailing the chronology of the investigation, Shelley took in the details. Detective Mulroney resembled a stereotypical old school detective, with a large Irish nose and small visible capillaries in his nose and cheeks, from too much Jameson's, she guessed. He looked to be in his forties, hair cut short and with a belly that pushed against his dress shirt. His partner, Detective Rock, was tall, slim, and muscled. A formidable-looking African-American woman, she was dressed stylishly in a black jacket, white silk shell, black slacks and pumps. She was extremely attractive, with high cheekbones and almond eyes, accentuated by her short haircut. But her expression was stone. Where Mulroney had thrown Shelley a look of surface friendliness, Detective Rock showed no emotion at all. Shelley guessed she was in her mid-to-late forties, though from her looks she could have been anywhere from thirty-five to forty-five.

Superintendent Boyle was slim and radiated energy, with dark brown, almost black eyes, black hair cut short and a commanding way about him. The Chief, in contrast, looked almost laid back, a misleading impression. The Chief's dark brown hair was graying and wouldn't stay put, a lock of it constantly falling across his forehead. He was a hulking bear of a man, slightly stooped from listening to so many shorter associates over the years. He looked at people intently with warm brown eyes, focused and kind. Shelley had learned that his mind was razor-sharp when it came to cases and he did not tolerate sloppy police work. When outraged, he resembled a grizzly at its full height.

"So, to summarize," Mulroney continued, "we still haven't located JaQuan Miller. It's likely he hid the gun with which Antwon accidentally shot Ishmael, since he's completely disappeared. If he did, of course, he would be an accessory to accidental murder. And of course, if he did hide the gun, we don't yet know why. It is unusual, actually unheard of, to hide a community gun in your house. The whole point is for the gun to be untraceable to any one person as well as for it to be findable and usable by any member of an agreed-upon group. This gun was used in several crimes, but the ones that have come back so far don't seem to connect to any members of The Deep, as the 33 Deep crew calls themselves. And they're young—fourteen to sixteen years old for the leaders, younger for their hangers-on. We're still waiting on more details with some of the gun matches."

"And that leaves us with a couple of initial premises that we're trying to make sense of," Detective Rock interjected. "The first is that Miller or a member of his crew stole this gun from another crew, the second, that they were sold it by a crew wanting to get rid of a hot gun, or, third, someone planted it." She looked around the room. "Obviously, there are very different implications depending on which, if any, of those scenarios are true. And the potential consequences go from an all-out gang war between two groups to someone in JaQuan's own crew wanting to unseat him, or simply having it hidden away in case something happens and they need it. We've been working with the gang unit to try to get a fix on what folks are saying on the street and which of these scenarios may start to make sense—if any of them."

The room was quiet for a moment as everyone absorbed this information. Then the Chief spoke to all of them.

"You can see this leaves us with some decisions to make, both in terms of proceeding with the investigation and in presenting information to the press. This story has stayed in the headlines longer than any killing since the random shooting of a suburbanite on Columbus Ave. years ago."

"Is there any possibility that JaQuan took the gun to keep it from being used in a crime?" Tentatively, Shelley threw the question out.

Detective Rock fixed her with a laser stare. Mulroney simply gaped, then said, "That has never been my experience with these gangbangers. I'd chalk it up to stupidity instead of a good deed."

Surprisingly, Rock added, "It's unlikely, but the thought had crossed my mind as well. If someone sold the gun to one of JaQuan's crew and he thought they were going to use it for something he didn't approve of, he might have hidden it. JaQuan has not yet gone the way of the Miller clan. The Deep is one of the newer, wannabe gangs. They mostly hang out, they sell a little weed. They've had their beefs, but tend to keep a low profile. They inherited most of their rep from the OG's who are long gone."

"Cassie, I have to agree with Mulroney." Paul Boyle fixed his black eyes on Detective Rock in a stare that would have unnerved her if she didn't know and respect him as well as she did. "In my experience it is highly unlikely the gun was taken for any altruistic reason. But," he went on, not looking at Mulroney, "I don't believe it was stupidity, either. It may well have been the only way of controlling one of his crew in the short term. These teens have a keen sense of what will bring on violence with other gangs—even if they can't always control their impulses. JaQuan Miller may just have wanted to prevent a gang war. Or he may have been expecting one, though the gang unit hasn't heard anything unusual. But that doesn't mean there isn't something here we simply don't understand or know yet."

"The gang unit shared some info with me yesterday," Cassie said. "Ishmael's mom has had a new boyfriend for the past three months. He goes by the street name Sticky, real name Richard Raines. He just got out of prison and he used to be a player. His presence raises the question of whether he had any involvement with the gun."

"Has anyone been able to locate Sticky?" Boyle said. Cassie and Mulroney shook their heads.

"The question, then," said the Chief, "is, how do we proceed in the search for JaQuan and Sticky; how do we minimize leaks and keep the press updated. Finally, is there any information we can give the press that would bring back information helpful to us?"

"Also," Shelley said, nodding to the Chief, "how do we anticipate events that might happen that we have no control over."

"Like what?" Cassie said.

"If JaQuan comes forward on his own, or with one of the ministers. If violence starts up between members of his 33 Deep crew and some other street gang, or between JaQuan and Sticky." Shelley looked around the table. "The press will jump on us then, and we need to be prepared. We don't want to look surprised or ignorant."

The Chief interrupted. "Let me back us up a bit. Detective Rock, why don't you lay out what you think of as next steps for the investigation. And start with your talks with the gang unit—is there anything in the wind about a beef with someone new, or about something bigger than the usual turf and girlfriend stuff?"

Cassie nodded. "First, we're talking to the gang unit and the teams investigating the earlier shootings linked to this gun. They have not been linked yet to any particular group, so there's no way to know yet where the Deep got the gun. They're pulling warrants, talking to folks and trying to up the pressure.

"Second, we've got a couple of undercovers sniffing around. Trying to get some info from JaQuan's boys, maybe up the pressure there a bit as well.

"We're setting up another round of interviews with his aunts, with his cousin Antwon." Cassie held a hand up as Shelley started to speak. "We're being very careful with Antwon. We're interviewing some of the older cousins and friends who were around the building that day as well. But my thinking is, we're really going to have to talk to JaQuan."

"Do you think he's left the state?" Shelley asked.

"No, actually, I don't. I think he's still around. Boston's home. It's what he knows. He might have enough friends to hide him for a while, but sooner or later he's going to have to come up for air, for money, and, if he doesn't want to lose his place with the Deep, he's going to have to get in touch with his boys."

Mulroney added, "There's even-money out there that some of our street informers will tip us off, even if the undercovers don't sniff him out."

"I agree with Mulroney," Cassie said. "But I wanted to bat around another idea with you and Shelley, John; if it's okay with you, Chief. I'd like to be a little more proactive in trying to flush him out and see if we can't use some of our media releases in service of that."

"It's fine with me, Detective. Let's hear your idea."

"Basically, Chief, I want to build on the work John and Shelley did interviewing the two boys' mothers. I think we should do a couple of stories re-capping the incident, replay some of the interviews with other mothers who've lost children, maybe put in some photos and end each series with a hint that in the tragic death of Ishmael Miller, we know it's an accident but that the gun was used in other crimes. We also put out that we're worried about JaQuan. Feeling guilty for his cousin's death, he might hurt himself. Finally, we put out that we're getting leads about where the gun came from and are about to put more pressure on his friends and associates to confirm where JaQuan might be staying. That it would be better for him to turn himself in and answer our questions before we have to exercise all that pressure on his friends."

"I don't know," the Chief said. "There's risk there when we rake it all up."

"There is risk, sir," Shelley said. "But I like Detective Rock's idea. I had been mulling something similar. It brings up all the sadness and tragedy, and shows everyone we're still active on this investigation and we're nailing down pieces. I don't see a downside. We're proactive and we control what's hitting the news."

John shrugged. "These kids don't even read, I don't think this will smoke him out."

"I disagree," the Chief said. "You make a good case, Shelley and Detective Rock. I think this will get the word out if we make sure to get it in the *Metro*, *Herald* and *Banner*, as well as the *Globe*. Work on it, but I want to see it personally before it goes."

"Right, Chief," Cassie and John answered simultaneously.

"One more thing," the Chief said. "I need you on some other priorities, John. I want to put Shelley with Cassie to sketch out this thing. Any objection?"

"None." John's affect was flat. Cassie kept her face impassive as well.

Chapter Fifteen

JaQuan

As he'd expected, Janet let him meet with his boys at her place. JaQuan could tell she was nervous, afraid one of her parents would come home early or that neighbors had seen them come in, and would tell. She'd ordered pizzas with the money he gave her, and tonic. She was sitting downstairs on the front stoop now, like he'd asked her to, keeping an eye out for her parents or anyone else who might walk in on them. It made her feel better and gave JaQuan the privacy he needed. She sat with her cell phone right beside her to call him if someone was coming. If she called him, he and his friends were to take the pizza boxes and tonic bottles and head out the back staircase.

His boys had followed his instructions. They grumbled, but were excited at having successfully made it to a new place.

"Word, Q—what's this plan we had to come all the way to the fuckin' suburbs to hear?" Cameron was a little on edge being in some-place new.

"Yeh, man, I'll be fucked if I'm getting on that fucking T anymore." Snake was usually quiet, calm, watching and listening. The subway and bus ride out had tensed him, he had too many enemies. He liked to choose his turf. The train made him a visible target with no control. He wasn't happy.

"What about you, J? MD?" JaQuan looked at his two other boys.

"Look, Q," J-Nice answered. "We're here, ok? You know none of us likes to take the T, we don't have to. We're sittin' targets, man."

"Or standing," MD smirked.

"Whatever," J-Nice continued, ignoring him. "Let's get down to it, Q. We're glad as hell to see you, man. But it's been hot down there. 5-0 is on our ass. We can't move anything. Sharena's missing the shit out of you and she's gonna be pissed, she hears about this white girl you're seeing."

"This white pussy, you mean, J," said MD. "Let's tell it like it is, man."

"Sharena ain't gonna hear about Janet, you got that?" JaQuan was starting to get angry. "You're my boys, right? We still tight?"

"Man, calm down," J-Nice said. "We don't mean nothing by this, Q. Having some fun with you's all. But you gotta know this has been tough. The cops are looking for you hard. They were all over the 'hood the first three days, and they still have two guys from the gang unit. Think they're undercover. But ain't nothin' we can do with them around. And you know, Q, when they finally give up looking for you, we gonna have some hungry players from H Block or Intervale, know you're away, challenging us for some of our trade."

"Yeah, Q, we gotta call in our allies," Cameron said. "Snake and I are setting up a meeting with Maurizio, from the Bloods."

"You're nuts, Cameron. Unset it," JaQuan answered, angrier now.

"Man, you left us there, we had to do something," J-Nice responded.

"You couldn't hold it together for a week?" JaQuan was up now, pacing the floor. "No one from H Block or Intervale is gonna want our business. They've got enough going on and we've had good relations with them."

"You only called us once, Q. We had no idea where you were, what was up, man. If you were even coming back. We had to start making plans to protect our territory." Cameron was defensive.

"Yeah, man, we don't even know now if you're coming back. How can you, when the po-po looking for you everywhere, keepin' watch on your aunts' place. They salivatin' for you, man." Snake spoke quietly, his eyes lowered dangerously, and then he stared at JaQuan.

JaQuan stood frozen, staring at the table and then at each of them in turn. Finally, he let his breath out and sat down.

They were in the dining room in this second-floor apartment of a two-story house. The walls were painted sky-blue. There was a framed prayer on one wall, "Lord, give me the strength"; fake china plates with blue willows and bridges on white backgrounds on another wall. A dry-sink with some hockey trophies. Two windows looked out at the ubiquitous trees that marched up and down this Everett side street.

"All right, you've done what you've done. I had to lay low, you know that, and I'm gonna have to stay on the down-low a little bit longer. I need to know you're still with me—are you with me?" JaQuan stopped talking and waited.

"Q, we're your homies, you know that," Cameron said.

"We're here for you, man," Snake and MD said simultaneously.

"You know we're one for all, man, like you said." J-Nice sounded hurt.

"Aight then, ya'll. You gotta stay disciplined. You gotta stay with the program. Aight? You know we ain't never started no beefs, we've held our ground with dudes, right. We've done some cutting when we had to. We've asked for respect, but we've given it, too. We don't want to wreck that. So, here's what we're gonna do."

They talked some, and then his boys left. When they'd gone, JaQuan sat for a minute in the dining room, alone. This was not good, his boys were panicked. They all talked a good line, like they were really tough, but he knew the only reason you act first is if you're scared, you're stupid, or you're such an angry, crazy son-of-a-bitch that you don't give a shit.

Snake had always had that potential, but he thought Snake was loyal above all. This meeting today really bothered him.

The door opened. Janet was standing there. "I saw your boys go, Q. Are you all right?"

"I'm good, babe. Come over here." He opened his arms and she walked into them. He kissed her, then ran his fingers over her face, down her neck, her back, her ass. He liked the difference in her.

"Q, not now. You know my parents are gonna be here any minute."

***

"This is wack, man," Snake said in a low, discouraged voice. It was dark and he was slouched in one of the many open seats on the T this late after rush hour. "How does he think he's gonna live in C-town and the 'burbs and run a crew in the 'hood. He think we like some multi-national corporation and he the CEO."

"Come on, man, it's Q. You know he can't come back yet," Cameron said.

"Yeh, man, but he's still talking this respect shit, like we can defend ourselves by being all talk and smilin' and shit. Those niggas gonna want our block, and they gonna take it. They think we're punks." Snake's face darkened and his voice got rough. "And Q moved the protection. I couldn't find it. You know that's the gun his little man got killed with. What he take it for, he don't trust us?"

"Why were you checking on it, Snake?" J-Nice asked.

"Just want to make sure it's there." Snake lowered his eyelids to slits again. "And it wasn't, was it."

"I'm not so sure about moving the business," MD put in. "You think these white yuppies gonna follow us to a new place for the mid-week feel-good? You aight about moving the stuff so far?"

"It ain't far, MD," Cameron said, "Not really. We do it in shifts, so 5-0 don't catch on. And the rest of us on the block start doing the rec thing with the younger kids, we look good, we look straight. It takes the pressure off us and off Q."

"Yeh, man," J chimed in. "And H Block, those dudes, we gonna keep our eye out, stay cool with them. They ain't gonna move in with po-po around and we'll be ready by the time the cops're gone. They don't really want our corner, it's just if they think they can."

"Yeh, well, you know, Morris starting to move on Sharena," Snake said. "I didn't want to worry Q, but he taken a liking to her and that be bad for everyone."

"He's old, man!" J-Nice said, making a face.

Snake shrugged. "It's what I hear."

They had changed from the Blue Line to the Orange Line trains at State Street, and their train pulled into Ruggles.

"We gotta make time, we wanta catch the early bus," Cameron said. "Let's go."

Chapter Sixteen

JaQuan

Back in Everett, JaQuan and Janet cleaned away the soda bottles and pizza boxes from their meeting, pushing them deep into the neighbor's trash cans hidden back behind the garage. When they'd finished, she walked him down to say goodbye, still nervous.

"My parents are gonna be here any minute, Q," she said. "You gotta go."

"I'm on my way, babe," he said, pulling her behind some rosebushes in the small yard. He put his hands on either side of her face. He had nice hands, she thought, they were big, strong hands that could do things, his hands always calmed her.

He kissed her, gently and deeply, holding her face. Then, watching her, he slowly ran his hands down her neck, over her shoulders, down her bare arms. He held her arms, still gently, but with strength—she couldn't move—and leaned in to kiss her again. He let his tongue roam, he bit her lips softly, he moved his hands over her back and then down. Then he stopped.

"OK, babe," he said softly. "I'm going." JaQuan held her arms loosely now. He loved the look of her, so different. Her hair was the color of golden straw, long and soft. Her arms were milky with tiny freckles here and there. Her eyes were a pale blue, her lips really reddish. She was a strange and sweet creature to him. He kissed her softly again.

"You are gonna miss this tonight." He could feel her melting. He touched her breast gently, then moved his hand down, massaging her belly.

They both heard the car.

"Oh, shit." Janet pulled away, then ran back and, standing on her toes, kissed him again. "Call me," she whispered hoarsely and ran toward the house. JaQuan melted into the next yard and came out as dusk was beginning, hands in his pockets, strolling slowly and happily, as if all was right with the world, down toward the streets that would pour him onto Main.

JaQuan walked a long way back toward Charlestown. He had a lot to think about. He stopped on Main Street, got an ice cream and ate it as he walked. He walked the side of the road past the rotary and the power station. He finally stopped and caught the bus that brought him to the community college.

He didn't know how he felt. This all excited him. He was good at planning, he thought. He liked to run things, have control, but he wasn't crazy to have it, the way some guys were. He didn't have to control everybody or everything. He was confident when he talked to people. He knew he could make them listen to him, he knew he could make them like him. He was heartbroken about his cousins, but he was glad not to be at his aunts'. It had never really been home for him. Neither had his moms'. If she hadn't ended up going to prison, he knew he would have eventually split. When he no longer had his grandmoms' place to go to, he'd felt like a lost boy and it was harder to put up with his moms. He knew what she couldn't do, her limitations, and he missed having someone he could talk to and love. Not that he didn't love his moms...

He walked across the bridge from Bunker Hill Community College into the heart of Charlestown. In front of him and atop Charlestown's great hill, the Bunker Hill Monument stared at him. He took a side street and climbed the hill, looking at the brick houses crammed together, expensive houses now, those little things. He peeked in the windows when he could, watching the warm lights glow and wondering what kind of lives were going on there.

JaQuan didn't like his life right now, but he couldn't see a way to make it something else. And he knew his boys were his responsibility. Snake and MD couldn't even get themselves out of bed in the morning for school. They were bored all the time. They weren't planners, they didn't want jobs where you made eight bucks an hour and stayed in one place all day taking orders. He couldn't blame them, he didn't want it either.

He had blown his chance for college, he thought, it would take too much now to catch up in high school. And he wasn't very good at school. Still, he felt trapped. Right now, having to plan how to hang onto his boys, save the block and do his business, that was exciting to him. Once it was back running smoothly, he hated the "same-old," and he hated the beefs with other neighborhoods. They got out of control too easily.

He flashed back to his conversation with Monique a few days ago. He didn't want to admit it, but he knew she was right. His life could have been something more. But he didn't see how he could change it now. He was a young black man, school had become a battlefield, he needed money, he needed protection. Even at fifteen, he wasn't a teen anymore, he had adult responsibilities if he was going to stay alive.

JaQuan had spent most of last night when he couldn't sleep, looking back over his life. He was sure he could pinpoint the moment things turned for him, the week his life changed. He had been twelve years old. That was the year Grandmoms died, suddenly, and it was the year he entered middle school.

Back living with his mother for the previous year, he still went to Grandmoms' almost every day after school—he'd been living with her off and on since he was four, and permanently since he was six years old. His mother had told Grandmoms that she'd gotten her life together and it looked like she had. Grandmoms was looking older and tired. It was the diabetes, she said. He remembered the day.

"How is it with you and your mom, Jakey?" Grandmoms asked him as she put a plate of homemade Tollhouse cookies down on the table. She wiped her hands on her apron and opened the fridge to pour him milk.

"Good, Grandmoms," he said, his mouth already full of cookie.

"Jakey!"

"I'm sorry, Grandmoms. I know—no talking with my mouth full." He was smiling. "But they're so good."

Grandmoms kissed him on the forehead and sat down opposite him with a cup of tea. "You are a charmer, Jake. That can be good and bad." She smiled at him. "But you always know just the right thing to make your Grandmoms feel good." She sipped her tea and continued, "Someday, someone's going to be onto you and that charm, and whoop you right upside the head."

They both started laughing. Then Grandmoms stopped.

"Your mom is really doing all right, Jakey? You need to tell me if she's not, boy, it'll just be between us. Your mom loves you, she always has, but she's been through a lot. All my children have." Grandmoms broke a cookie and absentmindedly began to eat it. "I don't want to have to worry about you, Jake."

"You won't, Grandmoms, don't worry, you won't." He reached across the table and took her hand. Her smile back at him had a tear in it, but she wiped it away and smiled strongly.

"So what is my young man learning in school today?" she said.

There were some days Grandmoms was like that, a little sad seeming, but always with some treat for him, and always ready to ask him about school, about current events, telling him what news from the neighborhood she had. His school was still in the South End but he didn't live there anymore, and he missed it. Some nights he stayed for supper or overnight. She always kept his old room for him and he knew, though they never talked about it, if he ever needed to come back, he could.

JaQuan didn't like living at home. He loved his moms, and he had missed her when she was away. But he didn't like how she treated him before she went away, and now, she was skinny and on edge all the time. But she was trying. She made him lunches some days, she made supper almost every night. He made the coffee in the morning for him and for her, and usually got some pastries and a microwaved egg sandwich from the corner store for breakfast on the way to school.

He was twelve years old and going to start 7th grade. He missed the breakfast chats with Grandmoms, but by the time he was leaving for school, his moms was just trying to wake up.

He wished he could have stayed with his grandmother, but she had bad days with her diabetes and it was getting harder for her to walk.

"Marlene, I am fine with JaQuan," she had told her daughter. "I don't mind him at all. He makes my life easier."

"Mama, I know you're just saying that 'cause you're not sure if I can take care of him. I'm doing good, now, Mama and I miss my son. I'd like him with me."

"Jakey, can you do me a favor?" Grandmoms asked when they had finished their snack. "Would you run down to the market and pick up a few things for me? When you get back, I'll help you with your homework and we'll have dinner."

"Sure, Grandmoms!" he said, grabbing his jacket. "I'll go right now."

"Here's the list and the money. I need milk, eggs, bread and some cheese."

"Got it, and I know the kind you like. I'll be back real quick." JaQuan kissed his grandmother on the cheek and went running down the stairs.

So he and his grandmoms finished their cookies and milk together. He ran to the market, did his homework while she cooked and they had dinner together. He didn't know then that it was for the last time. He was going to stay the night but Jimmy called and asked if JaQuan could go see a Little League game with him and stay over. Grandmoms helped him pick out school clothes from the spares he left at the house, and made sure he called his moms.

JaQuan and Jimmy had gone to Lenox that night. That was the night they were first threatened. The first time in his life he was afraid he'd be jumped. He went to his moms' house that night and did not get back to his grandmoms' for two more days. By that time, she was in a hospital bed at Boston Medical Center. Two days later, she passed. From that point on, his life changed. Looking back, he could see *he* had changed—that was the point. Faced with so many pulls, so many threats, he had lost his sanctuary, his heart was broken and his life began to move in a different direction.

Chapter Seventeen

His Boys

JaQuan *had always* loved the summer evenings most of all. He could hang outside with his friends all evening long. They had gotten close, his crew and him. They had a mission together—to make money, to keep their territory safe. Everyone in the crew had something he could do well. Everyone had specific tasks.

He stretched out his legs from the bench in the small park halfway down the block from his home. The sun was a couple of hours from setting and moving down behind the apartment buildings across from him. His boys had been doing a good business today with the after work and pre-evening crowd, everyone languid and friendly, enjoying the weather. He nodded at Snake, who stood relaxed at the corner of the street to his left, slouching against a four-story brick building, chewing on a toothpick. An older Saab cruised by, and Snake gave a slight nod. The car kept going but Q knew it would round the block and return. Snake nodded to J-Nice, who was at the other end of the park watching the cross street off to Q's right. J-Nice gave a nod to one of his younger cousins who was shooting hoops in the half-court. They always used younger kids as their runners—kids who were eight, nine or ten. They were fast and they were happy to make a little money, you didn't have to pay them much, and if the cops did catch them holding, they just got sent to juvie for a while—no prison, no record. The boy gave a final shot and loped away around the corner. He returned several minutes later at a casual saunter, going up to J-Nice and giving him an elaborate handshake.

J-Nice strolled down to shoot the breeze with Snake, and when the car returned they casually went up to greet its passengers. Snake followed just a heartbeat behind J.

Snake's job was to make initial contact, scope out who was in the car and what they wanted, keep watch for anything that felt off, or for any competitors who might choose to stroll through the neighborhood at this time of night.

J-Nice was the sales guy, the closer. He had a nice way with people, even people he didn't know. Q thought it was because he had some Spanish blood in him, his mom was Puerto Rican. He never seemed angry or edgy and he made the white guys who detoured through the neighborhood on their way home from work feel safe and comfortable. They came back to buy from them, Q was sure, because of that. Also, Q knew, because they always made sure they had a good product. It was a point of pride with him. If he had to do this to make money, he was going to do it right. He had another rule, too, nobody used the stuff while they were on duty. And members of his crew had to buy it if they wanted it. There was a discount for them, but it wasn't free.

Down the other end of the street, MD lolled, giving Q a smile every now and then. MD's job, with a couple other posse members, was to secure that end of the street and stay straight. He always did a good job at the first task. He could inspire people and they did the watching, and did it diligently. It was harder for him to stay straight. MD was a mellow guy, he said, and he wanted to stay mellow.

JaQuan watched the ballet of his crew. He was proud of them. They did their jobs like pros. He had come to know them, know their strengths, their likes and dislikes, and he used each of their strengths in this work, and made sure they felt like a family. They kept the neighborhood relatively safe. They made money. They had friends to chill with when home didn't feel right. They had friends to watch their backs. Sometimes he wished he could leave, explore the world, try something new, like he could when he was young. This was what responsibility did, he thought. How could he leave the Deep, they'd fall apart without him. He had Sharena. He'd do a little weed now and then to mellow out. He'd go ballin' with his boys down over the Y or the Shelburne, play a little five on five, perfect his shots from the line. Maybe sometime he'd want Sharena to be his baby's mama.

He stopped thinking. It depressed him.

Around 9 p.m. Friday, Q and his friends made their way to Cameron's mom's apartment. They had closed up their business for the night, chewed out some of their runners who had come on the streets high after doing a little weed after school. Q had a rule, no getting high on working nights. He'd noticed that was one way people got caught, those older dudes, some of them were medicated all the time. You could see it. It attracted attention, it attracted cops, and it affected customers.

Cameron's mom lived a block away from Seaver Street, a block and a half from the park. She had a second-floor right unit with the living room windows fronting the street, a bathroom next, the master bedroom, dining room and kitchen. In the back were two more bedrooms. Cameron's room opened onto the fire escape, which was pulled up from the ground. His two younger sisters shared the other room. Cameron's mom worked a three to eleven shift at the nursing home over near Walnut Street. His two sisters stayed next door at Mrs.

Richardson's until his mother picked them up when she got home. Sometimes if it was too late and she was too tired, Mrs. Richardson would keep them for the night. Mrs. R's family was grown or gone, she had room and it made her a little extra money. Shaliqua and Missy liked Mrs. R. and they were pretty, quiet little girls. It worked out for Cameron. He liked his sisters, but it would have cramped his style to babysit them every night. It was bad enough he had to pick them up from school each day.

The way it was now, he could chill with his friends and they always had a place to relax. He had a bought a fan, he would turn it on, open the window, get some music going and they could kick back and de-stress. School nights, though, as his mom put it: "None a your niggas better be here when I get home."

Cameron ordered some pizzas. Around him, the crew were laughing.

"You believe that white dude? Looked like he'd never driven in the 'hood in his life." MD took a hit.

"Hey, MD, who was that girl you were talkin' with by the court?"

"Yeh, man, spill. She was bootalicious!" J-Nice fell back, laughing.

"Fuck you, man." MD glared at him.

"Chill, dude."

"C'mon, c'mon. Gentlemen!" Q said, grinning as he and Cameron came in with the pizzas and soda. "I'm sure J meant that with nothing but respect."

J-Nice started laughing harder. "Fuck you, Q, you bring bacon pizza?"

"Oh, nasty," MD said.

"What do you mean, nasty, nigga? What do you know!"

Snake glared at both of them and opened one of the sodas. "Shut the fuck up, y'all, let's eat."

Sitting around in a circle, a little lamp in the corner giving out just enough light, they began to eat and talk. Cameron lounged on his bed, J-Nice took the window sill. JaQuan sat on the edge of a small desk and adjusted the fan that sat on it so it would blow most of the smoke out the window. Snake and MD stretched out on the floor, the pizza boxes open between them, lounging on pillows propped against the walls.

J-Nice was looking out at the lighted windows of neighboring apartments and could hear the yells of kids still down below playing basketball.

"You think we'll all be together in five years?" J was always thinking about the future and asking questions like that.

"We not in prison? Probably," Snake said.

"Dang, man. What you mean, we're not in prison...I ain't gonna do time ever. What's with that?" MD was adamant. "What, every black male gotta do time?"

"Shut up, fool," Snake answered. "You know's well as I do, you do this shit, you do the time. What y'all niggas laughing at?"

"You do the crime, you do the time, man." Cameron chuckled. "It ain't 'you do the shit.'"

"Well, fuck your shit, anyways." Snake took a bite of his pizza.

"No, I mean it, dog." MD came back into the conversation. "You know, it ain't no black thing to be proud of, all black men doing time. It sucks."

"Chill, man." J-Nice looked anxious.

"I'm chillin', dog. Now back off, I'm tryin' to have a serious dis-cussion. Those OG's, they come out like they big dogs, did their time, eff'd the Man. Know what I'm sayin'? Well, that's shit. They got to watch their ass every moment in there. They lose their women, they lose their friends. It sucks." MD took a breath.

"No argument from me, man," Q said. "This gonna look like a war, if we all make it a war. And I'm gonna raise the issue again, y'all, can we lose the N word here?"

"Yeh, fuck all, man, we know, we know, it's self-denigrating. Shows we don't respect ourselves or our race. Lighten up, Q." Cameron shook his head and took another slice of the bacon pizza.

***

Bookman Smith, known as Boo, ran drugs for Morris Coburn. Coburn was twenty-two and was known to some as Eightball, partly because of the drug but also because when Morris said so, the game was over. His street crew chief was Maurizio. Eightball had done time and was a serious player. His crew was Blood-affiliated. Boo was sixteen, about five-foot-eleven, skinny but muscled. He had a slight wandering eye that often distracted and disarmed people looking at him. He had a beatific smile but most people never saw that. He was a master of stealth and speed. His main function with the crew was getting in and out fast, whether making a drop or checking things out.

Boo knew JaQuan was heading up that little posse, 33 Deep, a few blocks past Egleston, on the way to Franklin Park. He didn't think JaQuan had seen him when he scoped them out. He'd hung around with Q back when they all called him Jakey. He'd considered him a friend, but after Q's grandmother died, they lost touch. Boo shrugged. It was a shame about Q's cousin getting killed.

Eightball wanted him to check out the Deep's action. Some of his crew had already approached Maurizio, then backed off. They were shaky, Boo thought. JaQuan was on the run and Morris might see this group of homies as an opportunity, but Boo thought they were too small-time. Boo didn't want to think about whether Jakey would see his actions as a betrayal. Time was, they'd been close. But the way he saw it, being a part of Eightball's organization might actually protect Jakey's crew, at least as long as they stayed on Eightball's good side. They were young, still pretty green. There wasn't really anything there for someone to move in on, it was a good little business for small change—only weed, and not that many regulars. But they were annoying people, and that was going to mean trouble. Jakey had kept good relations with homies on all sides of the hood. No power issues. But now, with Jakey on the run and a power vacuum, there would be some kind of trouble. Someone was going to move on this spot.

Darkness was coming and Boo stood about a block away from where one of JaQuan's boys lolled against a corner building. Boo'd come by the last couple of nights to just watch how the Deep did its business and protected their turf. No one had noticed him in the shadows. He was good at that. He moved forward into the street so the streetlights caught him, toward the boy guarding the corner. The boy stood straighter, though to most eyes he still would have seemed to loll against the building.

Boo nodded and the boy nodded back.

"Yo. 'Sup," Boo said.

"'Sup," Snake answered.

"I'm looking for Q. He around?" Boo gave his engaging smile.

"What's it to you?" Snake said, sullenness in his voice, and a touch of fear, Boo thought.

"Q and I go way back, man. He's been through shit, I wanted him to know his old homie, Boo, is here for him."

"Where you from? I didn't see no car."

"I had to take the bus and walk, man. How is Q doing?"

"It ain't your business, man, till Q tells me you're bonafide. Cool?"

Boo looked past Snake down to the other end of the street. J-Nice was talking to two men in a car.

"You know that's po-po in that car, right?"

"Stay out of our shit, man!" Snake's eyes threw rage.

"It's cool, man. Whatever. You tell Q that Boo is here for him, man. I'll be droppin' by. Aight?"

Boo walked off, back towards Blue Hill Ave. Snake stared after him, then caught Cameron's eye, over on the benches. He gave a quick cutting motion. And watched as Cameron, always within J's view, started pulling on his right ear. J-Nice said some more to the men in the car, then pulled back and shrugged, giving them a smile before walking over toward the ball court. He signaled MD on the courts. MD nodded, shot another hoop, then started off toward J's corner. Snake whistled for his young runners and posted them on his corner to keep an eye out, then went to join Cameron and J-Nice.

"What was up with that, Snake," J-Nice said.

"Guy is suddenly there with me on the corner. I didn't see him coming, he's just there." Snake shakes his head. "Says he's an old friend of Q's, wanted us to let him know, whatever he needs, his old friend Boo is there. Then he looks at you, J, talking to those guys in the car and says, 'You know that's po-po right?' So I signaled you, just in case."

Snake paused and looked around the playground, basketball court and the street. "He said he'd drop by again."

"Aw, shit," Cameron said. "Shit. We need Q here. He could always talk to those kind of guys."

"What kind of guys, Cam? He says he an old friend of Q," J-Nice said.

"Yeah, right." Snake looked at J. "I'm with Cam, man. This shit is trouble."

Chapter Eighteen

JaQuan

Coming back after meeting Janet the next afternoon at the TGI Friday's on Route 16, JaQuan realized he didn't want to head back to Emilio's in Charlestown. He knew he'd be out of there soon, once his plan with his boys got going, but it was already old. He was restless. It seemed like there was no place for him, no place he wanted to be. He didn't get off the train at Charlestown but stayed on until downtown and switched over to the Red Line. He rode that train all the way to the Quincy stop, then all the way back, just thinking and watching folks get on and off. Finally, he switched to the Orange Line to the Ruggles stop. This was old territory for him. He began to walk west. Behind him was the South End where his grandmoms had lived. The streets of lower Roxbury that he walked now were the first place he got jumped, and the place where his moms had lived when she was clean. He walked up Tremont Street, right past Boston Police Headquarters, toward Mission Hill and Fort Hill, keeping watch. The Mission boys were always jumpy. When he passed headquarters and Madison Park High, he turned up New Dudley Street, took his first right and climbed the hill past the Timilty Middle School, and the old Eliot Church. He remembered from school that this was part of the black freedom trail, a big part of black history that started in the days when all Roxbury was farmland. This was the heart of Fort Hill, which stared across the abyss of Columbus Avenue to Mission Hill, two drumlins standing like a sentry to Boston's current communities of color.

When he first met Sharena, she had lived on Fort Hill with her grandmother. It was how he got to know it. It seemed like a friendly neighborhood. Everyone knew everyone else and it was a pretty safe place. That wasn't the case anymore, it had shootings like everyplace else, but parts of it were still pretty calm. He walked down Centre Street until he could see Valentine Street. He turned and climbed the steepest hill yet. JaQuan wasn't exactly sure why he was doing this, but it calmed and exhausted him, the walking made his restless feelings still.

When he reached the water tower on the highest part of Fort Hill, he sat. He looked out on the backside of the city, though that's not what he would have called it. He looked north over to Mission Hill, west over Jamaica Plain and southward toward the streets of Roxbury and Dorchester he now called home. The sparkling towers of downtown, the golden dome of the State House, and the cobbles and red brick of the Freedom Trail—old Boston—and the Atlantic Ocean were all behind him. He had never really thought of it—Boston was surrounded by the sea, but everywhere he and his friends lived had their backs to it. From here, he saw the Roxbury streets he knew best. But it was behind him that Boston's downtown and harbor sparkled in the sun. Beauty seemed always behind him.

The view was beautiful and peaceful, all the same. Whatever direction you looked in. From up here you couldn't tell that homies were shooting at each other, tempers flaring, knives coming out. You couldn't see the girls giving it to dudes, thinking it would make them popular. Couldn't see the girls jumpin' each other over some boy; and the dudes, around their cars, ready to unload on the Harborpoint guy who disrespected them by coming onto a bitch who belonged to them.

Here, he was surrounded by grass and a quiet street, like he lived in the country and could spend his days cutting grass and catching grasshoppers. His grandmoms used to talk about spending her summers in the country as a little girl. That was the problem, he knew, this was why everything seemed wrong, why he was so restless. He missed Grandmoms in a way he couldn't even start to describe. She had loved him so much, he had felt it. And he loved her back. She made his world safe and happy, and he would have done anything for her.

When he went back to live with his moms, even though he didn't really want to, he didn't feel that badly about doing it, because he knew he could always drop by Grandmoms. She would always be there. He would always have a place to stay, so he could try anything, because he could always drop in, take a break, talk things out. Out on the street, in this new world of being challenged and jumped and disrespected, he could always come back to safety. Then suddenly, she was gone and the whole world of his childhood closed up. His moms, his aunts and an uncle he had barely seen, cleared the place out and sold it to a developer so fast, he didn't have time to understand what was happening. His grandmoms was gone and he couldn't stand by her kitchen table and remember her. He couldn't put out milk for the cat and sleep in his old room just one more time to say goodbye. When he walked into the South End after that, it was like a strange and hostile place to him. His grandmoms had shone her light on it, and that light was gone. He felt lost.

He had run into Monique and his friends at school that year. He went home with them sometimes for dinner, but after a while he stopped, it hurt too much to be that close and know Grandmoms wasn't there, would never be there. His pain made him angry and fearless. He was no longer afraid of being jumped, or in a fight. What did it matter if he got killed? The only person who truly cared about him and whom he had loved beyond all words was gone.

JaQuan cared about his moms, she was his mother after all. She meant well, and she tried as much as she could. When he thought about it, it was odd. He had friends who had brothers and sisters and cousins everywhere. He was pretty much alone. Until he moved in, he never saw his aunts and still didn't see his uncles. He did have cousins but he never saw most of them. None of them had ever come to visit his grandmoms, now he thought about it. When Grandmoms was alive, he didn't think about it. He didn't care. He had his friends and they were his cousins, his brothers and sisters.

The sun was beginning to sink over Jamaica Plain and Mission Hill, and mirrored gold in the windows of the Heath Street project and Back of the Hill townhouses on the hill above it.

"How are you doin' today, son?"

JaQuan looked up in surprise. He hadn't noticed anyone coming. He'd allowed himself to get lost in himself, a dangerous thing on these streets, but not so much here. He sighed. "I'm doing well, ma'am."

She was a well-dressed black woman, short and generously pro-portioned, with a close-cut natural, dangling earrings, and bold dark-rimmed glasses. She had a large black dog on a leash and she let him off to run through the hillside field.

"The city looks good from up here, doesn't it."

"Beautiful," JaQuan agreed.

"This is my favorite thinking spot," she said, hanging on to the leash and watching her dog run.

"I'm sorry, ma'am." JaQuan jumped up from his seat on the old stone wall. "Am I taking your place?"

She laughed, a hearty generous laugh. "No, son, you're fine. Sit back down. I'm sorry to interrupt your thinking time. I just got off work and Victor here needs to get out the minute I get home." She looked at him closely. "You live around here, son? Are you Catherine's boy?"

JaQuan looked at her again and she held his gaze. *She's not afraid of me*, he thought. *She doesn't think I'm going to rob her and hurt her.*

"No," he said. "I have a friend who used to stay up here with her aunt. I always liked coming here."

"It is a good place to figure out what you're feeling and just think about things. You just remind me of Catherine's boy. I think he's gone off to college now. I haven't seen him since Catherine moved. What school you go to?"

"Um," JaQuan hesitated. "I was at English but I'm taking a little break."

"What's your name, son?" She looked at JaQuan's face and laughed. "I'm not school police, I'm not going to report you—just being neighborly."

JaQuan laughed too. "Malachi, ma'am," he said, using his middle name, the one he'd used at the library with all his new white friends. He reached out to shake her hand.

"Good manners, too. Somebody raised you right."

"My grandmoms," he said without thinking.

"What's her name? Maybe I know her."

"She passed."

"I am sorry, Malachi." She hesitated, whistled for her dog, then turned back to JaQuan. "Son, you could do me a big favor. I don't want to put you out, so you tell me no if you can't do it."

"Okay."

"I just got off work and I am—no offense, Victor—dog-tired, so if you wouldn't mind running down to the Centre Street Market for me and getting me some milk and eggs, I would be grateful. I was going to walk down with Victor, but I'm about done in."

"I don't mind at all, ma'am. I came right by that store on my way up the hill."

She reached into the pocket of her jacket for some money and her list, then laughed. "Well, you have manners, Malachi, but I forgot mine. My name is Niecy Hoskins and here is the deal. You go to the store for me, then you need to let me give you supper, as my thank-you."

"That ain't...that's not necessary, Ms. Hoskins, I'll just do that for you."

"No, it's not necessary, but I insist. Unless you need to be somewhere now, Malachi, I didn't even ask."

"No, ma'am, Ms. Hoskins, I mean. I just don't want to put you out."

"I always make enough in case folks drop by, Malachi, and no one's dropping by tonight, so I insist. I live right up there, see that white house two down from the tower?"

"Yes, ma'am."

"There's a doorbell up on the porch, you just ring it when you get back, hear?"

"Yes, Ms. Hoskins."

"One minute, Malachi, let me call Victor before you go, so he knows you. Victor, come!" she shouted to the dog. After several shouts and a whistle, he came. JaQuan had always loved dogs. He'd befriended several in his South End days when his neighbors let them run in the park.

"Okay, ma'am. I'll be back."

JaQuan turned to walk down the hill. Niecy watched him go, hoping she had judged right. She'd know soon enough.

Chapter Nineteen

Shelley

Shelley finished scanning the *Boston Globe*, the *Herald*, the *Banner*, and a number of Boston weeklies. The Miller case had dropped from the headlines for the moment, but had spawned sidebar stories on the Impact Project, gun violence in the city, and the "no snitching" mantra in the black communities in Roxbury and Dorchester. Enough for today. Carolyn's plane was due in from Paris in about 30 minutes. She put the papers back neatly in her study, looked around the house as she grabbed her keys. She had given it a thorough cleaning, laid logs and kindling in the fireplace, made a large pot of sauce, and had the makings of dinner prepared and ready to cook in the fridge. She had a lot of making up to do.

She locked the front door and spent a minute, as she always did, listening to the gentle roar of the surf, smelling the salt in the ocean-clean air. Then she jumped into the Cooper, lowered the roof and took off. The drive to Logan from Revere was just 15 minutes, but she wanted to be there in plenty of time.

She timed her arrival well. Carolyn was stepping out to the curb with her roll-on and knapsack as Shelley pulled up. Early in their courtship, Shelley had always arrived early, parked, and greeted Carolyn at the gate.-- something she could no longer do since 9/11/2001 anyway. Even before then, as they got to know each other better, Shelley understood that when Carolyn arrived back in Boston from a trip abroad, she used the airport time to acclimate to being back in the States. She liked to be alone until she cleared Customs. By the time she made it curbside, Carolyn was eagerly looking for Shelley. If the flight was longer than seven hours, they went home. Under seven hours, Shelley left it to Carolyn to decide if she wanted dinner out and a plunge into the bright city lights or dinner at home by the fire, with the sound of the sea.

They put the luggage in the trunk, then shared a tease of a kiss in the car.

"Home, Scribe!" Carolyn whispered in Shelley's ear.

"Your desire, Madame Photojournalist, is my command," said Shelley with a straight face as she eased up on the clutch and headed toward Route One north. To their left, the Boston skyline sparkled as the sun sank slowly past the northwest horizon. "Does this mean I'm forgiven?"

"Oh, bugger off." Carolyn mock-glared at her. "But I'm serious about you getting out of that job."

"OK, then," Shelley said. "How was gay Paree?"

"Not so gay..." Carolyn said in her best Groucho imitation, "but lots of fun. Mackenzie sends her regards and is doing nicely. She still plays her violin zealously, and has begun to paint and write. She is seriously entertaining the idea of holding a monthly salon. I sat in on a couple of her practice ones.

"Practice salons? Give me a break, what do you have to practice?"

"Well, the food, for one, if you're not Gertrude Stein or Collette. I wish, my little potato-pie, that you could have been there with me. You know my French would be a lot better if we went more often."

Shelley laughed. "Oh, fuck off. You know my French would be better if I went at all."

"You're invited every time."

"I know, I know. I'm going to take time off—remember, I can't count these trips as work—but Italy is first on my agenda," she said.

"My sweet, times have changed, this isn't like the old days when you had to save for years for your one trip abroad. Your working-class roots are showing. You make enough already that you could join me for long weekends, at least a couple of times a year. To fly abroad doesn't have to be the plan of a lifetime anymore, honey." Carolyn had a smile in her voice. "I could call you, spur of the moment and say—ah, *ma cherie*, I cannot live without you—meet me in Paris, dahling." She gave it her best Bacall as she held an imaginary phone to her ear.

"*Mais oui, amour*, you could call, but would I have the courage to fly?"

"You're going to have to learn, because if the Republicans are running the country when we retire, we're becoming ex-pats and I know just the convent in Paris. Mackenzie's always asking for you, and we always have a place to stay."

"Yea, yea, yea, my exotic ex-pat." Shelley put an end to the discussion. "You're sure you want to go home? You don't want to head out for sushi or romantic Italian overlooking the beach?"

"I have all the romantic Italian I can handle, thanks. I want a fire, the sound of the surf and some very good red wine, then we can go from there."

"Paris always raises your standards."

"Xenophobe!"

They were relaxed when they pulled into the driveway. Shelley took the suitcase, Carolyn grabbed the knapsack with her notebooks and camera equipment. "When I get to the computer, I'll put up these pictures for you to see. They're something."

"Kids in the crossfires of war?"

"Pretty much, like the kids your folks are working with, but so different."

They walked to the front and up the stairs to the porch. As Shelley unlocked the door, Carolyn took in the smell of salt, the pounding of the invisible surf. The night was clear and cool enough for a fire.

Within fifteen minutes, Carolyn had the fire blazing and jazz pouring from the stereo. Shelley got the heat going under her sauce and the water boiling for pasta. She had uncorked one of their better bottles of red, and handed a glass to Carolyn. They toasted silently.

"What can I do to help?" Carolyn asked as she took a sip of the wine. "Mmmm! Nice. Very much up to standards."

Shelley laughed. "Get out of here, I'm all set. Go up and take a shower, change your clothes, whatever makes you comfy. I'll have dinner ready in fifteen."

"Good, I'm starving." Carolyn circled behind Shelley, put one arm around her as she stirred the sauce and kissed her on the neck. "I'm out of here."

Shelley laughed. "Good, no more disturbing the cook."

After Carolyn's departure, Shelley scatted along to Wayne Shorter's saxophone. She pulled a container of chopped vegetables out of the fridge and threw them into a waiting pan of olive oil and seasonings. She grabbed two chicken breasts she had washed and pounded, and set them in another pan with olive oil, wine, mushrooms and her secret seasonings. She set the heat on low for both and began to thinly slice layers of mozzarelle.

Life could be good, and they were both hungry.

***

The fire roared and candles flickered. Nothing could be more perfect than this moment, Shelley thought. She and Carolyn sat side by side facing the fire, surrounded by the sound of jazz saxophone, Dexter Gordon now, turned low and soothed by the ebb and flow of the ocean beyond the porch.

They laid their plates aside. Shelley took Carolyn's hand and kissed it. "How was it really," she asked. "Not Paris, Iraq. It sounds like this assignment was tough."

Carolyn took her partner's hand in both of her own, and gazed at the fire.

"It was tough," she said. "It was heartbreaking in so many ways. But it was also awe-inspiring. These kids are so resilient. On one level, their lives are being destroyed. They've lost parents, siblings, cousins, grandparents, aunts, uncles, friends. On another level, they seem to have a belief that what is going on is greater than they are, that it has a meaning, a large context relating to their whole civilization. They seem, most of them, to bounce back. But I have to wonder how they'll do in the long run."

She turned and looked at Shelley. "It also made me think a lot about all the youth caught up in violence in the city here. There is no larger context of meaning for these kids to hold onto, or to make sense of anything with. I can't imagine the level of misery and grieving in either case. And I can't imagine what the future will hold for them."

Shelley put her arm around Carolyn. "I'll want to see your pictures tomorrow, babe, and I'd like to get your thinking about whether we could do something using photographs like yours to bring this youth violence stuff home to people here. The police department has so many cases of youth shootings and killings right now, they're happening faster than they can be investigated. And of all of them, the one that's gotten the most attention is the accidental shooting with the little Miller boys. That was horrible, they were so young. But at thirteen, fourteen, even seventeen, eighteen—these are still kids. It's all a horrible loss, but the Miller case is the only one that keeps getting consistent coverage. Maybe photos of all the shooting victims would make people care."

"Let me think about it, Shelley. You know I don't want to encourage you to stay in this, but it's actually a good idea." Carolyn threw another log on the fire. "What's happening with that case? When I left, the older cousin was missing."

"JaQuan. He's still missing. But listen, that reminds me, I had to schedule something for this weekend."

Carolyn jammed the poker back into its holder and turned to face Shelley, arms folded tightly across her chest.

"I know, I know. Carolyn, listen...I kept the whole weekend free except for this. One of the officers investigating the Miller case is Harriet Denton's cousin. She doesn't seem to like me much, and I need to work with her. I thought I could get some insight from Harriet. When I called her, she invited us to Christina's opening at one of the South End galleries and dinner after at the Lebanese place over on Shawmut."

"So she knows you're trolling for info?"

"She does. It feels important, Carolyn, and we haven't seen Harriet and Christina in a while. I really wouldn't have scheduled it this weekend, but it fell that way."

"This has got to stop, Shelley. I really can't take this much longer. We make a plan and something from your job always screws it up."

"Car, come on. Please don't start this tonight. I am so glad you're back, this is one little thing, and yes, it's work, but it's always great seeing those two."

"That's not the point and you know it." Carolyn sighed and sat back down beside Shelley. "I know this whole job has gotten to you, Shel, and I don't mean to seem selfish. When this is over, we need to talk. For now, you're forgiven as long as the rest of tomorrow is mine and there's nothing more strenuous on the agenda Sunday than a very late brunch."

Shelley paused, and left everything she was feeling unsaid. Instead she deadpanned, "You got it, schweetheart. Now how about bed? You must be exhausted."

Carolyn blew out the candles.

Chapter Twenty

Shelley

Saturday night in the South End was like a party, Shelley mused. It was always like that. The South End was a moneyed area now, for the most part, and Saturdays *tout le monde* were out for galleries, theatre, ballet and the multitude of restaurants that gave Tremont Street the sobriquet "restaurant row," although there was no dearth on Washington Street or Columbus Avenue either.

Carolyn had decided if they had to come in to meet with Harriet, they might as well do it right. She had dressed for it, in the New York black that always drove Shelley crazy, huge gold hoops, low heels and a flamboyant scarf. They arrived early in the evening to restaurant row on Tremont Street for drinks and hors d'oeuvres. They both liked the energy of the area, though there were a few too many real estate moguls for their taste. Still, being here was a high. Shelley had dressed fashionably herself, in white linen pants, black silk shirt, white linen jacket, red and white dangly earrings, her favorite silver bracelet and rings. She liked the contrast the night would bring. Tremont Street was built up and snazzy. The gallery hosting Christina stood in the demi-monde of abandoned factories and old lofts south of Washington Street, and the

Red Fez had been on Shawmut Ave., serving up late night hummus, lamb and falafel for over thirty years.

After white wine and oysters, they joined Harriet at the Wareham Street Gallery for Christina's opening. Christina was dressed in white silk, with huge silver earrings and multiple bracelets, her blond-streaked shoulder length hair was pulled back stylishly in two large clips, a silver belt with a large turquoise clasp pulled in her white tunic style top at the waist and dramatized her harem pants.

"I can't believe you came! You have made this show!" Christina grabbed Carolyn, then Shelley, kissing them each loudly and solidly on the mouth. "Harriet said you would come, I didn't believe it."

Harriet stood beside Christina, dressed stylishly but conservatively in black jeans, black turtleneck and a loose black cotton jacket. Her close-cut natural, Shelley noticed, had a touch of gray in it, her large competent hands had several gold rings, her earrings were conservative gold hoops. She was quietly sexy and strong next to Christina's exuberance. She greeted Shelley and Carolyn warmly but with far more reserve.

"It is so good to see you both. It's been a while," she said. "Let me show you Christina's work."

"Don't you have to stand by your woman and greet potential patrons?" Carolyn asked.

Harriet laughed. "I hate these things. She'll sell a lot more without me by her side. And you know Christina; she can hold her own quite well. Let me show you the paintings, then we can head down to the Fez. Christina will either join us later if she can get away or I'll just come back for her."

They wandered the gallery. It was a second-floor space with two large open rooms painted white and divided by a three-quarter wall with two large entryways on either side, so art viewers could flow from room to room. Christina's show took up both rooms.

"This is a huge show for her," Harriet said. "It really does mean a lot that you came down. This is the first time she's had a solo show in a commercial space, and the first time she's ever shown in a space this large."

Christina's paintings were huge splashes of color on canvases that were approximately four feet by four feet, some slightly smaller, some appreciably larger. She used primary colors, concentrating on shades of red and blue. Shelley would have said, if she were writing a press release for the show, that Chris achieved a sense of urgency in the painting by using coarse brush strokes, looking almost like *impasto*, and a sense of calm in large flat surfaces using completely smooth paint that played against the brush strokes. The first room was hung with eight paintings, the second room with the largest of the series, an eight by eight canvas taking the side wall by the entryways. Four additional paintings hung in between two on the large wall and two on the end wall, along with a series of blown-up photographs showing the painter at work, and some of the paintings at various stages.

On the front wall of the second room, a slide projector showed the paintings, with the painter's voiceover narrative explaining her artistic choices, technique and what she was hoping to achieve in each work and with the series.

"It took Chris two and a half years to do this series. She's been working non-stop on it," Harriet said.

"What inspired her?" Carolyn asked.

"She says it was a number of things. We've been vacationing in Provincetown regularly, we took a trip to Italy, we've had all the violence and shootings going on in the city for years now, and, Chris says—and she's right—the South End has just changed so much. Except for IBA, Methunion and Castle Square, and a few token afford-able units, the neighborhood has completely gentrified. You saw the title of the series, *The Center Does Not Hold*? It's a quote from Yeats."

"She's right about the South End being gentrified," said Shelley.

"Don't I know it," Harriet said. "When I first moved here, there were tons of other black folk around. The markets were affordable, people were inviting neighbors for cookouts. You still had the old daughters and granddaughters of the black train conductors who'd bought homes on the undesirable train-track side of Columbus Ave."

"The side that now borders the very desirable park where the tracks once ran," Shelley added.

"Don't you know it. We still have some places we can afford and actually want to eat at—Bob the Chef's, Charlie's Sandwich Shoppe—but I don't know how long I give them. And black folk who move in now have to have bucks. You remember when Chris and I started seeing each other, she had a place on Albany Street she'd fixed with sweat equity—her own and a lot of ours. She got so good, she was making money as a carpenter."

"No kidding," said Shelley.

"I remember that," Carolyn said. "I'd just moved here and met you guys."

"So what do you think?" Harriet asked.

"I think these are amazing," Shelley responded. "I'm not sure I understand what she's trying to say about violence, gentrification and Italy..."

Harriet smiled. "Don't forget Provincetown."

"...but I could look at these again and again," Shelley went on. "The way Chris juxtaposes the colors pulls me in, then pushes me away, almost as if the paint is moving on the canvas. She creates these spaces that make me feel, first cramped and uncomfortable in one painting, then whirling out of control, then a huge painting of controlled tension and calm."

"Impressive," Harriet said.

"Shelley loves painting. I'm more drawn to photography," Carolyn said. "But I love these, they fill me with energy. They create spaces with simple strokes of a brush. They fill me with emotions, though I'd need more time to sort what those emotions are."

"With any luck, you'll get a chance to tell Chris. Are you ready to get a bite and have me spill the beans about my cousin?"

"Let's do it," Shelley said.

"I'm going to find Chris and say goodbye," Carolyn said.

***

They made their way over to the Red Fez on the very quiet back streets of the neighborhood. Once they left the bustle of the gallery district, the streets emptied, became mostly residential, and they edged their way over to the fast-shrinking Syrian, Greek and Lebanese section where the Red Fez sat. They entered the small restaurant, with nine tables in the middle of the room and two booths with high wood backs and red velvet curtains along each of the two side walls. They took an empty booth and greeted the waitress who came with menus.

"So, how did you find out that Cassie and I are cousins?" Harriet took a sip from her beer, as the waitress walked away with their orders.

"We were talking about a media strategy for one of our cases. I started thinking aloud about what neighborhoods we would want to have coverage in, since a principal in this case has dropped out of sight. I mentioned the South End and Cassie—Detective Rock—said, 'My cousin Harriet has some good contacts to talk to if we think we need to place something in their neighborhood papers.' I said, 'Harriet Denton?' and we were off. Once I told her how we knew each other, I'd come out to her. She didn't seem particularly thrilled. I really need to work well with her, Harriet, and there's something about her I like, but it's completely one-sided." Shelley stopped and drank some wine.

"Shelley thinks your cousin views her with contempt," Carolyn added.

Harriet burst out laughing. "Actually, Car, I suspect she does."

Carolyn laughed. Shelley did not. "Harriet, I need you to be serious about this." she said.

Harriet wiped her eyes and took a breath. Still smiling, she put a hand on Shelley's arm. "Girl, you have to lighten up. Cassie views almost everyone with a little bit of contempt, and distrust. But here's what you need to know...she is as professional as they come. It doesn't matter what she thinks about you, she'll do everything she can to get the job done right."

Harriet took a sip of wine. "Let me give you a little background on Cassie. She wasn't always a police officer, she started out in the financial field. She was making a lot of money, but she hated what she saw around her—growing drug use in the black community, and growing violence, first among adults, then among our youth."

Harriet paused as the waitresses began to bring plates of food. With dinner in front of them, she resumed. "Plus, her husband turned out to be a total jerk."

"It's hard to believe she was married," Shelley broke in without thinking. "I'm sorry, Harriet. Keep going, please."

"Well, I'll give you the short version—I don't want to betray all my cousin's confidences. Her goal was to make money, be happily married, and that she and Curtis would start donating money where it would make a difference in the community. Curtis wanted to move away, pretend he was white, live high off the hog and leave Roxbury behind. On top of that, he was abusive and an alcoholic. Cassie ended up divorcing him, which he fought. He made the divorce as miserable as he could.

"While this was going on, the daughter of one of their close friends was shot and killed in a drive-by. She was an innocent bystander, visiting some friends from school—she was at Boston Latin. The tragedy galvanized Cassie and she decided to join the police department.

"Once she got there, she was as talented and single-minded as she'd been in finance. That, and being a black woman at the right time got her to sergeant in only four years."

Shelley and Carolyn both stopped eating. Harriet took a few bites of her lamb couscous.

"I had no idea," Shelley said.

"Mel and Judy Plankhorn. Good friends of hers, and Shalia—the girl who died—was their youngest. It almost destroyed them."

The front door of the restaurant burst open. Christina, a whirlwind of pure and angry energy, surged in.

"Damn kids!" she said. She stalked to the table and sat in the seat they'd been saving for her. She grabbed Harriet's wineglass and drank from it, then put the glass down more gently and took a deep breath.

"They have this new thing," she said, "they zip by on bicycles, four or five at a time—holding up traffic, buzzing pedestrians, grabbing purses. I just got buzzed."

Chapter Twenty-One

JaQuan

JaQuan walked down the hill to the market on Centre Street. He had a good feeling about Niecy Hoskins, and he was hungry. It was tempting to bring her the groceries and stay for dinner. She had the kindness he'd felt in his grandmother. But she wasn't his grandmother. Once she found out he was a thief, sold drugs, was on the run, she would know she'd made a mistake in befriending him. And he had a feeling he wouldn't be able to con her with the web of stories that saved him at the library. But with the money she had given him, he could get some supper before he went to meet his friends.

"Can I help you?" The guy behind the counter looked hard at him. JaQuan hadn't realized he'd actually entered the store. The place had an old-fashioned smell to it. JaQuan could smell the wooden floorboards, and ground coffee.

"Ah, yeah, Ms. Hoskins asked me to pick up some stuff for her."

The owner, still skeptical, softened a little. "Let's see her list."

JaQuan handed it over.

"You can get the bread and milk over there. I've got the eggs, cheese, tomatoes and rice back here."

JaQuan paid for the groceries, took the change and the list, and thanked the man behind the counter.

"You say hello to Ms. Hoskins for me," the man said.

"I will," JaQuan promised. He gathered the grocery bag and turned to go, then stopped and turned back to the man. "Can I borrow your pencil for a minute?"

The man handed it to him.

JaQuan wrote for a few seconds and returned the pencil.

"Thanks," he said, and left the store.

At the top of the hill, JaQuan stopped to take in the view once more, then walked softly onto Niecy Hoskins' porch. He set the bag of groceries, with his note wrapped around the change, in front of the door, rang the bell, then leaped off the porch and ran down the hill.

He ran, feeling silly, until he knew she couldn't see him. He slowed, put his hands in his pockets and sauntered down Centre, taking a right on Linwood, past Romar Terrace, heading into Highland Park, and down the other side of the hill. He wanted to check a few things, later tonight. On the down-low. He wasn't supposed to meet up with his boys for a few days yet, according to the plan they'd made. But he couldn't wait that long. He trusted his boys' allegiance, but not their judgment, or their ability to stand strong together.

He felt energized, coming back into his turf. The Deep was his responsibility, he kept his boys safe, kept them in money, and they were his real family now. He was worried about Eightball and Maurizio encroaching on their turf. But he had deeper worries he hadn't shared yet. The reason he had the gun. He had trouble thinking about that. He wasn't ready to deal with the idea that he might be the reason his little cousin was dead.

The thought made him pause again. It was too early to head toward the 'hood. It was still daylight and the sun wouldn't be down for a couple of hours yet. He turned by the First Church and headed down toward Madison Park High School and lower Roxbury. He might still be able to find Monique and chill with her for a couple of hours in the South End. He didn't think anyone was looking for him there.

***

Niecy Hoskins opened her front door and saw, with disappointment, the bag of groceries resting on her porch. She sighed as she stepped out, making sure the dog stayed inside. The boy had gotten exactly what she asked for and left the change wrapped in her grocery list and the receipt behind the bag so it wasn't visible from the street. She picked up the change and noticed handwriting that wasn't hers. She brought the bag inside, closed the door, sat on the coat bench and opened the note. The young man had written on the back of her list. *I'm sorry, Miss Hoskins, I can't stay tonight. Maybe another time.*

Niecy counted the change. It was what she thought; he had bought the groceries, he hadn't taken any of the money, and he said, *maybe another time.* Just as well. She wasn't sure how she would have handled tonight, except to offer him dinner and a bed and try to think of other tasks that would bring him back. She had a suspicion she knew who he was.

Chapter Twenty-Two

JaQuan

JaQuan vectored through side streets, past the historic First Church, and down to New Dudley Street. He crossed near the Madison and O'Bryant schools and descended to the back parking lot, to zigzag across the streets of lower Roxbury, heading toward the South End. As he was leaving Niecy Hoskin's place, JaQuan had panicked. He hadn't thought through coming back to the city. He had just been restless. It was still daylight. There was no way he could head toward his home turf until night fell. Somebody would see him for sure and if Maurizio's crew was trying to take over his turf, one little call to po-po would be the end of his freedom. He should have gone back to Emilio's in Charlestown and laid low until darkness came. Truth was, he was bored and he was homesick…for his boys, for feeling needed and important, for being in charge, for having fun. *Man*, he thought, *I had nothing to do with Ishmael being shot, I shouldn't have to be running. It isn't fair.*

He remembered the day he saw Monique in the South End, his first day of running. She had said to call her. She'd been on her way to school. Monique had always been really serious about school. And they'd known each other almost all his life. He knew she would probably be home studying, or doing homework with her two schoolmates, Lakeisha and Kimberly. Lakeisha lived in Lower Roxbury, not far from where his mother used to live. Kimberly lived a few streets over from Monique in the South End. He'd started in that direction before the decision was conscious. He hoped she would be there, he felt the need to see her. Later, when it was dark, even though this wasn't the day for their planned meeting, he would head over to check out the action on his corner. He felt an urgency to be doing something. He was responsible for his boys.

Though his neighborhood had changed, the buildings remained the same and his heart broke every time he walked through the South End. He came down Washington Street from Dudley, crossed Mass Ave. and took a left when he got to East Springfield Street. He walked down until he reached Tremont Street, crossed it and the street became West Springfield. Kimberly lived halfway down on the left. He remembered, he hoped correctly, that Kimberly's parents both worked. The girls would probably be studying in the kitchen downstairs, so he went around the high stoop that led to the front door and gave a rap on the wooden door beneath the stairs. There was a bell as well, and he rang it. It took two rings before Kimberly's face appeared in the small square of glass. She turned away to talk to someone. He hoped she was talking to Monique and not her mother.

Finally, he heard the key turn, and the door opened for him. "Hi JaQuan. You looking for Monique?"

"Yeh, Kimberly. She here?"

"Come on in quick, JaQuan. She's here but my mom'll be home pretty soon, so you ain't got long."

"Yeh, OK. Thanks."

JaQuan walked into the long kitchen space. In one way, of course, it didn't look at all like his grandmoms' house. But on the other hand, built like all the townhouses in the South End, it did. All the South End homes had their kitchen in the basement, which was a ground floor entered under the front stoop and usually with a garden and small parking space by the back door. It had a large entrance/eating area as you entered by the front, often with comfortable chairs and a big dining table, and the actual cooking area, with a smaller table or breakfast bar, by the back door. The floor above was the large front parlor with a small back room, and the floors above that all had two bedrooms.

"Hey, Monique."

"Hey, JaQuan." Monique said it quietly, waiting.

"Monique, I'm going upstairs, lay out my stuff for school tomorrow," Kimberly said. "I'll be back in a bit and we can finish homework. Okay?"

"Thanks, Kimberly." Monique closed her math book, using the assignment sheet to mark the spot.

Kimberly looked at him. "JaQuan, you be careful."

"Yeh. Thanks."

Kimberly left. JaQuan looked around the room, taking it all in, then looked back to Monique. "I'm sorry, 'Nique. I really need to talk to you."

"It's okay, JaQuan. I'm sorry I couldn't stop last time you wanted to talk." Monique gestured to the long refectory table she and Kimberly had been working at. "Why don't you sit down. You hungry?"

JaQuan sat. "I ate this morning." He looked at the plate of sandwiches in the middle of the table.

"Have some. Kimberly and I always make too many, but they are so good." She pushed the platter toward him and he picked one up.

"What are they?" he said and took a bite.

"Bacon, lettuce, tomato with mayonnaise on toast. Kimberly's mom got us a whole pound of bacon. They're our new thing. What do you think?"

JaQuan nodded, mouth full. "Good," he said finally.

Monique got up and got him a glass. "Lemonade," she said, pouring him some. "It goes great with it. Makes summer last a little longer."

She watched him eat a sandwich and pick up a second. "Kimberly's mom will be home soon, Q, and you shouldn't be here."

"You think she'll call police?"

"No, I don't. But you'll get Kimberly in trouble, and you'll get me in trouble."

"Monique, I meant what I said last time I saw you. I need you to help me think through what I should do."

"What have you been doing the last two weeks?"

"I've been staying with people, like I told you, friends of friends, and I've decided I don't want to go away. There's no life for me in Providence or Springfield. It's been hard enough hiding around here. I don't want to run. And I know you don't get this, Monique, it's not your life, but I got my boys to think about. They really need me."

"Need you for what, JaQuan? I know you're Q out there, but I hate calling you that, OK? You lead your posse; the word is you're selling drugs—which is not the JaQuan I used to know—and everyone's saying you had the gun that killed your little cousin. You're in trouble and I don't see how you think you can stay around and do things like you used to."

JaQuan got up and began to pace around the room. "'Nique, we don't sell drugs, just weed, and we don't sell it every day, ok? My boys and me, we don't have any other way to make money."

Monique looked down at the table.

"And we need each other, we've made enemies. I got so mad when Grandmoms died, you know? I did a lot of things."

He paused and sat down facing her.

"And I miss my home, Monique. I walk by her house and it's closed to me. It seems like it should be the same, she should be there. I'd be coming home from high school, she'd be proud, and ready to help me with homework…" He stopped.

"JaQuan," Monique paused and looked him in the eyes, "you don't have to sell weed to make money."

"I knew you were going to say that, I knew it. OK, yeah, I could work at Mickey Dee's for eight bucks an hour, standing all day, smelling like burgers and fries. Yeah, I could do that. But why would I? I make as much money in a lot less time and I'm my own boss. And we take care of the 'hood. I help other homies make some money, a lot of them take it right to they moms. We make sure the streets are safe."

Safe from everyone but you, Monique thought, but couldn't bring herself to say it. She did say, "But there's a price, JaQuan, you know it. And there's no future. What, you gonna be thirty and selling your piece of weed? A drunk and going after young girls like those gangbangers, standing on the corner showing your biceps with a gun tucked in the back of your pants."

Suddenly angry, JaQuan stood up over her. "You don't judge me," he shouted. "What do you know about my life?"

Her eyes went wide and he stopped and sat back down, his anger giving way to confusion. "I'm sorry, Monique. I didn't mean to yell."

Monique looked away, and he looked down at the table.

"You remember when we were real young?" JaQuan spoke softly. "Remember how we had each other's backs, we swore to be blood friends. We ran all over this neighborhood. Remember the block parties and we all hung out at Sparrow Park, playing tag and kickball.

Sharon, Jimmy, Boo, you and me. Do you remember those days, Monique? I miss them. I was headed somewhere else in those days."

"Maybe it's not too late. I know you've missed your grandmoms, Jake. I know your mom had her problems and it was hard for you. But you're smart, and you're nice..."

"Monique..."

"You are, JaQuan. I know school was hard for you, but it was because you were always getting into fights, and falling asleep in class. Not 'cause you weren't smart. You feel good keepin' all your boys out of school too, so they ain't got no future either?"

"Not fair, Monique. They go, and I go."

"Sometimes."

"Monique, enough, OK? I need your thinking on what I should do now. I got a plan how I can take care of my crew without being 'round the hood all the time, and make some money, but I'm just tired of not being able to show my face.

"And what kind of man can't even go to his cousin's funeral. The way it is, I can't show my face in public ever again. I can't live like that, 'Nique. What do you think I should do?"

"Monique, JaQuan!" Kimberly's voice came from upstairs. "My mom is coming down the street."

"JaQuan..."

"Monique, no, don't even speak—I know what you think, I can see it. You think I should turn myself in. I can't do it."

"Jakey, I know some people you could talk to..."

"Appreciate it, Monique, but I can't. Hey, it was just good seeing you. I'm sorry I yelled. I gotta bounce out of here. Thank Kimberly for the sandwiches, aight?"

"Jake..."

He leaned over suddenly and hugged her. Then he went to the back door, unlocked it and let himself out through the back garden.

It was getting dark and time for his surprise visit to his boys, make sure this idea was going to work.

Chapter Twenty-Three

Cassie

It was early when Detectives Cassie Rock and Sam Mulroney commandeered the small conference room. Cassie had put on a pot of coffee using Peet's French roast, which Sam had brought from home. Sam lugged the file boxes in. By 7:30 a.m., they had laid out all the impact player files related to the Millers and were going through them one by one.

They'd been focusing on interviewing all JaQuan's friends, cousins and schoolmates, going to their homes as often as possible in the hopes of surprising him in someone's kitchen, and to find out how he'd secured the gun and why he'd hidden it where he had. The finding that the gun had been used in other serious crimes had upped the ante for finding JaQuan. The Chief had finally revealed to them that it had been the gun used in the accidental shooting of that suburban mom. He was not revealing it publicly yet but when it finally got out, as it would; as these things always did, they had to be prepared. It also raised the possibility that instead of being just another wannabe gang-banger, JaQuan had already followed the route of other adult Millers and their associates.

But to their surprise, they hadn't been able to locate JaQuan Miller. Usually they found a perp because he couldn't take the isolation anymore. He had to come back to the places and people he knew. No one would give him up—the code was against that—but usually the criminal gave himself away. So the fact that JaQuan hadn't been found after a week indicated that he was smart and had self-control—unusual both in a criminal, Cassie thought, and in a fifteen-year-old boy—or that someone very skilled was hiding him. Unless he left the city, though, he wouldn't stay hidden forever.

The Miller family was, unfortunately, not atypical, although their circumstances had yielded some serious criminal behavior. Cassie was beginning to understand that poverty, multigenerational and concentrated in particular areas, bred a lawlessness that came partly from hopelessness and desperation, and partly from an attempt to maintain pride and respect. She had come to respect Sam's perspective in working on these cases, because he shared her approach. They were both tough and unrelenting, but both also understood that none of these kids or young adults had been born "bad." Both Cassie and Sam had backgrounds that had made them the "other" and the underdog, and so both had empathy with people trying to overcome obstacles. But they had to stretch when trying to imagine overcoming so many obstacles with no tools at hand.

As an African-American woman who'd fought to make it in a largely white male industry—finance—and again when she chose the police, Cassie understood obstacles. And Sam, who in spite of his last name, was Jewish, understood being the underdog and despised. He had a Jewish mother and an Irish father. Growing up in Boston, he'd experienced more than his fair share of street fighting. What made them different was that they had succeeded powerfully in what they chose to do. What also made them different from the youth and families they came across in Homicide, Cassie understood, was that they both came from two-parent homes where people valued education, worked hard and steadily, and had strong extended families. They were poor but saw themselves on an upward social and economic trajectory, so they encouraged you to work hard and take a chance. There was disappointment, there were failures, but there was always hope, and always support: a place to go, feel valued, and lick your wounds before heading out again. She was pretty sure none of these youth had that.

"All right," Sam said. "I think I'm getting a sense of all these Millers."

"Getting a sense, but not understanding." Cassie put down a file and her pen. "I'm just beginning to follow the family tree."

"Yeh, understanding might be way beyond both of us, but let's take a crack at this on the whiteboard. You game?"

"Yup." Cassie pulled Sam's pad over and positioned it next to her own.

"OK. You have Anna Mae Miller, who married Darren Kipples and had three children by him. Darren Jr. in 1969, Antoine in 1972 and Marlene in 1974. Both Junior and Antoine had Kipples' last name, but Marlene was named Miller."

"Naming the girl after herself?" Cassie said. "Or marital troubles?"

"Looks like marital troubles. She divorces Kipples in 1975 and has two more girls, Miriam and Naomi, in 1978 and 1980, by a new boyfriend. She also names them Miller." He went on, reading from the file. "Anna Mae and her husband were real drinkers. Couple of drunk and disorderlies from some very public fights at the local, and there's one domestic, called in by a neighbor. This is all around the time Marlene was conceived and born, and just before the divorce in 1975."

"And Marlene is JaQuan Miller's mom."

"Right. Now here's what we have: Anna Mae graduated high school, got pregnant. She married Kipples and they started having a family. He worked as a bartender, and it looks like that's how they met. Junior, the oldest, did all right. Graduated high school, looks like he took the business track, went to college and got a job in a financial firm, he moved to the suburbs and never looked back. Married, three children, all did well in school. Antoine, the second oldest, not so lucky. Got in trouble with the law a few times, nothing too serious, barely finished high school, got a lot of girls pregnant—he has three sons and two daughters, all by different women—and eventually joined the army."

Sam added Marlene's name to the family tree he was building on the white board. Cassie handed him index cards where she had jotted the information on each of the sons. He taped them next to each name.

"Now Marlene was born in the midst of the troubles. She seems to have been a rebellious child, always in trouble in school. Dropped out when she was sixteen, ended up in a group home for drug use. Out again, she got picked up for prostitution and again for drugs. Got a suspended sentence for the prostitution, rehab for the drug use. She had two early miscarriages and got pregnant successfully with JaQuan in 1990—she was eighteen—and seemed to go straight for about a year, until she was finally arrested in a crack house, half out of her mind. She served a year and did some rehab, the child lived with one of her sisters until she got out and reclaimed him. It was back and forth for a couple of years, until she did some real time, this time for possession with intent to sell, and JaQuan went to live with Anna Mae."

"How long did he live with her?" Cassie asked.

"From about age four until he was ten. By then Marlene was out of prison, and Anna Mae was suffering from advanced diabetes. JaQuan went to live with his mom again, but that didn't last long. Anna Mae died when JaQuan was twelve." He tacked up the card Cassie handed him. "I have to say, looking at his school attendance and grades, that all the years he was with his grandmother, he thrived."

"She gave up drinking?" Cassie was looking at JaQuan's file.

"That would be my guess. And she was probably trying to redeem herself after doing such a bad job raising her own kids," Sam said.

"And she seemed to be from that generation," Cassie added thoughtfully, looking at Anna Mae's file, "that might have been drinkers and might have been fighters, but they held a job. She worked at the old Houghton Mifflin bookmaking plant in Cambridge right through all of this, and Kipples tended bar and was a partner in a luncheonette in the South End. They bought a townhouse on West Concord, back when only black folks were buying by the railroad tracks. Bought it for $2,000, which was a lot of money then. Anna Mae got it in the divorce and lived there till she died, renting out the upper two floors for some income."

"So it seems like JaQuan had a little stability for a few years," Sam said.

"Yeah. There were no problems with JaQuan until after his grandmother died. All his teachers write glowing remarks about his curiosity, his intelligence, his considerate personality." Cassie put down the file. "What happened to him when he left her?"

There was a rap on the door and it opened. "Good morning, Detectives." Shelley Colabro poked her head in. "I brought some coffees."

"You're a little early," Detective Rock said.

Detective Mulroney laughed. "You're fine, Shelley. Come on in, and call me Sam. And you can call Detective Rock, Cassie." He got up and took the coffees and a box of doughnuts from her. "Honey Dew, not Dunkin's—nice call, they make better doughnuts."

"We were just putting together the Miller family tree. We're trying to identify all the players from that family to see if we can get a line on JaQuan. We've canvassed his friends and schoolmates pretty thoroughly, and those relations we know of, and there's been no sign of him. Someone who knows what they're doing is probably helping him stay hidden." Cassie helped herself to a glazed. "And for the record, I try not to eat these."

"I, on the other hand, love them," Sam said. "Shelley, we're also going through the files to try to get a real sense of JaQuan and his family. If we're going to try to lure him, we need to know more about him."

"Do you want to bring me up to date so far?" Shelley sat at the table and opened the lid on one cup of coffee." She sniffed the air. "I see you two drink real coffee. We have no Peets or Starbucks where I live. I had to detour through Eastie even to find a Honey Dew. But the doughnuts are good."

"We'll backtrack in a few minutes, we just want to flesh out the links here, if you don't mind," Cassie said sharply. "Sam, you were just finishing with Marlene." She turned briefly to Shelley. "Marlene is JaQuan's mother. Sam, let's finish putting up the info on his two aunts, Naomi and Miriam."

"Naomi finished high school. Whatever else Anna Mae didn't do—JaQuan's grandmother," he said to Shelley, "—she pushed education. Miriam finished as well. But that's as far as they went. Naomi's school records show a lot of anger issues and fights. Her grades were erratic. Miriam was the youngest and seemed to be a decent student and fairly quiet in school. But both got pregnant as soon as they finished."

Sam added their names to the family tree.

Cassie read from the file. "Looking at this, it seems like Anna Mae got involved with another hothead in the boyfriend, Arthur Potts. He was the father of Naomi and Miriam. At least she didn't marry this one. Potts played the numbers—the lottery hadn't wiped them out yet. He drank and it looks like he fooled around. He had two children with Anna Mae, but several other children with several other women around the same time. About four years after Miriam was born, Anna Mae cut him loose."

"So what have we got?" Sam asked, stepping back from the board. Cassie gave him a few more index cards to tape up, then read from her notes.

"Okay—Darren Jr. and Antoine are out of the picture. Junior only re-emerged to help with probate when Anna Mae died, she'd named him executor. Antoine's kids by all the different mamas haven't done too well, as you can imagine. They've gotten into all kinds of trouble over the years, a few of them serious. They're all quite a bit older than JaQuan, so it's hard to know if they even know each other. Marlene's only surviving child was JaQuan."

She flipped a page. "Naomi had two girls and a boy some years before she had Antwon. They visit. The girls were always getting into fights, they both have young children now and apartments of their own. We've picked up her older son on drug and gun charges several times, but could never make it stick. He stays with her off and on.

"Miriam had two boys and a girl. Again, some years before Ishmael was born. Antwon and Ishmael look like last try children. Both of her boys still live at home, one has been in trouble time and time again, and seems to be a part of a local gang—though a different one than his cousin JaQuan's. The other looks like he's going to finish high school and has fairly good grades. He's linked with his brother's activities, but doesn't seem to be serious about them. Their younger sister is also at home, and helped take care of Ishmael and Antwon. But she's pregnant and only a sophomore in high school. She transferred to Egleston Community School last year, which is a good sign. They're small and give a lot of personal attention. When she has the baby, if she doesn't drop out, she'll have to transfer to Madison Park High because they have childcare. But they're a factory, that's not so good."

"Why are the Millers considered an Impact Player family?" Shelley asked. "They're not doing well, but none of their crimes seem major."

Cassie raised an eyebrow. "Just because we haven't gotten convictions doesn't mean they're not players. Naomi's girls almost beat another girl to death, we know it from the street, but there were no witnesses willing to talk. The boys are all linked to gang activity and drugs on some level. Antoine's children are all gangbangers, selling drugs, carrying guns. But it's one thing to know, another to prove sufficiently for conviction. They're all in and out of those two apartments fairly frequently."

"The older kids have all been implicated in drugs, knifings and shootings, Shelley," Sam added. "We just couldn't hold them. They all have sheets for minor stuff. Only Miriam's daughter and her oldest son seem uninvolved. Both Naomi and Miriam's previous boyfriends had records. Naomi's latest just got sent away for murder."

"And now Naomi, has hooked up with this character known as Sticky. Richard Raines, actually from a fairly successful black family in Boston. But he's as close to a sociopath as you can get and not be one. He's handsome, charming, but we think he murdered several people in robberies and street shootings. Problem is, nothing sticks to him."

"Hence the nickname," said Sam.

"So he's been living with Naomi, and it's a good bet that either he, or JaQuan, who has his own little gang and drug enterprise, brought that gun into the house. They're there the most."

"Are we looking for Sticky, too?" Shelley asked.

"Of course, but it looks like he's left town for now. The question is, has JaQuan left with him." Cassie looked at Sam.

"We think it's unlikely. Word on the street is, JaQuan hated him, and stayed as far away from him as he could."

"Give us a hand here, if you don't mind." Cassie handed Shelley a stack of files and another to Sam, keeping one for herself. "We've got the names and associations, let's get last known addresses for all these folks. Then we can spend time on your idea, Shelley. We'll put out this newspaper article, but it's a long shot. In the meantime, our detectives and uniforms can check out JaQuan's extended criminal family and see if we can locate him."

Shelley sat back and took a breath. "OK, so this family is bad news. But with all those impact players, why do we think JaQuan supplied the gun, and why are we focusing on him?"

"He disappeared, Shelley, that's the main reason," Cassie answered. "But the other is that he's still young and he doesn't have a criminal record yet. If we find him, we might be able to get more, not only on his activities, but on some of his relatives and the family hangers-on. Of course, he will have caught a case."

"And will then have a record. So, he's got a big reason not to come in," Shelley said.

"Yeah," Sam answered. "But he's also just a kid. He's fifteen, his posse is small-time. He hasn't stayed long with his aunts. He's probably scared."

"Remember your own theory, Shelley, that's why we're doing this. Sam doesn't really buy it, but it's possible JaQuan Miller moved that gun to prevent violence, not cause it. There's never been any hint of gun action with his group, 33 Deep. According to folks we've talked to, he only goes to his aunts' house to sleep. He still goes to school, though not steadily, and the teachers we talked to were surprised, they said he's polite in school, and responsive when he's there and not falling asleep." Cassie opened her first file. "Let's get this done."

Chapter Twenty-Four

Niecy

Niecy Hoskins finished her morning coffee and put the breakfast dishes in the sink. She had walked and fed Victor. "All right," she told the dog, "you be a good boy and Mommy'll see you tonight." She took her briefcase and a light jacket and headed down to Centre Street for the bus. She never drove to work if the weather was good. She liked the walk down to the bus stop, and it gave her some exercise.

Niecy had two children, both grown and doing well. She'd been lucky. She knew other black women with as much education and opportunity as she had, whose children ended up pregnant or on the wrong side of the law. There was a bit of randomness to what happened to children out here. Once they got to middle school, sometimes even earlier, there were so many influences that a parent couldn't control. Niecy had been a single mom for most of her kids' childhood, but she had some good neighbors who'd become friends, and were good role models. They had all helped each other raising the children. The neighborhood was changing, though, becoming much less neighborly. This had already happened to neighborhoods like the South End, but now it was creeping through Fort Hill, Roxbury,

Mattapan and parts of South Dorchester. It seemed as though soon there would be no place for working folks, it would just be the rich and the very poor—unless the very rich could find a way to get rid of them, too.

The very poor stayed because government programs paid private landlords a competitive sum to house them. But gentrification was already taking its toll on families, youth and the fabric of the neighborhood. There seemed no in-between for city planners. The neighborhoods were allowed to fall apart when poor folks moved in. Absentee landlords failed to make repairs, the city left infrastructure to rot. Families eventually created alternative economies and drug dealing crept in, then took over. Chaos and violence made sure no one stepped foot in these neighborhoods unless they had to. Violence became the signature: domestic violence, bullying, stabbings, now shootings. Violence had been bad in these poor neighborhoods of color since the '80s. Not that it wasn't bad before, but it had been isolated. Now it was everywhere.

She reached Centre Street and turned down it. It would be getting cool soon, but today was another seventy-degree beauty. Niecy was co-director with Michele Crane of The SAFE, a non-profit youth development agency Niecy and Mickey had co-founded about eight years ago. Niecy had worked for years at one of the city's oldest settlement houses in lower Roxbury, as an administrative assistant. The center worked with youth, elders, and families needing housing and jobs. About ten years ago, the youth violence in Boston, particularly in Roxbury, began to escalate. When the child of friends was fatally caught in crossfire, Niecy decided she wanted to be more hands-on, she wanted to understand how youth got caught up in the violence, and she wanted the chance to make a difference.

She'd applied to Simmons College, and over three years she got a master's degree in social work. One of the speakers in one of her classes was Michele Crane, a Protestant minister turned social worker/youth advocate. Mickey had worked with youth as part of inner city church ministries for years. But she had spent the last nine years doing street outreach in Boston and spoke passionately about the trauma many of the most violent youth had undergone as children, and what they needed if they were to have a shot at turning their lives around.

Niecy went up to her after class and took her card. They had coffee a few times, and when Niecy graduated and went back to her job at the settlement house, she spent nights and weekends learning outreach with Michele, and working with her on the steps to set up a new non-profit targeted toward these at-risk youth. In a couple of years, they had set up The SAFE, and gotten some initial funding. Niecy took a big risk and left her settlement house job to come on full time with Mickey. It wasn't much of a salary, but her house was paid for, she had some savings, and it was what she wanted to do.

The bus wheezed up and Niecy boarded, still thinking about The SAFE and how it all started. Mickey had two basic ideas she'd developed over years of working with youth. The first was that they had experienced complex trauma that acted as a stop button, affecting their ability to trust, to learn, to make good decisions. The second was, to create conditions for resilience to help these youth overcome their trauma and find hope and goals, you had to work with them on every level—whether it was learning to trust, learning to learn, to communicate, to talk honestly about feelings, to shake hands, to get up on time, to hold a job. And you had to do it over and over again. It was all exposure and practice. Like training as an athlete. It wasn't just battling depression or undergoing counseling. It was every day having small victories, mastering a skill, having support, learning that you really mattered—every day. It was every day coming to the program on time, participating appropriately, learning to speak up politely and articulately. There were plenty of mistakes, lots of attitude—but Niecy and Mickey had both learned it was all fear and lack of practice. Niecy also learned that many of the things teachers and parents called lazy and willful and attitude came from trauma and were the kids' attempts, on their own, to survive the big scary world around them with some dignity intact. And Niecy knew adults didn't understand the level of fear the youth carried: fear of dying, fear of failing, fear of being hated or invisible. Because these youth, for the most part, didn't seem fearful. They were loud, fierce, contemptuous, angry, quick to fight. But at The SAFE, she'd learned very quickly how much these kids wanted to let down their guards, to be cherished, to learn how to learn. How much they wanted to be something and succeed, how much they wanted to be part of the larger world, but how deeply sure they were that they never could be.

As always, Niecy and Michele arrived at work about the same time. They were almost always the first ones in the office. This morning their social worker, counselor and education coordinator were all there as well. Once a week they divided up school visits and went early to talk with teachers, counselors, and principals as needed to make sure their work after school was grounded in what youth were experiencing in school, if they *were* in school—dealing with youth who'd dropped out had another approach—and to find out if they were attending in any kind of regular way. They'd discovered that many youth with unstable family situations missed as many as sixty school days a year, or attended but slept through most of each day.

Niecy said hello to their small staff, poured some coffee and knocked on Michele's door. On the phone, Mickey waved Niecy in and pointed to a plate of pastries on the table. Niecy sipped her coffee.

Michele was white, in her mid-forties. She was slender, five-foot-eight, with blonde hair and a sense of edgy fashion. She didn't look like someone who spent all her time with young black and Latino youth on the edge. Niecy thought it was one of the reasons they were so effective as a team. Most people wouldn't expect them to get along so well. And most people assumed she was Michele's mentor. The truth was, they brought equal but different and complementary experience to the venture, and Mickey was an expert and a natural working with teens. The SAFE was still a young organization. They had a small staff, but one that reflected the diversity of the city they worked in, and possessed equally diverse sets of skills.

Both Mickey and Niecy believed passionately that youth were always open to people who were authentic, who cared about them and could help them take steps toward something good. In a racially charged city, neither woman believed race trumped everything. They both believed the youth wanted adults who walked the walk, who modeled the life they talked about and acted as adults, mentors and guides, not pals. So Niecy and Mickey used their differences to great effect. And they did their best to make sure The SAFE was representative of the world they wanted to see.

Michele finished her phone conversation and hung up. "Good morning!" she said, reaching for more coffee.

"Mickey, I think I found JaQuan Miller."

Chapter Twenty-Five

JaQuan

JaQuan paused at the end of the alley in back of Kimberly's house. He took a breath. He'd made a mistake, coming to see Monique. He missed her, he missed his old life, but these emotions were just messing him up. He fought back tears, he never let himself cry anymore. Forget it. He was going to go through with his plan. Even if he thought she was right and he could change his life now, what would happen to MD, Snake, J-Nice?

Cameron had a shot, if he wanted it, he did okay in school when he went and his mother had a real job. Cameron's real problem was keeping safe where they lived. Cameron's mom didn't get it all. She worked all the time. She wanted Cameron in an after-school program, but there weren't any good ones. You could go shoot hoops at the community center, but getting there and back you were on your own. If you could find a program, it was boring. Do homework, watch a movie, maybe shoot some pool. Unless you really wanted to do something like lacrosse or tennis. But that wasn't their thing. Cameron's mom also wanted him to be there every day to take care of his sister. Even when he dropped his sister off with the neighbor next door, he had to pick her up from school. How could he do both, even if he wanted to? But Cameron at least had a chance.

And then there were the wannabes—the younger kids just running loose around there, and some of his peers. They had nothing to do except smoke weed, play ball or fight. They'd taken up the newest hobby of kids their age, borrowing bikes and then harassing pedestrians by weaving through sidewalk traffic and almost hitting walkers. The more creative among them realized that with a quick lean on the bike, they could grab purses, zoom away, and have made a little cash. JaQuan had stopped his crew from that pursuit. He, Q, was the one who kept them all organized and made sure everyone got a little cash each week. They all had roles keeping the block safe and protecting their business from 5-0.

If he left, all that would fall apart. Snake was a hothead, MD was a pothead, Cameron was too laid back and J-Nice, well, he really was too nice. He liked people, he liked to talk to people, but left on his own he could talk too much.

JaQuan emerged on Tremont Street in time to catch the 43 bus that would take him to Ruggles. Night had fallen at last and it was time to check in on his boys. They hadn't been happy with his plan when they talked out in Everett, but they would go along. He had the details worked out now and it wasn't forever. It would take the heat off all of them. There were no cops visible when he got to Ruggles, so he jumped onto another bus to take him into Roxbury. He got off several blocks early and made his way quietly through the streets. A few people sat out on stoops smoking and talking, but most folks were inside finishing supper, getting ready for school.

JaQuan moved carefully, staying in the shadows and keeping an eye out for the cops. He zigzagged through the blocks, avoiding the streets near his aunts' building and his moms' last apartment. Finally, he emerged across from the park and the basketball courts. Standing in the shadow of the trees, he watched the action. There wasn't a lot. His boys didn't like the plan, but they were doing what he'd asked them to. Snake still had lookout on one corner. J-Nice would chat up passing cars, but there was no runner action. So he was actually following through and telling old customers how to find them next week.

JaQuan had been very clear. If J-Nice didn't know them, if they weren't already regular customers before Q went on the run, he would tell them nothing. Q figured the cops would be sending plainclothes guys to buy, not to bust them just yet, but to keep tabs and wait for him to slip up. He'd already told the boys not to sell to anyone new, but had no way of knowing if they'd followed his instructions. At their last meeting his instructions were clear and simple. Stop selling. Give your old customers the new site. Word of mouth would happen fast enough. The plan he and Emilio had cooked up was risky in some ways, because it took them away from the block and it assumed Q's lieutenants could really step up and handle things when he wasn't there. It also meant they had to come up with a different method to get stuff to the new location. But at least he could stay in touch with his boys regularly. They'd see him at least two or three times a week. This wouldn't go on forever and when the heat died down, they could get back to chilling, sharing pizza, buzzing around on their bikes, ballin', and chillin' with the chicks and other homies.

"Hoo-hooooo."

JaQuan saw Snake snap to attention. He called again. "Hoo-hooooo."

Slowly, casually, J-Nice finished chatting with the last car. Cameron moved from the bench to some trees behind the basketball court. MD passed off the basketball to some of the younger players, and Snake had vanished from his corner. JaQuan moved in the shadow of buildings and trees until he too reached the trees behind the court.

"Q, whatup, man!" MD was effusive, as always.

"Q, what you doin' here? We're not supposed to meet yet. We're just setting things up." Cameron was puzzled and a little nervous.

"You don't trust us?" Snake materialized behind him.

"What do you mean by that, Snake?" Q gave him a hard stare. "You doin' something I should be worried about?"

"Q, it's good to see you." J-Nice chimed in as always, cheerful, conciliatory. "Snake, man, why you say something like that?"

Snake stared at JaQuan.

"Chill, man," Q said quietly. "I was checkin' things on the other end and figured I'd drop by instead of using the pre-pay. That meet with your approval?"

"We changin' the meeting day?" MD asked.

"Naw, Wednesday like we planned," Q answered. "How's it going with folks, J?"

J-Nice thought for a minute. "Snake tell you some old friend of yours came by?"

"Fuck, nigga. I haven't had a chance, have I?"

"Chill, man, I just thought of it," J-Nice said to Snake. He turned back to JaQuan. "Our regulars seem OK with it. A couple were a little worried about being noticed. Most of them seem relieved we'll be closer to downtown."

JaQuan focused on Snake as he listened. When J-Nice finished, he said, "Who?" He stepped into Snake's space. "Who came by to see me, Snake?"

Chapter Twenty-Six

JaQuan

JaQuan was shaken up when he left his boys, though he was careful not to let them see it. Boo. He couldn't remember how long it had been since he'd seen Boo. Boo's family had been evicted and moved from the South End even before Grandmoms died. JaQuan never found out where they went. Boo had been part of the crew, all friends, back then. But for Boo to show up now looking for JaQuan...for him to even know his territory. It had to be related somehow to Eightball and Maurizio. He'd heard Boo worked for them. But why would he be looking for JaQuan now?

He couldn't seem to get hold of himself tonight. He felt trapped. Shaky. Even if he could make something of himself like Monique said, he was wanted by the police now, and he had to take care of his boys. But sometimes he felt like a little child, and wished his grandmoms was still alive and he could stay with her—tucked in, warm, safe, with a big breakfast in the morning and someone to tell him how wonderful he was. Someone to help him stay on the good path.

JaQuan realized he was almost at his aunts' apartments. Without even thinking, his feet were taking him in that direction. He stopped and leaned against a tree. He hadn't even thought of Ishmael tonight.

He was always trying not to think of him, dead, his little cousin, whom he loved, who looked up to him. Dead because of a gun he had tried to hide. He had a sudden urge to be with his aunts, his family. Even though he hated it there, it seemed like someplace where they would care about him, and take care of him for a little while. But would they even want to see him? Did they hate him? Were the police still waiting for him to come back there?

JaQuan sighed. He was tired. Confused. This wasn't him, he thought. He always had a plan for the next move. He felt now like he had right after Grandmoms died. He'd made some poor decisions because of his pain and his anger. But he got his control back. He put things together for himself and his boys so they had some money, they had jobs to do, they had each other. He'd always been strong when he needed to be. Now he felt...well, he didn't know what he felt. Was Emilio right about this plan? Was Monique right that he needed to change his life, that it wasn't too late?

He shook his head. It was easy for Monique to say. She had a family, she had someone keeping her on track. Her parents were there for her in a way that he didn't have.

JaQuan made himself start walking again until he could see his aunts' building. There was a black SUV parked in front. He could hear the boom of the bassline reverberating from it. He slipped into the shadows of the small grouping of city trees near the fence and edged his way toward the backyard. He stopped by the tree closest to the broken fence board. He could hear laughter, his Aunt Naomi's high and brittle from too much liquor; Sticky's, low and suggestive. He could smell dope, the boom box was playing a mix, and someone was grilling—probably Sticky.

JaQuan edged back until he could see through the decrepit fence. Sticky was grilling. *What is he still doing here*, JaQuan thought. *He should be gone. Why aren't the cops looking for him, too? He's done worse things than I've ever done.* JaQuan had never liked or trusted Sticky Raines. But JaQuan caught himself quickly—he had left the gun that killed Ishmael, not Sticky. He felt a sharp pain in his stomach. He felt it whenever he thought of the shooting. He'd hidden that gun so well, he thought.

The smell of a blunt drifted over to him along with music from a radio. Neither his Aunt Miriam nor Robert were there, and he wasn't surprised. It was a matter of time, though, before neighbors heard the music smelled the meat and joined the party.

His Aunt Naomi's voice was loud. "Well, fuck them, then, fair weather friends is what I say.... Fuck you, Stick," she said in response to something JaQuan couldn't hear. "Nah, I gotta get to bed early tonight. I got work in the morning. You know that."

JaQuan didn't see any police—plainclothes or cars. The dudes always thought they were blending, but you could always pick them out. Maybe he could stay here, in his own bed, at least for a night.

"You bitch!" Sticky screamed at Naomi. "I just cooked you dinner. Fuck you!"

Naomi hurled a beer bottle at his head. Miriam was nowhere to be seen.

It had never felt like home to him, what had he been thinking coming here? He loved his little cousins and always had fun with them. He had made friends with his homies here, and turned them into a team. But he'd never felt really welcome here.

Miriam had an extra room, and since he was Marlene's son they let him take it. That's how JaQuan saw it. How could they let him sleep on the street when he was family? But Naomi was usually outright rude to him, she always had attitude even when she was being loving. Miriam, who was the nicest to him, was never completely at ease when he was around. He always thought she was a little afraid of him, maybe judged him, because of his mother. That maybe any day now, he would go a little crazy like his moms was. But he took advantage of the fighting out back and slipped inside.

He moved quietly and opened the door to the room Antwon and Ishmael had sometimes shared. It was empty. If he was Antwon, he wouldn't sleep there either. JaQuan felt his whole body freeze. He had to see Antwon, he had to tell him it wasn't his fault. Maybe they already had. Maybe Naomi had made sure Antwon knew it was his older cousin's fault.

JaQuan went to his room, which was still empty, and grabbed a blanket and wrapped a pillow in it. He didn't know where he was going to sleep tonight but he would need these. It was too late for him to go back to Charlestown. On some very deep level, he felt, for the first time, lost. He had run out of ideas.

As he crept back downstairs, he noticed that Sticky and Naomi were done screaming. Sticky had her in his arms. The food was still cooking on the grill. He slipped out the door and moved back to tree cover. He saw Naomi pull away from Sticky and move over to the window.

"Miriam, that you?"

There was no answer.

"Damn. I thought I heard something, Sticky. Goddamn it—I'm not drunk! She's probably still at one of those Mothers' meetings. She needs to eat. Go take care of that chicken, will you..."

JaQuan backed further into the shadows and stopped. He felt someone watching him. He moved closer to the nearest tree, to use it as a shield if he needed to, and turned.

"Hey, Dog. I been looking for you."

JaQuan froze, then turned to see Boo in the shadow of the alley.

"I heard, man. I just heard."

They bumped chests and pumped their arms in a quick embrace, then did the handshake. Then Boo said, "It's all about to come down on you, man."

"What you mean, Boo. I know 5-0 still looking for me, but we got plans."

"Naw, I don't mean that, Q..."

"What you calling me that?"

"What, big man, you want I call you Jakey like back in the day?"

"Yo, man, we was close in the day. So what you doin' doggin' me wit my boys? And doggin' me here?"

Boo was quiet.

"I still got your back, man. E'en though I ain't seen you," he said softly. "That's more'n I can say for some of your boys."

Now it was JaQuan's turn to be still.

"What you sayin', Boo, man? You sayin' something against my crew?"

"Chill, man. I ain't dissin' your homeboys, I'm just tryin' make you see something you ain't seeing yet." Boo looked around, as he always did, to make sure no one was coming up on him. "What do you think's going on since you been gone?"

"I know Eightball's been eyein' my corner, man, now I'm not there to organize. I know he sending you down to see the what's what."

"Naw, man, that ain't it. Your little corner, man, meanin' no disrespect, it ain't worth shit. Naw, it's your man Snake. You know he going behind your back, talkin' to Maurizio...talkin' trash 'bout Eightball, like he all that, man. He doin' it on the QT, but he doin' it. And old Boo? There ain't no QT with me. I always got my eyes on what matter.

"Your boy, he takin' over. He tryin' to do it smooth, but the man ain't smooth. He's one angry nigga, man. You gotta watch out. The rest of your boys? They don't even know, they all trusting, man, like you. They just happy bein' small time, havin' fun, havin' some smoke and bling and all…. Naw, Q, cause Maurizio and them, they don't know he ain't representin' you…"

Boo stopped talking. He had already talked more than he ever did. But he still had feeling for Q, like a brother. Man, Jake'd always had his back, he was from back in the 'hood, back in the day, and Boo owed him this. Maybe only this…if things got bad, there'd be nothing he could do. But he owed him this.

"I gotta bounce, man, I just needed you to know. Nobody even really care about your block till your boy Snake started making himself all that and gettin' all paranoid. Now you do got a problem. Watch yourself, man. Aight?"

Boo had slipped off almost before JaQuan realized he was gone. Q could feel the heat rising in him, his eyes got hot, his eyelids half closed over them. His hands knotted into fists, he tried to still that awful combination of rage, fear, and confusion that always made him lash out. The reasonable JaQuan, the pleasant, smart young man that people saw, and so didn't understand the other Q; that JaQuan was always swallowed up by the angry Q, who needed to act or drown in his awful fear. He needed to act. Fuck Snake. Fuck his own life.

He melted back into the city.

Chapter Twenty-Seven
Emilio

Emilio Gonzalez made a point of knowing what was going on everywhere around him and with everyone he knew. It was how he stayed alive. It was also how he kept loyalty and kept his reputation as a someone who would hurt you if he had to. In spite of an incomplete and sporadic education, he was an intelligent man. He was also an emotional man, a born leader, and classically machismo. If he had been born into a wealthy, educated family, he would have been a daring entrepreneur and CEO, or, very possibly, the first Latino President of the United States.

Instead, at thirty-five, he was trying to retire from a way of life he'd used to survive, but which gave diminishing returns and less thrill as he grew older. He wanted different things now. He had kids, though none of them lived with him. He loved his kids. And he wanted deeply to make a difference in his community, for his kids, and all the kids. He wanted to be known for that. After his last state-ordered "vacation" down in Bridgewater, he was trying harder to figure out how. But for now, he helped those kids that he could, like JaQuan Miller.

He felt a special draw toward JaQuan. He could see the boy was smart, that he wanted to do things the right way. JaQuan cared about people and wanted to do something with his life. Emilio could also see that he didn't have the ruthlessness to survive in the life he was falling into. He'd heard things and he was worried for the boy.

He'd told Q, even while advising him on how to keep his little lemonade stand going by moving it away from the 'hood for a while, he'd told him: "It gonna be bad, man, your boys getting in Maurizio's sights. Dudes coming out of prison, want their corners, their corners gone. He want to give them something, some kind of action. They gonna be beefs to settle this and your boys gonna be hurt if they left out there on they own."

Maurizio was someone Emilio kept an eye on. He was friendly to Maurizio on the surface, but knew that Maurizio was ambitious and would have liked to take over for Eightball. Maurizio had serious *cojones*, but it was hard to tell what he thought about Morris Coburn. Bucking Eightball was suicide and Maurizio was shrewd, he showed loyalty. But Emilio knew him well enough to know he didn't like working for anyone. Maurizio wanted to run the show.

Emilio went out to wait for one of his baby's mamas, the one who had his car while his license was suspended. In return she drove him wherever he needed to go. He was going to meet with Maurizio. They had stayed close because Maurizio was tight with some of Emilio's boys from Mission. Emilio was hoping he could talk Maurizio out of going after JaQuan's boys. He was hoping Maurizio would do it out of respect, maybe even fear. Emilio would leave him a way to save face. Maurizio didn't need Q's corner or his boys. They didn't do business that way anymore, no one stood on the corner to sell. It was all phone calls and word of mouth. And Q's boys weren't players. It was penny-ante stuff, pin money. Kept them in slices, maybe sometimes a pair of sneaks. Maurizio was pursuing this to look strong, for the power. He was going after those young boys just because he could, and by intimidating them and pulling them in, he thought he'd make himself look stronger. Emilio was going to do this to keep JaQuan and his boys away from danger, but he wanted out of the game. Talking with Maurizio, trusting that Maurizio was wary of him, kept him in the game. But what else could he do?

Chapter Twenty-Eight

Mickey

Mickey Crane, co-director of The SAFE, had grown up on Beacon Hill in Boston but had been restless from the very beginning. She was a restless baby. In elementary school, she was curious, independent and always moving beyond the curriculum with her questions and ideas. She grew up acquiring a social polish, learned the politics of power and the skills of dealing with people diplomatically and, when needed, with kid-glove resolve. She grew up learning never to burn bridges if she didn't absolutely have to. She was a polite and accomplished young woman, with a certain standing in Boston, and she was desperate to get away. She applied to and was accepted at University of California, Berkeley. Her parents had wanted her to go to Harvard or Dartmouth, but she held strong. This was her chance to get out and discover who she was. And who she could be. She felt she was a cliché in her Boston circle—tall, blond, thin. She was fit and athletic and looked good in a little black dress. It was a prison for her.

At Berkeley she felt free. She made a slew of friends and she came to know many faculty members well. During her time there, she did a twenty-hour-a-week internship teaching basic journalism in a summer program with the Immaculate Heart nuns in an all-female high school in Hollywood, while working part-time as a stringer for the *LA Times*. It was her chance to spend time in Los Angeles before she went back east, if she went back east.

What ended up changing her life and direction—from journalism to what she did now—was watching how the nuns worked with their students, bringing out their best, drawing out and reinforcing healthy curiosity, growing their confidence, skills, and encouraging them to reach high. All of it done gently, with respect and caring. They made the whole school a fun and challenging place where the young people—whether from poor families or rich; whether shy or bratty—were treated as full human beings with valid thoughts and concerns.

The nuns did not yell, threaten, talk down or use corporal punishment. They reasoned, questioned, expected the best, and showed each student that she mattered. They didn't disparage or punish mistakes. They encouraged mistakes as a way of learning. They instilled a sense of a bright and wide-open future and encouraged their students to explore new things, and understand that they truly had some choices as they moved forward in life. Michele had had very few teachers or mentors like that. Here, it was a whole philosophy and the way every teacher acted.

And what she ended up loving best about her work with the *Times* that summer—doubtless because of what she was feeling and learning from the nuns—wasn't the actual getting and filing of her stories, but the poor neighborhoods she came in contact with as she did her stories, and the people she got to meet there. They assigned her mostly the feel-good features: "Priest opens work program in east LA—teaches gang member to bake". "Do-gooders create affordable housing and a farmer's market in South Central LA". "Mexican women become *promotores de salud* in their poor barrios"—the liaisons between poor immigrants, the doctors and hospitals. She had wanted to learn about gritty, and she did. But she also learned about hope and transformation that summer. She walked in worlds she'd never known existed. She saw the daily results of deep and pervasive poverty, the slow grinding down of pride and hope in families and children. The breeding of rage combined with indifference. She experienced what happened to families who had little money and no powerful connections.

That summer influenced her in two ways. First, she decided that journalism was not how she wanted to spend her life. Second, she wanted to take a closer look at her own hometown. Boston probably had whole neighborhoods where folks struggled like those she was meeting in California. Yet, in her childhood world, they had never been visible.

In the end, she left journalism and went to work with a community of nuns doing social service work in L.A. She apprenticed, she went back to school, she worked with homeless teens and gang-involved youth. She lived in California for fifteen years before she returned to Boston. When she returned, she trained in seminary and became a minister with a focus on youth and social work.

Michele sat now poring over newspaper clippings about JaQuan Miller and the shooting of his young cousin. She shook her head as she read the piece from yesterday's *Boston Globe*: desperate to find Miller, who had been on the run since the shooting occurred, the police—the paper reported—were planning to flood his neighborhood with cops around the clock, questioning and knocking on doors until they found him. They planned to bring his friends in for questioning.

Today, Niecy was meeting with the lead officer in the JaQuan Miller case. It turned out, fortunately she hoped, that Detective Cassie Rock was a neighbor of Niecy's up on Fort Hill. It would take all of Niecy's diplomatic skills to avoid ripping into Rock for this renewed approach to finding JaQuan. It might work, but it would set back trust and effective policing in the community for years. She thought, ruefully, as she heard Niecy's rap on her door and took her last sip of coffee, how The SAFE's goals and approaches for youth were not always aligned with methods employed by the police, or even most other youth programs for that matter—even though they worked together. Nobody talked about what these young people really were going through—they were living in a war zone in the midst of one of the wealthiest cities. They faced possible death each day, and the fear of losing housing, food, money and jobs was daily, and unending. Some had PTSD as deep as any war veteran, and it went unacknowledged. When would the powers that be begin to understand what really worked? It wasn't just jobs, or even counseling; it wasn't just school, or a mentor. It had to be all that plus a comprehensive, ongoing set of relationships, a safe and trusted place, consistency, helping youth grow a network of trustworthy adult mentors and guides.

It was taking the youth places they'd never been, experiencing new things, learning new skills so they gained confidence and were comfortable in the larger world. It was doing constant and meaningful community service that made youth feel part of the solutions. It was helping youth unlock and begin to understand themselves, and communicate.

But that whole package wasn't politically sell-able. It took money and time. But what could you expect when a child had been on his own since toddler-hood, or sometimes even infancy, and had to make his own rules and his own way?

Niecy came in, and Michele managed a smile. "Good morning, Niecy. What's your thinking on this?"

Chapter Twenty-Nine

Shelley

S helley rapped on the frosted glass of Cassie's open door. Cassie, with reading glasses on, looked up. She frowned.

"I brought you a copy of the *Globe* story." Shelley said.

"Have we gotten any calls from it yet?"

"I just thought you'd want to see it."

"I have other cases you know, Ms. Colabro. Just drop it there." Cassie indicated a hard chair by the back wall of her small office. "I'll look at it when I have a chance."

Shelley held her ground. "I thought we had progressed to first names." she said. "Look, you won't have to work with me forever, but I'm here now and we are working this case. Do you want to tell me what I've done to offend you?"

Cassie sighed and pulled off her glasses. She indicated the seat beside her desk and gestured for Shelley to sit down. "It would take much too long to tell you that, and you, personally, haven't done anything. Let me see the article."

Shelley handed it to her. She put her glasses back on and read:

POLICE TO CRACK DOWN IN MILLER CASE

Detective Cassie Rock, lead detective in the shooting death of Ishmael Miller and the search for his teenage cousin, JaQuan Miller, announced yesterday that the Boston Police would step up neighborhood patrols and the interrogation of Miller's family and friends in an attempt to find him.

"We have been aggressive in our attempts to locate JaQuan, but respectful of the mourning his family is going through," Rock was quoted as saying. "The gun used in the accidental shooting of his nephew has been involved in a number of serious crimes. We can no longer move with kid gloves. If the gun was not left by JaQuan, he has no reason to be on the run. If it was, we believe he and others associated with him may be in danger.

"We are looking for him only for questioning and urge him to turn himself in. We will be obtaining search warrants for a number of spots where we think he might be hiding."

Cassie looked at Shelley.

"This should work," she said, and looked down to finish reading. The article concluded with a brief summary of the shooting, contact numbers to be called and a final quote by Detective Rock urging JaQuan to turn himself in.

"I just hope somebody turns him in before we really have to deploy that level of force." She took off her glasses again and looked at Shelley. "Thanks, Shelley."

"I'll let you know if we get any responses, or you let me know if you hear them first." Shelley turned to walk away, then turned back. "Maybe when this eases up a bit, we can get some lunch and get rid of some of this tension between us."

Detective Rock put her reading glasses back on. "Thanks again, Shelley."

She lifted the phone receiver and turned away.

***

"As I told you on the phone, Cassie, I'm pretty sure I had a conversation the other night with JaQuan Miller." Niecy and Mickey sat with Cassie in the cafeteria at Boston Police headquarters.

"What took you so long to call me, Niecy? You know we've been looking pretty intensely for him. Did you see the *Globe* article this morning?"

"We did. It was good you put in that you're not looking to charge JaQuan with anything. But Cassie, you know no one in the community will really believe that. And threatening intense scrutiny of all his friends and family... Don't you think that might push him farther away?"

Cassie took a long drink of her coffee. Then looked long at Niecy.

"I know this won't sound cop-like to you, but we strategized over this approach for a while. We think there's a real possibility this young boy did nothing wrong. He's appeared on our radar as part of the 33 Deep gang, but they haven't been involved in much violence, and none of it gun-related. They're a wannabe gang. Now his extended family is definitely part of our Impact Player group. Violence of all kinds, drugs, crime. But JaQuan hasn't been involved directly in any violence. We think he might've squirreled the gun away to keep it from being used. If that's the case, he might well come forward to take the heat off his homies."

Mickey Crane looked at Cassie, her eyes twinkling. "Did I just hear a police officer acknowledge the assets and not the deficits?"

"Excuse me." Cassie turned a stony glare on her. "Who are you again?"

Mickey held out her hand. "Mickey Crane. Niecy and I work together."

Cassie sighed.

"It was an accidental shooting, Cassie. Why the push?" Niecy asked.

"We're getting a lot of pressure to prosecute someone for hiding a gun in the building. A young child was killed—that gets to us all. And, as you've read in the press, that gun was used in other crimes, so we might be able to make some connections."

"We'd like to work with you, Cassie," Niecy said. "It won't do that boy any good just to be hustled into the system."

"What are you proposing?" Cassie finished her coffee and waited.

"We're proposing that when you find him, you refer him to our program for at least six months. It doesn't make sense for him to have a record this young, or even get into the system."

"He may have been in possession of a gun, Niecy. At the very least."

"And if he was, do you think sending him away is going to help him?" Niecy pleaded with her. "I know you have some sway with the Commissioner, Cassie. This would be a good experiment. Instead of having youth referred to us after they've gone through the system, this could be an alternative sentence, pre-booking and pre-trial. If he goes through six months, or even a year with us, with good behavior and no incidents, it all goes away."

"And what does that do?" Cassie stared at Niecy, and ignored Mickey completely."

"You know what that does." Niecy said, staring back. "It gives him a chance. A real chance."

Chapter Thirty

Emilio

Emilio had seen the story in the *Metro*. He picked one up at one of the free boxes every day. The police were looking for JaQuan, and they were going to put the pressure on his boys. And on anyone they thought he might be staying with. Would they know about Tyrone? He didn't see how. And they couldn't possibly know about him.

They were probably just going to put heavy surveillance on his 'hood and start harassing his family again, and probably his boys' families as well. Emilio pondered it. Well, it could keep Maurizio and Morris away from little man's turf for a while, but it also meant if po-po or the D-boys picked him up, Morris would know the area was wide open. He'd recruit Q's crew, they'd want to keep getting some money, and their little drug corner was not going to be casual anymore, the area was gonna go into the hard stuff.

What would that do to Q's new plan to move the business? Would one of his boys rat him out to Maurizio? Emilio'd seen it himself, it was why he was trying to get out. When the pressure was on, your homies eventually folded. And if you went away, you were completely alone. Nobody came to see you.

But Emilio knew he still had a rep, he'd been a shooter once, and people still feared him. He might be able to help Q out of this with Maurizio. With the cops, though, little man was on his own.

Chapter Thirty-One

Cassie

"Detective, you want me to give orders for this boy not to be processed if he's picked up?"

"He's technically wanted for questioning, we don't have to process him immediately."

"He's wanted for potential gun charges, he fled the scene of a shooting and he's been obstructing an investigation. Not to mention his little drug-selling business. If he's not guilty, the charges will go away."

"They won't and we both know it. I have six other shooting cases going right now, none of them accidental, and three of them by youth under fifteen, over stupid things—you not from here, you looked at my girl. With old gangs, at least there were rules. There are none anymore. These young kids are deeply angry and they don't know how to handle their rages when they come."

Cassie stopped and took a breath.

"I know why we want to close this thing with the Millers and the potential leads from it, but he's a kid, Chief. He's never been in serious trouble that we can see. His stuff is penny ante. We have no evidence of that rage and violence with his group. And whatever's going on, he's kept his little area and his crew free of violence until now. And you and I both know that if he's put in the system, even if he's eventually cleared, the damage is done. The charges stay on his CORI sheet, he'll have done pre-trial time..."

"All right, Detective. I see your point, but this could be a precedent."

"I don't think so, sir. First, this is all related to an accidental shooting as far as we know. Second, if it did become a precedent, I'm not sure it's a bad one. We can work on the details, though," Cassie said, watching his face, "so it doesn't become one."

"Work up the details, quickly. If they make sense to me, we might try it, Detective Rock, but I'm not promising anything." The chief sat down at his desk. Cassie took that as dismissal. As she turned to go, he looked up. "You're sure about these women?"

Chapter Thirty-Two

JaQuan

His bedding stuffed into an old knapsack, which he slung over one shoulder, JaQuan wandered. He kept away from the main streets and zigzagged through the quieter residential streets. Anywhere he heard voices, or music, coming from porches, backyards or corners, he avoided. It was up to him now to decide what he was going to do, but he couldn't think. He walked. He looked at lights in the windows. They looked so warm and inviting. But those warm lights behind drawn shades and curtains could be deceptive. He knew. Was it a single mom, tucking her children into bed, exhausted and ready to sleep herself, work the next morning? Or a mom and dad admonishing their middle school son to finish his homework, the dad kissing his baby's mom goodnight, since he had to be at the garage early the next morning for his job? Or were the parents, or boyfriend/girlfriend, swearing and fighting, doing drugs; or partying so loud and late a child couldn't do homework and couldn't sleep? Or were they just screaming at the children to shut up and go to sleep?

JaQuan realized he was walking back in the direction of Fort Hill and that woman who reminded him of his grandmoms.

Those were the times in his life when he was happy. At his grand-moms', where behind those lighted windows he'd really been safe, warm, loved. His friends in the South End, the first neighborhood that really felt like his. He and his friends owned it. It felt safe, he knew neighbors. He felt like part of the bigger city. His grandmoms took him to Chinatown. They went to museums. They went to the beach, they watched the sea. Then his first crush, in middle school, eleven years old, on Sharena. He realized that had probably been a close neighborhood like his, lively, with all sorts of folks. He suppressed all the times he was scared, hungry, cold and unhappy. Most of those times involved his moms, sometimes his aunts. Almost all the time before and after his grandmoms. He felt like a baby thinking about it at all.

JaQuan squared his shoulders as he walked. *Fuck, I can't be thinking of this, I've got to be strong for my boys. I've got to be strong to make it in this world.* He felt the tears on his cheek and shrugged them away. He had to be a man now—it was up to him. He saw Niecy Hoskins' house ahead of him and moved quietly toward it. He needed to feel safe for a night.

He curled up in a darkened corner of the wide front porch. The lights were out, the corner was hidden from the street, Ms. Hoskins had probably already gone to sleep—he saw no lights. He pulled his blankets around him and made a sort of pillow with the knapsack. He heard her dog bark, and froze. The barking stopped. He couldn't keep walking around the city, and he couldn't think anymore. He knew he had to make a decision. He had to make a move. But he couldn't. Seeing Boo, talking with Monique, watching his boys guard the block last night, realizing he'd never again be able to stay with his aunts. He felt disaster in front of him and for the first time since Ishmael was killed, he felt confused. And overwhelmed with a sadness that enveloped and opened up his grief. He fell asleep.

***

He was a good problem-solver. He knew it. He'd identified one problem: stay clear of the cops. He'd focused on it and solved it. With that purpose, and having to be on the move every day, he'd been able to push his feelings about Ishmael away. But right now, he didn't know what problem he was supposed to solve. And, right now, having feelings was painful in an even deeper way than he had known before. Maybe this was why his mother stayed high all the time—it helped her not to have any feelings. He shuddered. A window opened inside him and he understood that it was about feeling with his moms. But her not being able to handle those feelings had made his life painful and hard. With his grandmoms, feelings had been a good thing. He'd enjoyed being able to feel joy, love, happiness, excitement and anticipation. He could hardly remember those feelings now.

JaQuan was reflective enough to understand, now that confusion had let feeling back in, that he had squashed his ability to feel in order to get through his days. He had blown off school, he had no future now. He could feel loyalty for his boys—he thought that must be a feeling. He could feel pleasure with a girl, or in chilling with his boys, eating a hot slice. He felt powerful when he made a plan and it worked. He felt pleasure when he solved a problem. He felt pleasure whenever he was successful.

But he remembered when he felt love and warmth for other people, when he felt pleasure at seeing something beautiful—like the sea, or a painting at the museum. When he felt excitement about what he might do when he grew up. When he felt joy at learning something new. That JaQuan seemed gone. Q—tough, smart and focused—had taken his place. But today he'd lost Q as well. He had no idea who he was.

And he was haunted, all the time now, by Ishmael. Seeing him the way he'd been, when they played or joked together. JaQuan was sure he had hidden that gun well. He'd been so careful because he was afraid of someone finding it. Not his cousins, really—but Sticky, or Robert, or frankly, even his Aunt Naomi, whose temper was short. Sticky, he hated—guy was a con man, but he was dangerous because he only thought about himself. If Sticky didn't get his way, he might hurt someone with that gun.

JaQuan respected Robert, almost liked him. But in some ways, he was afraid of Robert, too. There was something deep there, something he didn't understand. He felt that Robert would never use a gun lightly, but if he ever felt a need to carry one—someone would end up dying. JaQuan had never for a minute thought his little cousins would find it, he couldn't even imagine how they had.

He shouldn't have brought it into the house, he knew now, but he had to move it. He knew Snake was eager to carry the gun, and JaQuan had to hide it somewhere Snake would never find it. Snake would end up using the gun if he found it, JaQuan had been sure of that.

Chapter Thirty-Three

Niecy

Niecy Hoskins was still asleep when her phone rang. She knocked it from the cradle as she tried to answer it, but got it swiftly to her ear.

"I'm sorry to call so early, Niecy. I drove by your house on my way to work this morning. It looks like you have a person curled up in a blanket at the far end of your porch. I'm guessing it may be JaQuan Miller. I've sent a team to pick him up, if it is him, and I wanted you to keep him calm. They should be there in five..."

"Cassie? I thought you weren't..."

"I'm going to do my best to keep him out of the system if gun possession is his only offense. But we have to talk to him, Niecy, he hid a gun that ended up killing a little boy. Don't forget that."

"Cassie, I hear something else in your voice. What's going on?"

"Niecy, please just go outside and wait with him. The team is on its way and I don't want him to bolt. Then get yourself some coffee and I'll send someone by for you."

The line went dead.

The call knocked away the fuzziness of interrupted sleep. Niecy sat up and dialed again.

Chapter Thirty-Four

Shelley

As they approached from Commonwealth Avenue, Shelley could see through the open shutters of the first-floor windows, old wood paneling and soft lighting. She imagined the tinkle of the wine and champagne glasses the guests were holding. The large mahogany door opened to usher them, or Shelley at least, into another world. The young man who opened the door was dressed in a tux and white gloves. Across the room, Shelley caught sight of a city councilor talking to a state representative, who was laughing. She thought she heard the Mayor's laugh and she prayed the Police Commissioner wasn't among the attendees. She was standing among the social elite of Back Bay and Beacon Hill tonight because their hostess chose every year to honor the three recipients of the Copley Awards, given annually to a visual artist, a writer, and a musician. Carolyn was a recipient this year, chosen because of her photographs of children caught in the web of war. It was a high honor. To Shelley, this event and the world of the Bischoffs was a world she only read about in books by Edith Wharton or Henry James—at least, that's how this gathering appeared to her. Even though it was the 21st century, she wasn't sure what would be different. The other two honorees were a viola player and a fiction writer.

"Can you believe this!" Carolyn whispered to her as they walked in.

"Thank you for coming, Carolyn, dear, this is such an honor!" Bitsy Bischoff was tall, slim, very blond, and somewhere in her fifties. She'd taken it upon herself to be Back Bay's culture queen for the last twenty-five years and was spotted often in the *Globe* and *Herald*'s party pages at theatre openings, literary events, and, of course, the symphony. She was a member of the Athenaeum, a trustee of the Museum of Fine Arts, and had hosted the celebration of the Copley Awards every year since they were first devised.

"Thank you for hosting this, Bitsy. I am honored to be here."

"No, Carolyn—it really is our privilege to celebrate you. Your photos moved me to tears."

"Bitsy, I'd like you to meet my partner, Shelley."

Bitsy was effusive in her welcome, and after grilling Shelley about her work and congratulating them on their relationship—"two people committed to each other and doing such meaningful work"—Bitsy waved over a waiter with the champagne tray. Carolyn and Shelley each accepted a glass. Bitsy air-kissed each of them and whirled off to greet another honoree.

Across the room, Mickey took a fresh glass of champagne and turned back to her brother, Ned. "I know this is unorthodox..."

"Mickey, stop. You're always unorthodox, but I think this is downright illegal. And what am I to do with a fifteen-year-old city kid for a week?"

Mickey took a sip of champagne and turned to survey the room. "Congratulations, Ned, this is a big honor."

"Don't change the subject," her brother said, turning himself to see who was in the crowd.

"I mean it, I'm proud of you. I shouldn't have brought this business up now, but time is a factor."

Ned Crane was a solid and fit six-foot-three, a redhead. Contrary to all the stereotypes, however, he was extremely good-natured, flexible and a natural problem-solver. He was also an accomplished author and had three novels to his name, numerous short stories in respected literary magazines, and had just begun to publish a small literary journal that was gaining a solid reputation. This was his first Copley Award. His plan was to enjoy the party tonight, then leave for a month at his cabin in Becket. Something he did three or four times a year to give himself concentrated writing time.

"First, Mickey, I'm heading up to the Berkshires to get away, to write. Not to babysit. Second, this boy is wanted by the police. Third..."

His sister rolled her eyes.

"Mickey, professionals don't roll their eyes. Third..."

"You're being pompous."

"Pompous!" Ned bellowed. A few nearby heads turned. He raised his glass and smiled, then turned back to Mickey and lowered his voice. "Pompous? You want me to take a fifteen-year-old, urban male you haven't even met, who is wanted by the law, to my place..."

"It would be a week, tops, and Niecy will be there. You don't even have to cross state lines... This is a higher good, Ned, you have to help us. Just think about it. Now go, mingle with your admirers."

Before he could respond, Mickey had moved off to greet Bitsy and be introduced to some of the *haute monde* as the radical sister of the celebrated writer.

The Bischoffs' parlour had been designed to entertain when the home was built over a century ago, and they continued to use it for that purpose. Shelley was in awe that this was a private home with two people currently living in it. It looked like the reading room at a venerable club or a room out of an ancient library or museum. The parlor occupied the entire first floor front of the house and had a fireplace at one end, blazing now with a welcoming fire; three small conversational areas of love seats and armchairs, and one wall almost floor-to-ceiling books.

Shelley and Carolyn wandered around, scrutinizing the antique furniture and the art on the walls. Formally dressed waiters crossed the room with plates of appetizers or flutes of champagne. Admiring what Shelley thought might be a Miro print, they each accepted a second glass of champagne and found themselves listening to a conversation among several well-dressed men and women.

"I think it's time the legislature created a curfew for everyone under eighteen in that part of town. It's impossible to know who has a gun these days and it's scary to think of someone else getting caught in crossfire." The woman speaking looked to be in her thirties, wearing a sleeveless gray dress that looked like silk, her hair in an elegant French twist. Her male partner, in bowtie and dinner jacket, nodded and took a bacon-wrapped scallop from one of the waiters.

"More than a curfew, I think. It's time to call in the National Guard and send them door to door with the police searching and confiscating all the guns. This is ridiculous. The shootings are increasing every year. It's bad enough that all the young men are killing each other and killing young children, but now it's clear that any of us can get caught in the crossfire. And the parents have no control over their children. We're losing the city to drugs and crime."

An earnest young man standing next to him added to the conversation. "There are such things as civil rights, you know. You can't just go barging into people's homes. That is too extreme."

"You would say that, Bowditch. But sometimes the situation calls for desperate measures."

"Martial law?"

"I think," an older woman added, "that we need to start licensing people to become parents. They clearly don't have the training to raise children correctly. And with no jobs and everyone on welfare, children don't even know better."

"You know, Gertrude," Bowditch broke in, "that the majority of people on welfare in this country are white."

"In this country, maybe," she rejoined, "but not in Roxbury."

"And what does color have to do with raising children?"

"For God's sake, Bowditch, it's not the color, it's the poverty and lack of education."

"And that's your answer?"

Carolyn took Shelley's arm just as she started to step toward the group, and pulled her out of earshot. "Not our conversation, and not the time..." Carolyn whispered. "Please."

"But they don't know what they're talking about!" Shelley whispered back.

Small plates of finger sandwiches had been placed on tables between the large windows facing the street, and Carolyn guided Shelley toward them. They stood by the windows taking in the whole room as Shelley calmed down.

A podium with microphone stood, unoccupied, at the far end of the long room. Mahogany wainscoting came up waist-high on the two long walls, and the wallpaper was a soft powder blue, elegant with a barely noticeable pattern of slightly raised fleur-de-lis. Four chandeliers and a number of table lamps gave the room its soft golden glow, and numerous side tables were filled with photos of authors and artists the Bischoffs had met, interviewed or supported over the years.

The Bischoffs had done the work of assuring that the Copley Award was endowed so cash prizes could accompany the honor of winning.

"We should find a way to nominate Christina for this award," Carolyn said. "Her paintings at that South End exhibit were just amazing!"

"Yes, they were, and nice subject change. But tonight, we're celebrating your work, Car. Our host is right, your photos are beautiful and so moving."

"And this place, huh?" Carolyn looked around then back at Shelley, her eyes sparkling.

"You grew up like this, didn't you?" Shelley said.

"Not exactly, not quite as Back Bay, but similar, and you know I ran from it as fast as I could. But the people in this world do some good things—like this event tonight."

"Yes, and they have some fascist ideas," Shelley responded.

She took in the details—this room, this house, was very far removed from the Revere circles in which she grew up. Even with her father as police chief, the fanciest they ever got was a ball at the Mayor's house. And Shelley was only second generation college-educated. Her father had been the first. His father and those before him hadn't felt the need for book learning when they could be making the money they needed to build their families through construction and the trades.

"I don't know the viola player, but I've read stories by Ned Crane," Shelley said. "I'd like to congratulate him."

"You want to meet my brother?" The tall blonde woman startled them and they turned. "And I see you were getting an earful of something across the room, from the Markhams and the Farrs. No, don't protest, I saw you run away. Don't worry, they're probably the most conservative and out-of-touch of everyone here. I'm Mickey Crane, I'll introduce you to Ned after Betsy gives out the awards."

Carolyn reached out her hand. "I'm Carolyn Parker."

"The photographer! Your photographs are amazing. Congratulations on winning a Copley Award."

"And this is my partner, Shelley Colabro."

Shelley reached out to shake hands with Mickey.

"Shelley manages Special Communications for the Boston Police Department."

Before Shelley could object to the word "manages," Mickey became even more enthusiastic. "Then we have to talk, Shelley. You must be familiar with the JaQuan Miller case."

"I am, but it isn't something I'm authorized to discuss." Shelley answered quickly and tersely. This had been her fear, that someone would want her to talk about the police response and lack of progress.

"I respect that," Mickey said, surprising Shelley. "Maybe when the awards have been presented, you can just listen to my thoughts for five minutes before you both leave. One of the reasons I love Carolyn's photos so much—aside from the fact that they're beautifully composed and deeply moving in the way she caught the plight of young people in a war-torn country—is that I work with young people here in Boston. They're caught in the middle of a war here, too. And it's not one most people see. They only see it when a stray bullet hits a commuter's car, or kills a little child..."

"All right." Shelley stopped her. "After the awards are given out—you introduce us to Ned, I'll give you five minutes."

"Thank you." Mickey flashed her a warm smile and walked off, grabbing an hors d'oeuvre from a passing waiter.

"I liked her," Carolyn said.

"I did, too," Shelley responded, surprising herself. "But you know I can't share anything about the case."

"Aren't you intrigued about what she wants to tell you?"

"Of course." Shelley laughed, unexpectedly. "What a small town. Now, let's get back to celebrating you!"

Betsy Bischoff stepped up to the podium and tapped the microphone, signaling for quiet. "Thank you all for joining us tonight. As you know, every year we're are privileged to host these awards to honor some of Boston's most talented young artists. Tonight we are celebrating three of them. Brian Stephens, composer and viola player, whom you've been lucky enough to hear tonight. Carolyn Parker, whose photographs you've been admiring, and Ned Crane, novelist and short story writer, whose work you've read.

"Let me begin by thanking some of the supporters who make this annual award possible..."

Chapter Thirty-Five

Niecy

Niecy Hoskins drove the last few miles down a road curving through unrelenting forest. JaQuan Miller hunched quietly against the front passenger door.

"Beautiful here, isn't it?" Niecy asked, as she looked over and smiled at JaQuan.

"There's nothing here but trees," JaQuan said quietly.

"Take another look at that map for me, will you?"

JaQuan sat up straighter and reached for the hand-lettered map on the dashboard.

"There should be a little dirt road on the left at the top of the next hill."

As she spoke, the little car began to climb. Just as they could see where the road leveled, JaQuan shouted, "There it is."

Niecy slowed and took the left. The road was unpaved and rutted. The trees were even closer to the road here and towered above them. In about a quarter mile the little road opened into a clearing, and a modest two-story cabin stood before them. Niecy felt her own shoulders relax and could see JaQuan move forward slightly in his seat.

Niecy pulled the car over to park and JaQuan turned to her. "Can't you pull right up to the front door?"

She met his eyes and he turned away.

"It's safer." He looked at her again and she could see him putting on his leader role. "Ms. Hoskins, it will be easier to unload and there will be less chance of bears, wolves or anybody coming after us. We have nothing to defend ourselves with."

Niecy started to reply to him and thought again. *Of course, he should feel safer here, but how could he know that, this is all strange to him. Fear is a daily part of his life and it's possible he's never been out of the city. No gangs, no handguns, just the sounds and beauty of nature, but he's imagining horrible things with all this silence and these great woods.*

"Don't worry, Ms. Hoskins," he said then, "Victor and I'll protect you if anything jumps out at us."

"Thank you, JaQuan," Niecy said. "I appreciate that.

***

The ride out to the Berkshires had only taken a couple of hours. JaQuan was sleepy and stunned as they bundled into the car. Victor had taken his customary place on the blanket in the back seat. Niecy gave him the stay signal. He put his head down and as the car started up, decided to sleep. JaQuan put back his seat and lay very low in it until they were on the Mass Pike. Only then did he dare sit up again.

"Where are we going, Miss Hoskins, and why did we have to leave so fast?"

"I got a call this morning that the police were on their way to pick you up."

"You said that, but I don't understand who told them I was there and why you didn't just call a lawyer and turn me in."

Niecy turned and met JaQuan's eyes for a moment. "Let's just say I thought we needed a little more negotiating room before you turn yourself in."

"So where are we going?"

"A friend of mine has a place up in the woods that's pretty isolated. We'll stay there for a couple of days."

JaQuan sat back and looked out the windshield while they drove. "Don't take this the wrong way, Ms. Hoskins, but why are you doing this for me?"

"You remind me of someone, JaQuan, and I think you have a lot of good in you. You need a chance."

"How did you know it was me out there? I mean, that I was JaQuan, not Malachi."

"The police have been looking for you pretty intensely. They put the word out everywhere. You looked like the description."

"I still don't understand how someone knew it was me on your porch—I was all covered up!"

"I'm not a hundred percent sure myself, JaQuan, but I have an idea. We'll talk about it when I know a little more."

JaQuan had looked at her and waited, but when she said nothing more, he straightened out in his seat and went to sleep.

***

Niecy and JaQuan unloaded the car, while Victor bounded around to check out the surroundings. As they moved his bundle and Niecy's hastily packed bag inside, JaQuan began to relax. Obviously, the dog didn't sense any danger. When they were safely inside, with the car and front door locked, Niecy crossed the living room and opened a set of French doors onto a screened porch.

"Come on out here, JaQuan."

She heard him suck in his breath as he stepped on to the porch.

"Beautiful, isn't it," she said.

A thick forest had surrounded them on the ride up, but now the view opened to a vista of gracious old oak trees on the back lawn, open meadows further down the hill, and a view of the Berkshires in the distance.

"Wow," JaQuan breathed.

"Let's take Victor for a real walk. He's been cooped up a long time.

JaQuan hesitated.

"There's no one around here but us, JaQuan. My friend's brother owns this place and it's surrounded by conservation land. I've been here before, it's really very lovely, peaceful.

In the silence, Niecy walked back to a small closet by the front door. "JaQuan, you could also do me a favor." She opened the closet door. "The owner keeps a walking stick here for the steep hills. Would you mind carrying this for me in case I need it coming back up the hill?" She handed him the sturdy shillelagh stick.

"Of course," he answered finally, straightening a bit.

"Come on, Victor, walk!" Niecy yelled, though Victor had never left JaQuan's side.

JaQuan and Niecy started out through the porch door and walked slowly across the broad back lawn. The view in front of them was green and lush. The trees were widely spaced, tall with thickly leafed branches. They followed as Victor led them through the trees.

"What was the hardest thing, JaQuan?" Niecy asked him after they'd been walking for a bit.

"What do you mean, Ms. Hoskins?"

They kept following Victor, JaQuan walking just a bit ahead of her. Niecy kept silent for a moment.

"You've been all by yourself, JaQuan, on the run. Your cousin was killed and the police think the gun that killed him was yours." Niecy hated herself for having to say it.

He walked ahead of her now, faster, not even waiting for the dog. He stopped, his back to her, and leaned on the walking stick with one hand while he grabbed a small birch with the other.

"Don't make me weak now. I can't be weak now." JaQuan strangled the sob in his voice and straightened, still holding the tree.

"JaQuan, you're not weak." Niecy spoke just above a whisper and didn't move.

"You're not weak," she said again, louder. "You've had to mourn your cousin without even being there. You've had to stay hidden from the police, and you've done it. That is not weak, that is strength. But it is hurtful to you. You have feelings that you're trying to control, JaQuan, so you can survive this. But feelings are what make us human, not weak. This is a safe place. It's all right to let your feelings come out while you're here."

JaQuan stood rigid for a minute and then a sob escaped. He dropped the stick and slowly slid down the side of the tree. Though Niecy could not hear anything, his shoulders shook. Victor had been sniffing trees as they talked and now went to JaQuan. He stuck his head in between JaQuan's arms, trying to lick his face. Finally, he fell down beside him and leaned his doggie self into the crying boy while looking back at Niecy and tentatively wagging his tail.

Chapter Thirty-Six

Emilio

Emilio had no license right now and usually had one of his baby mamas drive him. Today he decided to drive himself and risk a stop, rather than put his baby mama in any danger. He slid out of his ride and strode up to the small group standing around Maurizio.

"'Sup, bro." They shook hands and gave a quick shoulder hug.

"You lookin' good, man. Haven't seen you 'round here in a while."

"Yeah, been busy where I am. You lookin' good, too. Your boys, too. All copacetic here?"

"Yah, you know. A little pressure from 5-0 now and then, but it's cool. Try'na get these guys to stop rappin' on YouTube, you know? They antagonizing all they's neighbors." Maurizio laughed, and the five guys around him smirked.

"C'mon, *'sito*," Emilio said, laughing, "you know I've seen your shit up there. You inviting po-po to come and find you?"

They all laughed.

"You know it's good stuff, man, but you be waving your piece and when you walk away, you take that kerchief down, the whole world sees your face."

"True that!" one of the guys said, laughing. "I been tellin' this little m'fucker that, but he don't listen to me."

"Hey, M, man. Take a walk with me, okay, want to get your thinkin' on something," Emilio said.

Maurizio looked hard at him, then nodded. "Y'all keep things under control till I get back, you hear?"

Slouching against the bricks of the building they stood in front of, his men nodded back at him.

"Y'all watch my ride for me, too," Emilio said. They all looked at Maurizio. He nodded.

"Yup, do what my brother asks." He turned to Emilio. "Let's walk, man."

***

"You gotta be jokin', man." Maurizio looked back to where his boys were leaning against the bricks, watching Emilio's car. "You think I want to take over that piss-ant spot? You smokin' something again."

Maurizio laughed, then stopped walking and turned to Emilio, all laughter gone. "I'll tell you this though: Q got a problem with one o' his homies, and that's what's going on over there. Your little man's homeboys be challenging me. That's a problem."

"Man, they're kids, you hear me? You supposed to be the adult, man. You leave them alone, especially Q. Anything happens, I'm going to have to do something, and you don't want me to have to do that."

Chapter Thirty-Seven

Cassie

"Dammit, Rock, I thought you had a line on him." The Commissioner paced in front of his large office windows at One Schroeder Plaza.

"I did, sir, but he was gone when we got on-scene."

"Where's that social worker whose porch you thought he was sleeping on?"

"Her colleague tells me she's at a conference."

"At a conference. What conference?"

"I don't know, sir. I didn't ask," Cassie answered. "But we went by the house. He wasn't there. We were following a tip, sir."

"And this has nothing to do with you asking me not to book this kid for possession?"

"Are you accusing me of something, sir?"

The Commissioner stared at Cassie Rock for a long minute.

"No, Detective, I'm not. But we need to wrap this up, do you understand? The shooting was accidental, but a little boy was killed because this teenager—or someone—brought a gun into his house. A gun that's been used in other crimes. We believe this fifteen-year-old is running a young gang and selling drugs. He's on the run and an entire police force can't find him. We need to resolve this and somehow make the point that we can't have teenagers or children running around with guns. There have to be consequences of some kind, and we can get him help."

"And a shooting that was very high-profile, we now know," Cassie responded.

"Yes, Detective. And I hope you're not implying that I'm bringing pressure because the victim was a while suburbanite," the Commissioner said.

The pause was stiff with tension and challenge on both sides.

"Whatever you feel, Detective, understand that the news will leak at some point and it will up the pressure to find this young man. Better to do it before the leak happens.

"Wrap this up, Detective." The Commissioner nodded to her and moved back to his desk.

Her eyes and voice like steel, Cassie answered. "Yes, sir."

Chapter Thirty-Eight

Cassie

Cassie slammed her fist down on her office desk, having been careful not to slam the door. Swiveled her chair toward the one piece of art she had in the office, a photograph of the Harbor Islands and the sea beyond, shot from her attic window. She was angry at the Commissioner's response, but the truth was that Cassie found herself deeply conflicted by this case. Five more shootings had happened since JaQuan Miller's gun killed his young cousin, but this was the one that had stayed in the news. The fact that Ishmael Miller was so young and had been accidentally shot by his brother appalled people, but the news that the same gun had killed a suburban commuter last year as she drove to work had the public—she amended her thought—the largely white, professional public clamoring for JaQuan's arrest and justice for the commuter.

She didn't blame them, of course. Kids, from teens to twenty-somethings, were killing kids and sometimes innocent bystanders. And, yes—*say it to yourself, Cassie*—they were largely youth of color killing youth of color. And she wanted justice, too. She had become a police officer to make her city safer.

In one way, she was slightly encouraged that the city's white elite were appalled by the shooting of a young black boy. Often it seemed to her that if the victim wasn't white, the victim didn't matter. On the other hand, why weren't they equally appalled when any young person was shot? And she suspected they blamed the shooters' color, not the poverty that was the ultimate cause.

The cop in her agreed that poverty was no excuse—the killing was wrong, period—but she didn't really understand it either. Why were these young men of color killing each other? The city was finally providing summer jobs, youth organizations were trying to keep youth occupied and off the streets. Some of the young felons were from families she knew and liked—some poor with a single mom trying to hold it together, some poor with two hard-working parents.

But there was no excuse for killing someone. Yet, Niecy's description of young JaQuan and her conviction that she could provide an alternative that could alter the boy's life, had moved Cassie. She'd been sure the Chief would be receptive to a pilot alternative for JaQuan and was surprised and embarrassed when he wasn't.

There was a tap on the door and it opened before she could respond. She swiveled back to face Shelley, standing just outside, her hand still on the knob.

"Not a good time," Cassie said and turned away.

Shelley entered the office and closed the door. Cassie turned back and stood up. "Shelley, this is not a good time." Her voice was stony.

"Well, at least you called me Shelley. And let's face it, Cassie, it's never a good time. Right?"

Shelley sat in the visitor chair on the opposite side of the desk. Cassie sat as well. "News travels fast around here." Shelley said.

"Shelley, what do you want?"

"You know, I had dinner with your cousin a couple of weeks ago. I was trying to figure out why you're so hostile toward me."

"This is not the time for this. And I am not hostile."

"You are, but you'll be relieved to know that I still have no idea why."

"Ms. Colabro, you are wasting my time."

"With all due respect, Detective, please listen to me. I am as upset as you are that JaQuan Miller is still missing. I am as horrified as you are about what happened to those young children and now this news of how this gun's been used. I have been working as hard as you have to find a way to convince him to turn himself in. And I thought we were very close to making that happen. Maybe we still are. And..."

"Your point, what's your point." The anger had left Cassie, but the resignation it left behind seemed worse to Shelley.

Shelley blew out some air. "If we're going to work together. If we're going to find this young man and be able to make this city understand his story—which is my part of this job—we need to be in sync. We need at least to have a good working relationship, and I feel you fight me at every turn."

"Why do you care if the city understands his story? And how do you even have a clue what his story is?"

"Don't pull that crap with me, Cassie. You are no more street than I am, in fact, probably less so. I grew up in a pretty rough working-class neighborhood before my father moved his way up in Revere. And I come from a cop family. I've seen a lot. I understand a lot."

"Again, Colabro, what is your point?"

"My point is that nine times of out ten, these kids just fall into something. They're in over their heads. I want JaQuan to have a chance as much as you do. I don't understand what it is to be black in this country, but I understand what it is to be gay. I understand what it is to have people look down on you and think you're less than. I know what it is to have to work harder than anyone else..."

"Stop it. Stop it now." Cassie strode angrily back and forth. "We're not having this conversation now. Or probably ever..."

"And I think I might know where JaQuan is."

Cassie stopped short and whirled around in a fury. "Not another word. Come with me. Now. And say nothing to anyone else."

"I need to let John..."

"Now."

Cassie grabbed her briefcase and her keys then walked with Shelley down the hall to the elevators. "If anyone asks, we're getting some lunch."

Chapter Thirty-Nine

Niecy

Back inside after their walk and moment on the hillside, Niecy had made up a bed for JaQuan and given him a cup of cocoa courtesy of a box of Swiss Miss she found in the cupboard. It reminded her that she had to go down to the village to get a few groceries. JaQuan had settled into his room with Victor snuggled up beside him. Niecy brought in some wood and kindling from the woodbox and arranged them in the fireplace. She got a strong fire going, made herself a cup of tea and sat down to make a quick shopping list. She began to feel her spirits lift a bit. She wanted to check in with Michele, but made herself wait. She didn't want to risk giving away their location if anyone was checking the phone's GPS. She would have to nip down to town, though, to get them some food. If JaQuan didn't wake in a half hour, she'd wake him. She wanted to go before it got too late.

The plan was for Mickey to reach out to Cassie and negotiate a plan for JaQuan to turn himself in and put himself into their custody informally, through The SAFE, without filing charges. She didn't know what Mickey would do if Cassie denied their request again, or if the Commissioner ultimately vetoed the plan. The only ray of hope she had was that Cassie had called her before they came to pick up

JaQuan. It may have been only a courtesy call, but Niecy read it as an apology of sorts that she hadn't been able to get the Chief to agree to keeping JaQuan out of the system.

The news that hit the *Globe* a week ago, about the gun that killed young Ishmael being used in the shooting that had wounded a suburban commuter last year, had increased the pressure to bring JaQuan in and get answers on where the gun came from. That news had looked bad for Cassie and the police department on two fronts. First, it had leaked and they weren't sure how. Second, the initial ballistics tests had made the link to some drug-related crime but not to that particular shooting at first. That raised issues around the state of the department's record-keeping. She understood that until proven otherwise, the police had to assume JaQuan was involved on some level. There weren't many people that understood the forces working on a young man like JaQuan.

She heard Victor bark and the door to JaQuan's room open. He walked into the main room, rubbing sleep from his eyes and yawning. He stretched as he looked at the fire.

"Nice!" he said.

"Feeling a little better?"

"Yes, thanks." JaQuan kept his gaze on the fire. Victor had come to sit beside him, and JaQuan petted the dog absently. He looked up at Niecy. "How long do you think we have to stay here, Ms. Hoskins?"

"I don't know, JaQuan, but I hope only a couple of days." She finished her tea. "I'm going to head into town and pick up a few groceries. Why don't you come with me? We can leave Victor here to take care of the house."

The dog's ears pricked up.

"Sure. You don't think I should stay hidden?" JaQuan said.

"I honestly don't think anyone's going to think to look for us out here, JaQuan. I think we'll be all right."

***

The town was small but had a breakfast restaurant, bar, hardware, a clothing store, bank and grocery. The stores on each side of the street were in brick or stone buildings, each fronted by a wooden walkway. Instead of parked cars, JaQuan thought there should have been horses tied to railings.

They parked and walk up the steps into the small grocery store. When he stepped inside, JaQuan stopped as Niecy moved forward to take a small cart from the row beside the door. He closed his eyes for a second, then opened them as he heard her roll the cart up beside him.

"Are you all right, JaQuan?" she asked.

"I am." he said, and smiled. "You go ahead, I'll follow."

Niecy headed toward the vegetables. JaQuan followed at a distance. He sniffed the air as he walked, and smiled. He hadn't been inside a grocery store that smelled like this since he was a young boy. He could smell the ground coffee, and there was a smell of wood plank floors and sharp cheeses.

***

"JaQuan, will you grab me a pound of coffee? Can you reach it all right?"

"Yes, Grandmoms! Of course I can."

"All right. I'll get butter and maple syrup. Will you get me a box of eggs and check them, make sure they're not broken?"

***

"JaQuan?"

"Sorry, ma'am."

Niecy looked at him quizzically but didn't press. "I was asking you what you'd like for supper."

"Anything's fine."

"How about some macaroni and cheese, chicken and broccoli? And I'll bake some cornbread."

"That sounds great!"

"Will you get me a dozen eggs? And check to make sure they're not broken?"

JaQuan stared at her.

"Are you sure you're all right, JaQuan?"

"I'm fine, Ms. Hoskins." He smiled again. "Sometimes you just remind me of someone.... Can we have pancakes for breakfast?"

"I was thinking that, JaQuan, that sounds just right! I'll get some bacon, milk and coffee too." She paused. "And after breakfast tomorrow, we have to have a long and honest talk, all right?"

He nodded.

Chapter Forty

Cassie

Cassie and Shelley exited police headquarters and walked to Cassie's Prius in the parking lot. The sky above headquarters was a rich, deep blue, like a summer sky, and the air sparkled with sun and freshness. What few clouds floated by seemed playful.

"The top goes down on my Mini," Shelley said.

"This is not a fun trip, Shelley, just get in, please."

Cassie started the car and moved out onto Tremont Street. She shot straight up past Roxbury Crossing, where it became Columbus again as Tremont angled right toward Mission Hill. They passed the Jackson Square Station in Jamaica Plain and veered off on Amory Street before they could hit Egleston. This part of Boston was a nexus of several neighborhoods. In a half mile area Roxbury, Fort Hill, Mission Hill and Jamaica Plain interwove or conjoined.

Cassie pulled into the parking lot of the old Haffenreffer Brewery, which now housed a café, Sam Adams Brewery and the well-loved Veggie Lunacy restaurant.

"I think we can talk here without interruption," Cassie said. "Wait until I can take notes." She had said next to nothing on the ride over. They got out, walked inside the restaurant and claimed a table. Cassie ordered a kale Caesar with chicken, Shelley the bean burger with Vermont cheddar.

When the waitress brought their food, Shelley said, "OK, this is feeling like a spy novel. Why all the clandestine activity? What's going on?"

Cassie picked up her fork. "This case is very touchy with the Chief. You probably know we sent a car to pick JaQuan Miller up this morning, on what I thought was a good tip. All we found was a couple of blankets on a front porch."

"So we're eating lunch in JP because he wasn't there?" Shelley took a bite of her burger and washed it down with some Sam Seasonal ale.

"We're here because the Chief came down hard on me for missing him, and if you think you know where he is, I want all the details and I don't want anything leaking around the department." Cassie took a long drink of her iced tea. "I'm not implying you'd leak anything," she continued, anticipating a comment from Shelley. "But people overhear things, and you'd have to report to John eventually."

"And what about Mulroney, where is he today?"

"We have other cases."

They both ate their meals, and then Cassie pulled out her notebook. "Okay, lay it on me."

"I was at an awards ceremony in the Back Bay last night—the Copley Awards. My partner Carolyn was receiving one for her photographs of children caught in war."

Cassie waited, pen tapping softly against the notebook.

"I met a woman named Mickey Crane, whose brother was also receiving an award."

The pen stopped.

"I wanted to meet her brother because I like his writing."

"Shelley, get to the point." Cassie's voice was soft and strained.

"When she heard I worked for the police department, she asked me if I was familiar with the JaQuan Miller case, said she wanted to talk to me for just five minutes."

"Shelley, you can't talk about cases."

Shelley took a breath. "Cassie—Detective—will you get over yourself? Do you think you're the only professional in this room? I told her I could not discuss the case. She said I wouldn't have to discuss it. If I would just listen to her for five minutes, she'd introduce me to her brother. I thought she might have some information I should know, so I agreed."

"And?" Cassie still had not written a word.

"She told me she thought she could find out where JaQuan is and bring him in for questioning if the Commissioner agreed not to charge him, but to release him in pre-arraignment custody to the youth program she runs."

"And what did you say?"

"I said we couldn't promise anything, but that I'd be willing to set up a meeting between her and you. I also said if she actually knows where JaQuan is and doesn't tell us, she's obstructing an investigation.

"She said she certainly didn't want to obstruct the investigation and she wants to meet with you. In fact, she'd like to meet with you tomorrow."

Cassie wrote intensely in the notebook, then stared out the window for an uncomfortable moment. "And you couldn't just tell me this? You had to make this big production?"

"First, Cassie, you are not easy to talk with. You have some issue with me and it's not even subtle. But, second, I'm not done. I met Mickey's brother Ned. She introduced me, as she promised. It was a thrill, though I'm sure you don't care. But I noticed a tension between the two of them. Anger or exasperation, I wasn't sure which, coming from him." She ate another bite of her sandwich and took a long swallow of her ale, then looked up into Cassie's glare. "The tension bothered me, so I decided to do some research on Ned Crane. It turns out he owns some property in the Berkshires."

"So?"

"What if the tension came from the fact that Mickey has JaQuan staying there?"

"Jesus, Shelley. Do you write fiction as well as press releases? Do you have any evidence that's what happened?"

"Of course not, but think about it. You thought you knew where he was this morning, then he was gone. He disappears the day after my conversation with Mickey Crane. It all seems a bit too coincidental, don't you think?"

"No, I don't." Cassie signaled the waitress for the bill. "Finish up your lunch, Shelley, and not a word of this to anyone else." She softened her tone. "I will look into it and see if there's anything there. I appreciate your bringing this to me."

Chapter Forty-One

Boo

Boo didn't know what to do with the information he'd discovered this afternoon. JaQuan was nowhere to be found and things were heating up. His street loyalty was to Eightball. His heart loyalty still extended to JaQuan. When they were young, JaQuan was always the first one to invite him to play, the first one to defend him, to invite him home for supper. Boo couldn't always stay, but he felt that JaQuan had always stood by him and treated him right. Though there were things in his past Boo couldn't talk about, he was sure they wouldn't have mattered to Q. The two of them hadn't seen each other in a long time, but part of that was because Q had gone to live with his moms, and his grandmoms had died so suddenly. Then Boo had stopped going to school and hooked up with Eightball's crew, much earlier and much deeper than Q had started in the life. It wasn't JaQuan's fault they lost touch.

But this was going to start a war. JaQuan had missed a meeting with his boys. His team was demoralized and scared. Snake was determined to grab the power and had gotten hold of a gun. He had publicly disrespected Maurizio, and that was reckless. Then Boo found out from a homie in the crew that an old OG from the other side of town was a friend of Q's and had threatened Maurizio if he harmed any of the 33 Deep crew. Maurizio was now between that rock and hard place. Boo understood that Maurizio was also ambitious and clever. He wouldn't make any move in the Deep's home territory, the cops were watching it too closely. But the minute they moved away from there, it was anyone's guess.

Chapter Forty-Two

Mickey

"Niecy, I found an ADA willing to give this a shot, and a hot-shot of a defense lawyer willing to make sure the agreement sticks. There are some rules JaQuan has to agree to, but if this works, he will not have a record, and will have a chance to stay clean. Can you start back?" Mickey listened for a minute. "Yes, we'll meet at her office." Mickey gave Niecy the necessary information, then hung up the phone.

When she finished the call, she put on a fresh pot of coffee and opened the box of doughnuts she had brought in for the meeting with Detective Rock. This morning's group of young people had eaten all the rest. The timing of the meeting was interesting. She'd been about to call Rock yesterday when the phone rang, and it was the detective asking for a meeting this morning. Mickey's guess was that the woman she'd met at the Copley Awards had contacted Rock.

Mickey flipped on the lights in the office. The new turn of events made the meeting much easier, they weren't asking the Commissioner for anything now. But she wanted Rock's cooperation and agreement to the process. Plus, she wanted Rock to make the apprehension. From Niecy's discreet comments, she suspected this would help Detective

Rock as well as JaQuan Miller. She wondered, though, what Cassie Rock wanted.

The doorbell rang, and she walked through the large meeting room to answer it. She introduced herself to Rock, who shook her hand and started talking before they'd even reached the office.

"You know, Niecy's a friend of mine. She tells me The SAFE does good work, though I have to tell you I've never heard of it before." She entered Mickey's office and put her briefcase down. "Still—I took your proposal to the Commissioner and, as I told Niecy, he said no. I'm not sure what we have to meet about."

Yet you called me, Mickey thought. "I've made some fresh coffee. I'm having some, can I pour you a cup?" she said, pouring both cups before she got an answer. "And forgive the cliché, but I bought doughnuts for a youth meeting this morning and we have some left."

She brought the box and a cup of coffee to Detective Rock. "Please, help yourself."

Mickey let the silence build as she selected a doughnut, took a sip of coffee and watched Rock stare at her.

Rock put her unsipped cup of coffee down. "You know where he is, don't you? I need you to tell me."

Chapter Forty-Three

Niecy

It was another beautiful day in the Berkshires. Not yet far enough into the season for the heat to become lazy-making and the thunderstorms to become a weekly occurrence. The clouds were fluffy and high, the grass a dewy emerald green that sparkled, the sky a deep washed blue. Niecy and JaQuan sat at the kitchen table, each with a plate heaped with pancakes, fried eggs and bacon. JaQuan's plate was slightly more heaped, and generously adorned with butter and maple syrup.

Niecy sipped her second cup of coffee. Victor waited politely near the table in case anything should spill and need to be cleaned up.

"Wouldn't you love to live in a place like this, JaQuan?"

JaQuan looked at her, startled. He'd been wondering almost the same thing. He ate some more before answering and decided to be honest. "I was just thinking that, except, to be perfect, there would have to be mountains where they are now, and ocean down the hill on the other side; a few houses with families and children, and the town would need to be bigger and have a movie theatre."

Niecy laughed out loud and JaQuan's face closed down.

"I'm sorry," she said reaching out to touch his hand. "I'm not laughing at you, I'm laughing because I couldn't have said it better. You just described a paradise I'd like to live in, too."

Embarrassed, JaQuan looked away but felt better and said, "The only problem, Ms. Hoskins, is that I can't live someplace like this right now. I know you won't understand this, but my boys depend on me. I was going to ask you if your friend found a lawyer yet, because I have to get back to them today, just for a little while."

"Why don't you explain more to me, JaQuan, about how they depend on you so I can understand it. But finish your breakfast first."

JaQuan nodded and ate some bacon.

"Would you like another cocoa?" Niecy asked.

JaQuan nodded again. How could he tell her, he thought, that he'd almost tried to walk home this morning? He'd risen earlier than usual and Victor rose with him. He'd left Ms. Hoskins a note saying he'd taken Victor for a walk, but, taking both his walking stick and Victor's leash, had left the cabin with a determination to keep on going and hitch a ride back to Boston. Ms. Hoskins had no idea how important it was for him to get back and hold that meeting with his boys. He'd already seen that Snake's nerves were on edge. And Boo's warnings had stuck with him. It wasn't just him anymore.

Being here, away from his fears, he'd thought, *maybe I can go back to school. Maybe I can do something that would make Grandmoms proud.* But he realized when this was over and he was back in Boston, it would be just him again. The one thing he could do, even though it meant staying on the street, was make sure his boys didn't get themselves hurt and had enough money to help them out.

He and Victor had started down the hill away from the cabin, Victor looking at JaQuan, then back at the cabin every now and then.

But when JaQuan said, "It's okay," Victor would move forward again. It was almost as if the dog were saying, "Are you sure?"

The sun was bright and it wasn't as scary as it had been the night before, but when he'd gone a mile, or at least it seemed like a mile to him, he realized he couldn't do this to Ms. Hoskins. She would be upset when they didn't come back. She would get in the car to come find them. He would feel like he had betrayed her.

He and Victor turned around, and when they got back to the cabin the smells of coffee and bacon almost made him cry.

He told Niecy how he met his boys when he went back to live with his moms and ended up with his aunts, and how they all had messed up home lives. He had come up with a way they could all earn a little money, he and his boys were too young to work real jobs, and in turn, he felt like he had a family. He started to explain to her why this meeting today was important when the cabin's phone rang and she picked it up.

"Excuse me, JaQuan, I have to get this but I want to hear the rest of the story."

Chapter Forty-Four

Emilio

E milio cursed and ran out the door, jamming his baseball cap on as he moved. He jumped into his car—he'd taken it back from his baby's mama. He'd had a feeling he might need it. He gunned it and took off toward Egleston. He'd just gotten a text from one of Q's homies. He already might be too late.

He arrived as the ambulance was leaving. He slowed and parked a distance away. The cops were still there and looked like they were taking statements. He texted back to meet him by the Y and drove away to park. There wasn't anything else he could do right now.

Twenty minutes later, Jonathan tapped on his window and opened the car door.

"What's up, man?" Emilio said.

"Q said you were the one I should call if there was any trouble."

"Who got shot?"

"MD. Matthie."

"How bad?"

"Don't know. He got hit in the side, they just took him away. This car just came by, slowed down, and started shooting. Don't know who it was. Snake thinks it's Maurizio and he's already making plans. He's just mad crazy right now."

"I'm gonna need to talk to him," Emilio said.

"Yeh. He took off, though. He grabbed one of the bikes and just took off."

"You let me know when he back, man, okay? I'm gonna talk to some other people I know."

Chapter Forty-Five

Niecy

It didn't take them long to clean the dishes and cabin. Niecy and JaQuan were packed and on the road within forty-five minutes of that phone call. Niecy felt good that they had left some groceries for Ned and would make sure Mickey let him know.

On the ride in, keeping close to the speed limit to make sure nothing would trip them up, Niecy explained the details to JaQuan. He would have a lawyer, the famed Rosaria Scotto—though she didn't tell him that. ADA Jerrold Ross had agreed to try a pilot project where JaQuan would be arraigned but nothing put on his record—he was the test case. He was only wanted for questioning right now, though there were possible gun and obstruction charges. Those were the charges ADA Ross had agreed to hold back on, unless there was other evidence that JaQuan had been involved in any crimes linked to the gun.

"When you talk to Attorney Scotto, you have to be absolutely honest with her. Everything you say to her is confidential, but she can't help you unless she knows everything."

"I'm telling you, Ms. Hoskins. There's nothing, I swear."

"I believe you, JaQuan but I'm not the one you need to tell. And you need to think about anything else you might know about that gun, however small, and tell your attorney."

"I will.'

JaQuan was quiet after that. Niecy noticed him once or twice taking out his phone and looking at it. She had completely forgotten about the phone. There had been no cell coverage where they were. The only contact was the landline at the cabin. But he made no comment and put the phone away.

They arrived in Fort Hill in a little over two hours. Niecy parked in front of her house. "Let's just get Victor inside, JaQuan, and we'll head down to the courthouse."

"All right, Ms. Hoskins."

They brought Victor and their belongings inside. When she had given Victor fresh water, she called out to JaQuan. "Let's go!"

It took her a minute to realize he was gone.

Niecy stood frozen, her hands clutching the back of a kitchen chair. Then, in a voice even she didn't recognize, she rasped, "Victor. Come." She stepped onto her porch, locked her door, and said, "Find JaQuan!"

To her surprise, Victor took off at a run. Her first instinct was to call him back. Instead, she got into her car, which still sat in front of the house, and took off, trying to follow the dog. Less than a quarter mile away, next to the small market, she found JaQuan sitting on the curb, his head in his hands. Victor was leaning up against him, trying vigorously to work his muzzle in between those hands.

After several minutes, JaQuan flung an arm around Victor to quiet him, looked up at Niecy, and wiped his eyes.

"It's my fault," he said.

"JaQuan, please stand up and look at me," Niecy said.

He did and looked so miserable, Niecy stepped forward and held him tightly for a moment. Kindly, she said, "Get in the car. We'll talk as we go, we can't miss this appointment."

Once she started up the car and both were seat-belted in, she said, "I know how tempting it is, JaQuan, but at some point you can't run from problems anymore, they always follow you."

He turned his head toward the window, wiped his eyes again, and turned back to her. "I wasn't running away, Ms. Hoskins, I was going back to my boys after everything that's happened. Then I realized I didn't know where to go. I've failed them. I didn't do what I was supposed to do."

"After what happened, JaQuan?"

"There's been a shooting. There's a war now. And I could have stopped it. It's all because of me."

"How do you know that?"

"You know there was no cell phone service out where we were. As soon as we got in range, I checked my texts."

"So what happened, JaQuan?"

"I don't know exactly. No details, just there was a shooting, and one of my boys was hit. You know there's another gang trying to take over our territory. I could have stopped it if I was there. I told you, I take care of them and they take care of me. They get nervous without me. But I didn't take care of them. I wasn't there."

"But you couldn't have been with them anyway, JaQuan, even if you were here. You know that. You've been hiding for a reason..." Niecy stopped and looked at him. "You know what, though, let's stop for a minute—let's have this meeting and try to get you straight, then I promise you we'll find out exactly what's going on and figure out how to help."

JaQuan was quiet. He turned back to face her. "With all due respect, Ms. Hoskins, you don't know my world. I know you want to, but I don't think you can help me."

Niecy reached out and touched his shoulder. "Well, let's take this one step at a time, JaQuan. There's almost always something I can do. Let's drop Victor back at the house again and see if we can make our meeting on time."

Attorney Scotto's offices were not far from Fort Hill. She had a suite of offices in Dudley Square as well as a small office at 14 Beacon Street downtown, which she used mostly during trials and appeals. Niecy found a parking space on Washington near the Tap Room.

Mickey was already there. "I'm sorry we're late," Niecy said as they entered. Had a couple of delays on our way back."

JaQuan looked at her, but that was all she said.

"This is JaQuan Miller. JaQuan, this is Attorney Scotto and my colleague, Mickey Crane, who runs The SAFE with me."

JaQuan solemnly shook hands. Scotto gestured to a seating arrangement of comfortable chairs and they all sat down.

Her office was large, with big windows looking down on the square. The walls were painted a federalist blue, the window frames white and the windows had wooden blinds. A large wooden desk covered with papers stood in front of one window. Their seating arrangement, a large sofa and four chairs around a cherry coffee table, stood in front of the other large window. JaQuan could see the Urban League building, and he knew some locally owned stores, like Nubian Notions and Stash's Pizza, were out of sight but down below. He thought it was interesting that Scotto was white but chose to have her office here.

A young black woman stepped in and took orders for coffee, water and soda. *Please*, he thought to himself after she left, *let's just start*. He felt jumpy inside, the kind of restless feeling he always had just before he fought someone.

"All right, JaQuan. I have been hired as your attorney. From this point on, we are in this together and you don't talk to the police or anyone else without me there. Everything you tell me is confidential because of attorney/client privilege. When I ask you questions, I need to know the truth so that nothing surprises us. I am on your side, so you need to trust me. Okay?"

JaQuan looked at Niecy, who nodded, then said, "Do you understand what Attorney Scotto is telling you? She will keep anything you tell her completely confidential—secret—unless you tell her she can share it. But she needs to know everything that's happened so she can make the best decisions to help you."

"I understand," JaQuan said.

Scotto looked at Mickey then said, "Good, JaQuan. You'll need to completely trust me, because it's become even more complicated. Ms. Hoskins, you haven't heard this yet either, but the police are contemplating serious charges now."

Niecy looked at her and Mickey. "I thought you told me the ADA was willing to hold back on the gun and obstruction charges unless there was evidence JaQuan was involved with the older gun crimes."

JaQuan looked panicked and stood up.

The lawyer spoke. "Please sit down, JaQuan. I'm telling this so you know why we have to work together. You can't run any more, it will look bad."

"Yes, JaQuan," Niecy said. "Please sit down. I was just surprised. Let's figure out a strategy."

"Niecy is right," Mickey said. "We need a strategy and you need to know you have a whole team on your side. You don't know me yet, but you need to know that Niecy and I both care very much what happens to you, as does Attorney Scotto. So, Ms. Scotto, where were we?"

Chapter Forty-Six

Rosaria

"There are two things," Rosaria Scotto said, "that make this more complicated than it was a few days ago, and that's why we have to know exactly how you obtained the gun, JaQuan, and where you hid it to keep it safe.

"First, of course, the police want to know how your cousin found the gun, and that's one reason they've been looking for you—they know the actual shooting was an accident.

"Second, their ballistics department tried to match the bullets that fit the gun with previous crimes. When they ran it, they thought they had some matches, and we've been waiting for them to run down details of the specific incidents. And now they have..."

Rosaria stopped to take a sip of her tea and JaQuan felt his insides go completely cold.

"First," she continued, "they found that a fingerprint on the gun matched a fingerprint from a recent armed robbery site—a robbery that happened a few days before your little cousin found the gun. They want to see if that fingerprint is yours, and if not, they want your help to figure out whose it is. Second, ballistics found that the bullet matched one taken from what they called the Westwood shooting.

This was back a few years ago, when a woman from Westwood was driving down Columbus Avenue toward Egleston, and a bullet from a building near Academy Homes struck her car and severely wounded her. You'll all remember this because it was in the papers for weeks."

Mickey was up and pacing. She stopped and put a hand on JaQuan's shoulder. He spun and shook her hand off. "That's impossible. I hid that gun, no one could have used it in a robbery and I don't know anything about anyone getting shot."

"Who sold you the gun, JaQuan?" Rosaria asked.

JaQuan sat back down. "I can't tell you that."

"JaQuan, why did you buy a gun? What did you need it for?" Niecy asked. "You never finished telling me the story."

JaQuan was completely silent now.

"What about my boys," he said finally, his voice low and tight. "You said we could find out what's happening with them."

Chapter Forty-Seven

Emilio

This time the text was from Maurizio, and Emilio was pissed. Emilio had found Snake. He'd sat the boy down and spent his own time talking to him about how he needed to play this, and the key thing he told him was to lay low and wait until Emilio got more info. He had it from Maurizio himself that this hit had nothing to do with either him or Eightball. Emilio believed him because Maurizio would have to be crazy to cross him so blatantly and disrespectfully.

Emilio put the word out on the street, and he knew he'd hear something about what went down with MD. Fuck this. He'd just met some women and he liked what they were doing for kids. He thought maybe this was the way he'd like his life to go now. Doing something for kids on the up and up, not just the way he'd always done. Maybe it was a new career for him. But if he got involved with this, he might screw it up. If he didn't, these kids were going to get themselves killed.

Maurizio and the rest of Eightball's Bloods were fronting with the Villa. That was a dangerous combination. Somehow Snake had used his crew's profits to get himself a gun. Q hadn't shown up for the plan, but Snake and J-Nice had pulled it off anyway, making some money down near those colleges but far enough away from Jesse's spot to not get into trouble. They'd gone down on the bikes, just about five of them, and made some sales. Then Snake got it into his head to do a buzz down near the Villa. He was feeling all that and they blocked traffic at Mass Ave. doing figure eights. Held up traffic down Tremont, weaving all over the lanes, then they peeled off by Castle Square, then through the Villa toward Cathedral before anyone could call the cops—they figured they buzz through, reppin', maybe grab a purse or two on Washington Street and head back to their block. At least that was the plan.

At the last moment, after picking off two shoppers on Washington, Snake broke away and zipped back through the Villa, pulling his piece and firing it at a group of homies. Emilio was guessing he didn't know they were allies with Maurizio now. Or maybe he did. Probably out of pure anger in retaliation for Matthie, Emilio thought—not caring whether these guys had been the shooters or not. So either Snake had completely ignored his warnings, or he was just being stupid. Either way, it was a war now. Unless he could do something.

But Maurizio was neither stupid nor disrespectful. He'd texted Emilio right away: *Nothing you can do now, bro, this homie really dissed us. Giving you the heads-up is all.*

Emilio was back in the car. *If I get stopped without a license*, he thought, *Snake is dead because I'll kill him myself*. He was headed straight back toward the Deep's block. He'd text Maurizio from there. If he could get Maurizio to hold off until he cooled down, maybe he could set up a meeting and get Snake to apologize enough to squash this. If Snake wouldn't do it, there was nothing more Emilio could do. Thank god the m'fucker didn't hit anyone.

Chapter Forty-Eight

Mickey

"It was your friend Matthias who was shot," Mickey said. "He was hit in the leg. He'll need time to heal, but he's going to be okay. But, JaQuan, this is all the more reason to tell us who you bought the gun from. Things are escalating and all your friends are in some danger."

"I don't snitch," Q said, his eyes hard, lids half lowered.

The room was quiet. Rosaria had sent out for sandwiches and drinks. She, Niecy and Mickey sat patiently but strategically around the room. By now, Niecy understood that JaQuan's first action in a situation, whenever he felt troubled or confused about what to do, was to run. The ADA, Detective Cassie Rock, and her partner John Mulroney, were all expecting JaQuan to turn himself in, so there was nothing to do but be patient until JaQuan began to understand the forces around him and the most likely outcomes.

After ten minutes of silence, the door opened and Scotto's executive assistant brought in the food, waters, sodas and more coffee. "Thank you, Keisha," Scotto said to her.

Keisha nodded and went out, closing the door behind her.

Scotto broke the tableau by getting up and taking a sandwich. "We're going to need our strength. I suggest everyone eat something."

Niecy rose and took two sandwiches. She gave one to JaQuan. "Ham and cheese for you. Tuna for me. Let's all take a break and eat. Maybe we'll be able to think better after some lunch."

Mickey nodded. "Sounds good to me." She rose, chose a turkey with cheddar and avocado and poured more coffee. "Great sandwiches," she said to Rosaria, and gestured toward a corner of the spacious office. "Can we do a little brainstorming?"

JaQuan looked at Niecy with alarm and made as though to rise. Niecy put a hand on his shoulder. "Let's do a little brainstorming ourselves while we eat."

Chapter Forty-Nine

Mickey

Mickey's phone pinged with a text as she sat with Rosaria. It was from an OG she'd been cultivating in Mission, a guy named Emilio. She'd met him in one of her regular canvassings of the project streets in Mission Hill. She'd found that the best way to get the really high-risk youth into the program was by just hanging out and talking. At first they thought she was a narc, then a social worker. Now they knew her as a worker from The SAFE, and that was cool. They were hearing from other kids that it was a cool hangout spot and the people there actually could help you.

Emilio was a gangbanger—ex, he said when they finally began to talk—that the youth really looked up to. He was tough, people feared him, but she found he really cared about the youth, and they knew it. For them, he was a soft touch. She and Emilio finally started to talk when she had a small group of the younger children going around with cameras to do a photo journal on where they lived. Some of the active bangers cornered her and wanted to take the cameras. Emilio had watched from the side as she convinced them this was a youth project, nothing bad. He watched as she took instructions from the gangbangers on where not to take pictures. She'd kept calm, not seeming at all frightened, and that must have impressed him. He strutted up later, asked her what she was doing there, just for good face, then he got her card. He'd been meeting with her off and on since, testing her. She kept confidences. She was honest.

She'd figured Emilio was tired of living on the edge and on the run. He had children now himself, with several baby mamas, and he wanted a new way to make a living. And he was good with young people, he knew that. They feared him, but they also liked him. He really wanted to help them so they didn't end up dead or in prison.

Emilio's text said *Please call me*, and gave a number.

She excused herself and stepped outside.

***

"I got a situation here," was the first thing he said. "You remember me, right?"

"Of course, Emilio."

"I need to strategize with you. I been working with some youth from a little crew they call 33 Deep. You know that kid JaQuan that's on the run?"

"Ah, yes, of course." Mickey couldn't believe the timing of this call. She'd had no idea Emilio knew JaQuan, but she was fast learning that Boston's drug- and youth-gang world was really very small.

"Well, the Deep is his crew and without him they've been getting reckless. One of them—this is confidential right?—has been out there threatening another, bigger gang. I'm going to try to squash it, but I'm not sure I can. This kid really disrespected the other side in a big way. I wanted to see if you had any ideas I could use. I know he ain't Mission, but I know you care about all these kids."

Mickey had been getting Emilio to volunteer in small ways. He had some skills that would be helpful, but she was fairly sure he was out there dealing since he didn't seem to have any other work. When she got to a point of really trusting him, she would offer him a job and see how he did.

He was psychologically a very perceptive man, even though he had no training. And on this psychological level, he seemed honest and sincerely caring about the young people he encountered. This phone call—if she was reading it right—was a reinforcement of that. She put those thoughts aside and concentrated on the problem he'd put in front of her.

"Emilio, tell me what you're thinking..."

Chapter Fifty

Rosaria

After she finished her call, Mickey stepped back into Rosaria's office and returned to her sandwich at Rosaria's desk. Rosaria looked at her expectantly and Mickey quietly filled her in.

Once they all finished eating, Rosaria pulled them into a tight circle of chairs—Mickey, JaQuan, Niecy and herself.

"JaQuan," she said, "after talking to Mickey, I think it would be helpful to you if you understand how I work. Usually, I only take cases where folks have already been convicted and are in prison. Somebody, usually someone who loves them, is able to convince me there's enough evidence that didn't come up at trial to prove them not guilty.

"Once I take a case, I use all my resources—investigators, sources, colleagues, forensic experts—to investigate just as deeply as I can. Usually, I find evidence that wasn't used, and often more. I am a bulldog.

"You have people in this room who care about you and they have convinced me to take your case before you're found guilty of anything, before you're even booked, so you won't end up in jail or with a record. They believe in you..."

JaQuan shook his head.

"JaQuan, I'm not saying they think you're perfect. Or that you haven't made mistakes. What they do think, and tell me if I'm right ladies," she looked at Niecy and Mickey, "is that you have a lot of goodness in you, a lot of potential to be something in this world and that you've been trying to do the right thing."

JaQuan could not lift his eyes from his shoes.

"But in spite of all this support, JaQuan, if you can't trust me with the truth—your truth and the facts you know—there is nothing I can do. And I'm not sure there's anything I want to do.

"You have to care about yourself, JaQuan, and you have to be willing to help make things better."

Mickey spoke up. "JaQuan, I need you to tell me where you got the gun."

Rosaria looked over at Mickey, and Niecy realized some information must have come in during that last phone call. Mickey locked eyes with the lawyer, then they all looked back at JaQuan.

They could hardly hear him when he spoke.

"There is no way they should have found that gun." His voice filled with tears. "I took it apart, I shoved it so far down."

"JaQuan, I asked you a question."

His voice went even lower.

"Snake bought it. I told them no guns. We don't need guns, we're not into that. We had some knives, you never know when you might need them, but I said no guns. I don't know where he got the money.

"He brought it out one night when we were having pizza. It really scared my bros. You know, they still young, they don't think that what we're doing is bad or anything. It's just to make a little cash, you know. The gun, though...

"Anyway, we fought and I took it away from him. I told him—Snake, as long as I'm running this, no guns. I'll put it somewhere safe, OK, I told him, in case we ever need it, but no good is gonna come from having this around. But Snake doesn't like to listen. I had to hide it."

JaQuan looked up again, defiantly now. "I told Ms. Hoskins I'd come in to talk with you, but only if you all help me find out what's going on with my crew. I need to help them so, if you're going to help me, I need you to help all of us."

He stared at everyone in the room, then bowed his head.

"JaQuan," Mickey said softly, "here's what we can do together. As we told you, you need to turn yourself in. We've made an agreement with the district attorney's office—no charges on you, unless you were involved in any crime using that gun—and so far, it seems you were not.

"In return, you have to start coming to The SAFE, you need to get back in school and you need to stay out of trouble. We'll help you.

"And we'll help with your boys. We're setting up a meeting with them right now, in fact. And you're going to need to help them by getting them to agree to come to The SAFE as well."

Rosaria spoke then. "So, JaQuan if you're serious about this, if you're willing to take this deal so you don't have to keep hiding, let's get down to business. We have to go over paperwork with you and make sure you understand it. The district attorney and one of the judges will be ready at the courthouse in two hours to sign off on these agreements. This makes sure you don't go to jail and you don't pick up a case. This is up to you, now, JaQuan. Do you want to do this or not?"

JaQuan looked up, held her eyes for a moment, then nodded.

Niecy looked across at Mickey, who signaled that she'd fill her in later on all the details. Niecy and Rosaria sat with JaQuan and went over the papers he had to fill out and the contract he would sign agreeing to get back into school and to attend The SAFE. Niecy had to keep bringing JaQuan's focus back to it, though, because his eyes were on Mickey as she paced with her phone, and his questions kept repeating: "But who's setting this meeting with my boys? Can I be there? What's going to happen to them?"

Chapter Fifty-One

Cassie

Cassie hung up the phone after speaking again with Mickey. Cassie was beginning to get really angry about this new relationship. She was the police officer, she was open to helping JaQuan Miller as much as anyone, assuming he hadn't been involved in a crime.

"I have some information." Mickey had said. "If you want to stop a potential shooting, you have to get some officers patrolling around Seaver over to Humboldt for a while. It's possible something will be going down there in the next few hours."

We don't do concierge policing, Cassie fumed. Then calmed herself—*she's just giving me a heads-up.*

But what bothered Cassie was that it felt like Mickey was telling her exactly how to do her job. She had to make sure the officers seemed just to be casually patrolling. They couldn't say they got a tip, it would compromise her source, Mickey said—whom she wouldn't reveal. Worse, it had to do with members of 33 Deep, just as Mickey assured her that JaQuan Miller was about to turn himself in.

"But he won't do it," Mickey had said, "unless he believes we're going to help his crew."

Then, thought Cassie, *I'll just send my folks over to storm Scotto's office and pick him up. Since when do the civilians get to tell us how and when to do our jobs?*

She took the plasticene stress ball she kept on her desk, squeezed it twice, then threw it with fury against the office wall. The throw was less than satisfying. Then she made herself breathe. They wanted the same thing. She was as tired as Mickey Crane was of arresting young black men for practically anything at all. Crane had engineered a nice solution that gave this boy a second chance. One that Cassie hadn't been able to make happen.

She picked up the phone, then put it down. She'd go down to operations herself and make sure the order was put out correctly. Then she'd head down to Scotto's office, as they had agreed earlier, to pick up JaQuan. He'd agreed to the terms and was signing all the papers. Grimly, she picked up jacket and keys, and locked the office door behind her.

Chapter Fifty-Two

Shelley

Shelley got the call from Cassie and sat now at her computer to work on a press release on the surrender of JaQuan Miller. She would do several versions from the straight "he has turned himself in," to one with more details: he had not bought the gun, was simply hiding it so others wouldn't use it; the shooting was a tragic accident. She had to be careful not to raise more questions than she answered.

In the meeting with the Chief, they'd played out all the pros and cons of mentioning these details and details of the diversion. They hadn't reached a final decision, so she would write a version for each possibility. As the Chief had pointed out, they hadn't yet verified any of JaQuan's assertions. Yet Shelley felt strongly that it was important—if this new diversion idea were to hold—that people be convinced of JaQuan's good intentions in hiding the gun, and innocence in any of the crimes this gun had been used for. Cassie had pointed out, however, that they still had no idea who had taken and replaced the gun in the hollowed-out newel post. John warned that this diversion agreement might confuse or upset people.

If Shelley believed what Mickey Crane had finally told her and Cassie, JaQuan had hidden the gun so well, it would have been highly unlikely the cousins would find it. Yet they had. A recent, as well as an old, crime had been committed with it. And ultimately, a young child was killed by it.

After several drafts, Shelley decided on a succession of press releases. This story was going to have to unfold. People would react, would have questions, would not be able to take it in all at once. Most people would read one story and be done if the press left it alone. But the press had kept the story alive and would keep digging—why did it take the police so long to find JaQuan, why did he have the gun, why did he run, and who had committed the crimes using the gun. And with JaQuan not charged, there would be no trial to get these answers out to a hungry press corps. So if the press kept pushing, she would have a strategy and templates ready to go. And she would have to spin the agreement with JaQuan—why was he not being charged with any of the crimes linked to the gun?

Then she'd have to talk to the Chief about getting social workers back out to talk to Ishmael's mom and aunt. They had to have the heads-up about this agreement. They might need some help coming to terms with it, but they'd have to be relieved that any eviction procedures their landlord might be contemplating were moot. Being poor was hard enough. Losing your apartment because a relative was accused of a crime seemed cruel and senseless, but it was the policy.

Chapter Fifty-Three

Mickey

Mickey walked down with Niecy, JaQuan and Rosaria to the parking lot and waited with them for Detective Rock to arrive. When she did, Mickey wished them luck as they got into Cassie's vehicle.

"You're not coming with us?" JaQuan and Cassie asked simultaneously, and both a bit angrily.

"I have one more thing to do. I'll meet you there," Mickey said.

Mickey drove off in the other direction, after Cassie's car pulled out. In her conversation with Emilio, they had agreed on a longshot strategy and he had an hour to pull it off to stop potential retaliations. She knew Cassie wouldn't approve, but she felt their idea had at least as good a chance, possibly better, than the plan she and Cassie had put together. Hopefully, one of them would work.

Chapter Fifty-Four

Emilio

Emilio had jumped into action as soon as he got off the phone with Mickey Crane. Once they came up with a plan, that was all he needed. He was skilled at getting things done once he knew what he needed to do. He had to find a place where Q's boys wouldn't bolt when they saw a white woman walk toward them. And where the meeting would be relatively private. He knew how to lure them—he had information on Matthie's condition and he knew where JaQuan was.

As soon as he figured out the meeting place, he texted Jonathan with the information. He ended the text with: *Make sure Snake comes if he's there.*

At Sammy's House of Pizza, he grabbed a Coke and a slice, and a table at the back. All the boys knew the place. He'd texted Mickey, but told her not to come in until he texted again—he wanted all the boys at the table and eating before she arrived. He'd ordered a whole pizza for when the boys arrived. He took a seat facing the door.

Emilio was fairly sure Snake wasn't around and wouldn't show. It would be a different discussion if Snake did show, but Emilio was ready either way.

Eating his pizza, he reflected on his last meeting with Maurizio.

"You gotta be fuckin' kidding me, bro. I did what you asked, I backed off. Now I gotta retaliate or I look weak."

"Man, they're fuckin' kids. They didn't know Snake was going to pull a gun. Look, some of them boys are family to me. You go after them, man, I gotta pull my crew together, go after you." Emilio had pulled himself to full height and made his face and eyes go dead. He knew Maurizio was thinking, *What crew? You been outta the game.* But he didn't dare say it. Emilio had a reputation and Maurizio couldn't be sure. And Emilio knew he could pull a crew together in an hour if he had to.

Finally, Maurizio had shrugged. "Fuck, this is the last time, bro. We go back a long way and I have mad respect for you, so I won't go after this little 33 Deep crew, but this kid Snake, he has to come to me personally—you can bring him if you want—he has to apologize and show me some respect. If it was a mistake, I'll give him a chance. I can't speak for the Villa, though."

Emilio glared at Maurizio.

"But I'll see if I can get them to hold off. Two days, man. That's it."

Emilio was just finishing his Coke when the boys walked in—Q's lieutenants, J-Nice and Cameron, and two of the lookouts, who were taking on some new responsibilities with Matthie and Q away. Snake wasn't with them.

"We put the word out, man. But Snake, he either didn't hear or he's just not into it," J-Nice said. "So, you gonna update us?"

"Yeah, my brothers, sit down. Let's get some food and I'll fill you in."

He went up to the counter and with his back to the boys, texted Mickey to give him fifteen minutes, then come in. He brought over the two pizzas the counterman had waiting and a two-liter soda.

When Mickey walked in, they were deeply engaged. She came up to the table and all the talking and arguing stopped. Emilio was grateful Snake hadn't come by, he would have stood up now, said fuck this, and walked out, maybe taking all these boys with him. But without him, they simply stopped eating, put on their dead-eye faces and stared at Mickey.

***

The boys rode with Emilio. He followed Mickey back to The SAFE. The SAFE had a small house next to the center that they used for boys who had no place to stay. Mickey had called the night staff and they were ready. She got numbers for the parents and began to make calls. Emilio had the boys text the rest of their crew, telling them to stay off the streets for the next two days—po-po was looking to grab them. Not true, of course, but it would work better than talking about Maurizio or the Villa. As soon as he let these boys out and got them settled with Mickey, he'd meet again with Maurizio, and put the word out for his people to let him know if they saw Snake. Then he'd head home for a couple of brews. This had been a long but good day. He dared to think it might also be the beginning of a new life. He would talk to Mickey tomorrow.

Chapter Fifty-Five

Epilogue

The sun was dropping like a shiny quarter in the west as officers Coombs and Moriarty cruised down off Seaver Street through the neighborhoods, on alert for a kid named Snake as well as members from a local crew run by a guy named Maurizio. They would alert the Anti-Gang Squad, who were undercover tonight all around the area, if they saw them and before they took any action. The situation was, as the Chief was fond of saying, fluid.

Cassie and Rosaria sat silently in the front seats of Cassie's black Prius. Niecy and JaQuan sat in back. Cassie had promised Mickey she'd make one spin through JaQuan's neighborhood to see if he could spot any of his boys. Cassie had promised him she would radio some of the gang squad with orders to bring any of them down to Area B2, where she was bringing JaQuan. If they were willing to turn themselves in, she might be able to help them, find them a safe house. JaQuan slouched in the back, but stared steadily at his territory as they cruised around. He couldn't see any of his crew, which made him feel relieved. It also made him anxious. It was strangely quiet in the park and on the streets. Cassie turned the car and headed toward Dudley.

JaQuan imagined his boys in the days ahead, huddled in the park, waiting for Snake to come back; fearful that Snake *would* come back. They wouldn't talk about Matthie, because they didn't know how he was. They'd be afraid to know. He tried to picture what would happen to them if he never returned.

But where were they now?

"JaQuan, we're almost there."

He looked up to see Niecy staring at him, with that kindness in her eyes. He didn't know what was next and nothing made sense to him, including what he was about to do—turning himself in to the police. He could tell Niecy understood. He felt himself crying and smashed the tears away with his fists.

"It's scary, I know." She spoke softly. "But it can be a new and good beginning for you, and you're not alone."

He turned and stared out the window again. He didn't know how to feel not alone. Even with his boys, he was apart, the leader. With his aunts, he never felt he belonged. The sky was clear and a bright blue, he noticed. He never noticed the sky these days. There were a few soft clouds hanging high, making the sky seem bigger. As they neared the police station, he tried to remember which way the ocean was. He closed his eyes and saw his young cousin dead again. He could try to jump out of the car, but he knew Niecy would expect that. But maybe if he jumped hard enough, he might not have to make this choice.

In his mind he saw his grandmoms at the old stove in the South End kitchen, making him pancakes. He saw Boo again, running for the ball, slicing those tires. JaQuan wanted to choose the right thing, but he was ashamed. He had messed things up. He had not protected his boys. He had not been able to save his grandmoms. He hadn't even been able to stay in school. She'd always thought he'd be something.

He thought back on his time with Niecy in western Mass. That life would never be his.

Niecy reached over and touched his shoulder. He stiffened. He looked straight ahead and saw Cassie looking back at him in the rearview mirror. He felt trapped.

"You're safe now, JaQuan." It was Niecy. He didn't know how she knew what he was thinking. His grandmoms always had, but he was young then. He thought about when he last felt truly safe and it was only a faraway memory. When his grandmoms died, all his safety had gone with her.

Cassie pulled her Prius into the lot. They all got out and walked—JaQuan still with them—into the station. The day began to fade as calls were made, judges consulted, more papers signed. Finally, JaQuan was placed in an unmarked police car with two officers and driven away to a night center run by city, holding tight to Niecy's reassurance that she'd see him tomorrow when the judge would finalize their agreement. "They have to hold you tonight," she told him, "because you've been on the run so long."

As JaQuan was being driven away in the back of the cruiser, he passed young people hanging on the corners, families going to shop at the bodega on Washington Street, people going into the CVS. He knew the young white professionals and off-duty cops were hanging out with beer and food at Doyle's, just a few blocks away. He was headed someplace he'd never seen in South Boston, a neighborhood he'd never seen.

Five miles away and over the Zakim Bridge, Emilio sat on a stoop and sipped a beer with some new friends in the Charlestown projects, aware of everything around him. The bricks of the buildings were a dull blood red except where the sun got in to paint them. Doors were propped open and metal stairs rose up to the apartments, sickly green walls in the hallways and stairwells. Kids were shooting hoops or playing in the project streets. Emilio knew everyone and was loyal to his old friends, he felt at home—but everyone had beefs, so he was always on the lookout for that car coming too slow around the corner. Two streets away from Bunker Hill Street and over by High, well-to-do professional couples were picking up their children from daycare or school, or firing up the grill on their rooftop decks, uncorking a $40 bottle of wine for dinner, or hitting a restaurant down by the refurbished Charlestown navy yard.

In Fort Hill, on the edge of Dudley Square and Highland Park, Niecy Hoskins was returning home, hopeful that what they were doing with JaQuan Miller would actually help him, and maybe set a precedent.

Mickey Crane, back at The SAFE between Jamaica Plain and Mission Hill, was debriefing the day staff and making sure the evening staff had everything they needed.

In the South End, Harriet and Christina were heading out for dinner before meeting up with their writer friend, Arnetta, and catching a play at the Boston Center for the Arts. They walked down Tremont Street from their rowhouse up near East Springfield Street, remarking on the continued gentrification of the neighborhood.

In the Back Bay, Betsy Bischoff and her husband were hosting a cocktail party for a famous Harvard professor to hear his theories on combating urban poverty, before heading out for a much-needed vacation in Italy.

Detective Cassie Rock sat on her third-floor porch with a vodka tonic and watched the rays of a slow-falling sun reflect from the skyline and the section of harbor visible from her house in landlocked Roxbury. Her hand kept straying toward the telephone, but she wasn't sure who she wanted to call, or what she wanted to ask. She felt a restlessness that, for once, she was not able to repress.

Shelley and Carolyn, the day done for both, sat in beach chairs by the sea, a bottle of sauvignon blanc chilled between them, watching a tanker cross Broad Sound, while the setting sun fired the waves and reddened the island of Nahant. Shelley's mind was reeling with the options and possibilities of what came next, but she couldn't share these thoughts.

As night truly fell, JaQuan Miller sat miserably by the window in his room at the group shelter in South Boston, not far from Castle Island, fronted by the sea and by the end of a beautiful fiery sunset, painting a rasher of cirrus clouds. He reminded himself that he wasn't in jail, and he tried to hold on to the hope that Mickey and Niecy had given him that he would be out of this shelter tomorrow, and free before the end of the week. Though he wasn't sure where he would go. He heard the taka-taka-taka of helicopter rotors above him and, craning up, he could see the copter silhouetted against the sunset.

The traffic helicopter was ending its rush hour run and its pilot marveled at how calm and beautiful Boston seemed—this little city by the sea with its sparkling skyline, the city lights just beginning to blink on, the traffic finally slowing. It was amazing, he thought, how the skyline was growing and how modern and wealthy the city was becoming and how its problems finally seemed to be receding.

With one last wink at this town, the sun set; the ocean turned dusky blue; the sky darkened and one young man—not yet sixteen—sat worried about all the people he was supposed to care for and wondered whether life really held anything good for him. He stared out at the invisible sea and tried to hold hope steady.

About the author

Nikki R. Flionis has worked with diverse staff, youth and families in low-income neighborhoods of Boston for over two decades. A graduate of Mount Holyoke College with an AB in English,, she also earned a Masters in Public Administration from Harvard Kennedy School and a Masters in Fine Arts from the Stonecoast MFA program at University of Southern Maine. With fellow HKS graduate, Anne Carrabino, she co-founded MissionSAFE: A New Beginning, Inc., a youth and community empowerment organization, in 1997. She is a longtime Boston resident and has been active in issues around affordable housing, community safety, youth and community empowerment, Flionis resides in the Fenway neighborhood. This is her first book.

Afterword

This book is based on what I've experienced and learned working with urban youth and families for over twenty-five years—but it is a work of fiction. This story will show, I hope, what drives many of us to work together to beat down the obstacles to hope, happiness and nurturing communities. It should also show that the world, with all its violence, can be larger and kinder than it seems. As Boston activist, mayoral candidate, state representative, and intellectual, Mel King, always reminded us: "We may have come on different ships, but we're all in the same boat now." The issues of violence, and fear of the "other," touch all of us; as does the need to discover our identity and place in the world. What we need is kindness, empathy and an ability to not let fear rule us, as well as respect for—and celebration of—difference.

The condition of ongoing urban and national violence that forms the spine of this book has not improved as much as we would have liked in the last decade, in spite of reduction in the number of fatalities. There is so much to be done to eliminate the violence, and the hatred of the other that holds us back: white, black, Latino, Asian, Native peoples, immigrants, women, gays; those who are economically poor, or face racism, xenophobia or other forms of hatred. We citizens of the

United States should be glorying in our diversity, but we are still far from being fully realized humans—in feeling, empathy, and policies.

Edward P. Jones, in a book dedication to his mother that still breaks my heart, noted that when she left the South to come north for something better, she found "far less than even the little she dared hope for." I am not sure we have come much further.

Again, this is a work of fiction. I have taken liberties with time and the workings of various organizations in order to better tell the story. No resemblance to any living person is intended and, in spite of the assistance of many readers and colleagues, all mistakes are mine.

Acknowledgements

This story was made better through the insights and support of a number of early readers, my Stonecoast workshop mates, and generous and accomplished writers of the Stonecoast faculty—all of whom made helpful suggestions at every level.

Special thanks to those readers: Stefanie Flionis—who read early and often—Stacey Altieri, Amy Michele Alvarez, Mark Flionis, Sherri Richardson, Anne Carrabino, who gave the support so crucial in the early stages (and still later!) and helpful suggestions; my Fenway friends—especially Joe Kenyon and Mat Thall—who gave encouragement and (thank you, Joe) did serious copy editing; Boman Desai, whose wise advice helped me with issues of structure; Elizabeth Searle and Patricia Smith, whose insights, suggestions and unreserved enthusiasm helped with the final piece; Joan Connor, Suzanne Strempek Shea, and Michael White, who gave, knowingly or not, encouragement at crucial points. Thank you to Maria Cheevers of the Boston Police Department who steered me in the right direction with police matters. Thanks to Colleen Farrell, Nancy Galloway, and Frances McNamara, who read the final draft. Thank you to Detective Nina Boynton and Melissa Trumbore for asking me again and again when this story will be finished and humoring my Moxie connection. Thank you to all who helped with research, advice or suggestions to make this a more readable story. In spite of all this assistance, the author made choices and played with time, place and circumstances to make the story flow—errors, of judgment or fact, are mine.

To better tell an urgent story and to give a sense of the Boston leading up to it, I have played a bit with time and geography. Though set—story and back-story—roughly between 1982 and 2002, I have added a few more current touches to give a realistic feel to the ways folks live and the issues they address. The Boston of 2016 and beyond grew very much from the changes that began back in the 1980s, with condominium-based gentrification and the condo's ability to create extravagant and quick profits, the beginning of our "new" era of widespread greed and constant change; "disruption" both productive and not. I want also to point out that the backdrop of violence affecting the heart of communities of color didn't really touch many of the city's white residents. There was, and is, an economic divide in Boston. There were, and are, racial inequities. In the time period this book covers, Boston went from a reserved and somewhat stodgy city of traditions—good and bad—to a city of whip-fast change. The high-end restaurant where you proposed to your life partner may not be there next year. The built landscape and feel of the Boston then, and Boston now, are quite different. But this is not a historical tale. The issues here remain very real, even if how and where they play out has changed. But by playing with time, I hope I give a thoughtful look at where Boston and its people were, and where we are today. This is a work of fiction and all its characters and happenings are fiction, though they are drawn from the experiences of a quarter of a lifetime working with young people and in neighborhoods hit hard by poverty and violence.

Boston 2025

www.ingramcontent.com/pod-product-compliance
Lightning Source LLC
Chambersburg PA
CBHW061803190726
48289CB00007B/2048